CW01210117

The Solution?

By Tim Dowling

The Solution?

This is a work of fiction. Names, characters, places and incidents either are the product of the author's imagination or are used fictitiously and any resemblance to actual persons, living or dead, business establishments, events or locals is entirely coincidental.

The Solution?

ISBN: -13: 978-1481897266
ISBN-10: 1481897268

Acknowledgements

I got by with a little help from my friends:

Author and apologist, Dr. Ravi Zacharias, Dr. John Lennox, the RZIM Team, and Just Thinking Broadcasts, thank you for tremendous inspiration!

My new friend Judith Rohan, thanks a million! It was like attending a great summer camp with you and Bill at Beachwoods. There may be editors as skillful as you, but none better.

No way could I have done this without knowing you, Father Bob.

Carebear, thanks for your imperturbability.

And Keels, Timmy D. and Doctor Marie, you were my motivation. Love you guys!

Table of Contents

Chapter 1

Past and Present

It is all but impossible. How can my country, any country, compete with America's technological advantage? Whatever this closely guarded secret is, we cannot depend on our countrymen's skill to reverse engineer the weapon—if it is a weapon. The Director of Defense for one of America's most important rivals was contemplating his next move.

"We can effectively acquire the desired information once we identify the principals. Detention won't be compulsory. Simply *motivate* their friends or loved ones by gaining their trust. Revealing the secret will come about much easier; work smarter, not harder!" One of America's longtime and trusted allies instructed his elite operatives prior to their clandestine deployment to the United States.

"Carefully hear me. Failure is unacceptable. Our intense training has prepared us for this mission. We must use whatever means necessary. Once we possess the data, eliminate the subjects and destroy all proof of our activities. Nothing less than absolute triumph is expected of us." The trained enemy undercover agent was addressing his team of infiltrators prior to launching their attack. "Be prepared to suffer the consequence if we fail."

“Assassinate? Kill the American President? He has lost his mind! Conceivably, if it were thirty years earlier or even twenty, but to carry out this order in these times?” The second in command of a notorious terror group confided in his subordinate after receiving orders to murder the President of the United States. “Perhaps our experienced Mideast comrades can be helpful, yes?”

~~~ Thirteen Years Earlier ~~~

The Space Shuttle Columbia disintegrated over Texas and Louisiana during re-entry into the Earth's atmosphere, resulting in the death of all seven crew members.

The loss of Columbia was caused by damage sustained during launch, when a piece of foam insulation the size of a small briefcase broke off from the space shuttle’s external tank under the aerodynamic forces of the launch. The debris struck the leading edge of the left wing, damaging the shuttle's thermal protection system, which shields the vehicle from the intense heat generated from atmospheric compression during re-entry. Some engineers suspected damage while Columbia was still in orbit, but NASA managers limited the investigation, on the grounds that little could be done even if problems were found.

Just minutes earlier, a report had been delivered by the director of NASA’s Jet Propulsion Laboratory impersonally over the phone. Max, Bud, and Jack discussed the conference call, critiquing it amongst them, as they sat huddled around a large, custom-made conference table.

“Did it sound to you like the Director was reading from a script drafted by NASA’s cover-your-ass
~~~

bureaucrats?" Layman "Bud" Parker spoke in his habitually adroit manner. Bud continued to wonder out loud why conscientious scientists would have authorized re-entry, if even the slightest chance of failure existed. "The liftoff video clearly shows that a large chunk of something came loose from the spacecraft. Every single one of those engineers knew that if the leading edge sustained even minor damage, the shuttle might not survive. Why can't the world's most sophisticated space agency rid itself of its chronic cranial rectumitis?"

"I agree, but I'm not sure we would have done anything differently. What options did they have?" Jack Thompson realized Bud was more of an expert on this subject than he was, but believed Bud was being too critical.

"Be careful, Jack. Nothing is so self-defeating as asking a question that has not been fully thought through." Jack got the mocking answer he'd expected from Bud.

"Don't make me turn the hose on you guys," Max Quinn interrupted his two associates and close friends. Bud and Jack repeatedly confronted each other every chance they got, and kept score too. "I'm surprised JPL is involved. This is way out of their bailiwick. Most of its projects are planetary exploration—you know—unmanned stuff. At least, that's all I've ever observed when I was in school out there." Max was uncertain why this side of NASA would ever be involved with the Columbia accident. "Sounds like the agency could use all the help it can get on this one. I'm kind of surprised they called us. What's your read?"

"Hey, after eighteen years, they know what our shop is capable of," Bud bragged. "They finally learned that good ain't cheap and cheap ain't good. Besides, maybe the bureaucrats are close to admitting the space shuttle and ISS (International Space Station) were terrible mistakes that cost a quarter of a trillion dollars so far and now fourteen astronauts' lives. Unfortunately, the culture at NASA believes if a flight is successful, then nobody will ask how much it cost."

"The shuttle was supposed to be a horizontal lifting-body combination spacecraft." Jack was already beginning the process of finding a solution to NASA's problem.

"It was supposed to overcome the waste of single-use rockets, like the Mercury, Gemini, and Apollo capsules, but funding cuts made that goal impossible," Max weighed in. "Instead, all NASA got was a crude, oversized glider that still had to cling to disposable, single-use boosters and fuel tanks to reach orbit."

"The very idea of the shuttle, which requires disposable cargo and an indispensable crew be sent into orbit simultaneously, is a bad one," Bud added. "Worse, the shuttle is actually less safe than Apollo or Gemini capsules because it's launched parallel to the disposable counterparts, rather than safely on top of them, where the capsules could be preemptively jettisoned in the event of trouble. That way you don't have to worry about being killed by a crummy piece of insulating foam."

"Not only that, the controlled glide re-entry is less safe than the parachute-mitigated descent of the Apollo capsules. The only technical advantages are larger crew sizes, its potential as an orbital construction platform, and the ability to ferry cargo back from orbit." Jack moved to a whiteboard to illustrate his claim. He thought the shuttle was a bad solution to all these issues. "Larger crew sizes could have been better accommodated by larger, improved capsules. Almost no one wants to bring something back from orbit. It's easier to design the object with self-contained re-entry and recovery in mind, rather than risk craft and crew on a go-fetch mission."

"The shuttle was a good orbital construction platform, but this shouldn't have been necessary in the first place." Watching Jack shake his head in agreement, Bud continued. "When modular components are sent into orbit, they should be designed with orbital construction in mind, so that you don't need a two billion dollar spacecraft to insert Tab A into Slot B. But we now know the intent was to build a let's-all-join-hands-and-sing-politics-over-science international space station, with too many countries building a dozen or so parts independently, so a shuttle *will* be needed to bolt the end-product together."

And as for ISS, all three men believed there was pretty much no legitimate scientific reason to build a space station in low earth orbit, other than to study the long-term effects of microgravity on human beings.

"Why weld a telescope onto ISS when you can build a Hubble? ISS is *not* a way station for eventual ferries to the moon. It wasn't built for that, can't handle that, and won't solve that. Good, cheap, fast; you can pick any two, but you can't pick all three." With his usual flair, Bud kept firing his one-liners. "Let's get to work boys. I'll put the team together. You two plan on the usual."

* * *

Six months later, Max read from an August 1, 2003, press release to his company's team responsible for searching and developing the solution for NASA's shuttle launch problem.

"'The Columbia Accident Investigation Board's recommendations addressed both technical and organizational issues. Major changes to shuttle operations will include a thorough on-orbit inspection to determine how well the shuttle's thermal protection system endured the ascent, and keeping a designated rescue mission at the ready, in case irreparable damage is found.' Well done everyone! Thanks to all your hard work and dedication, I've got a feeling next year's Retreat may be our best ever. Thanks to all of you and thank you NASA! Party at Brennan's on Sixth Street after work." Holding his two thumbs up, Max finished his attaboy by pointing out Solution's conference room window in the direction of Austin, Texas' famous major entertainment district.

* * *

Solutions, LLC opened for business on St. Patrick's Day in 1985. The Austin based company was founded by Max Quinn and Bud Parker. Both men were thirty-three when they began operations. The two met in England after graduating from their respective colleges in 1974.

Max and Bud's business became known as TC, short for "The Company." TC's first client coined the nickname as a way of proclaiming Solutions, LLC to be the gold standard in the problem-solving business worldwide. Over the past twenty-eight years, TC developed an unmatched reputation for its ability to find solutions employing creative technology for mainly government and industry clients; especially the defense industry. New weaponry was TC's specialty.

The Company's latest claim to fame was the development of an upgrade to the intelligent personal assistant feature of the most popular smartphone on the market, manufactured by the largest maker on the planet, Integra, Inc. An Intelligent Personal Assistant is a mobile software agent that can perform tasks or services for an individual based on user input, location awareness, and the ability to access information from a variety of online sources.

The application employs a natural language user interface to answer questions, make recommendations, and perform actions by delegating requests to a set of web services. TC engineers programmed the software to adapt to the user's individual preferences, and included a voice which could give the operator almost unlimited information when prompted. Integra named its voice "Alf" after the funny and lovable character featured in a '90s sitcom.

The upgraded technology enables the device to pick up electrical impulses from the optic nerve and the inner ear and transfer them into data that is then translated by the phone's servers into audible sound. This new discovery allows the smartphone maker's famous voice to warn the device's owner to "stay awake, dummy" by inserting an ear fob that receives a trickle current synced with the owner's inner ear.

Integra sold millions of the next generation device and was accredited with saving thousands of lives by Alf's voice alerting the user while driving, operating machinery, or performing other tasks requiring the person in control to "stay awake, dummy."

Prior to the Integra home run, The Company's team of problem solvers discovered a way to quickly identify contaminated water. Knowledge of water quality issues in a given area starts with the ability to test it. Unfortunately, many areas lack the financial resources to regularly test water supplies.

The Company changed that by developing a device which puts data in the hands of those who need it through an inexpensive tool. The device lets anyone test water with the push of a button and then wirelessly submits the results along with location data. The Company's findings identify problems much more quickly than chemical-based testing. It requires minimal training and almost no education, including literacy, for its operator.

By allowing basically anyone to use the simple, inexpensive tool to test and submit data about the quality of a water supply, it can provide an early warning system for potential outbreaks of water-borne diseases or poor quality drinking water. The tool is especially useful in areas hit by natural disasters to help governments and NGOs know where help is needed most for restoring access to clean, fresh water. With the apparatus to collect and analyze this data, important decisions can be made at an administrative level before time and lives are lost. TC's invention analyzes water samples by using light and measuring wavelengths to draw conclusions, which Max discovered utilizing nanotechnology. The finding greatly enriched Solutions, LLC.

But not all of The Company's solutions relied on newly discovered processes. Internal factors and self-inflicted problems have been the major causes of poverty throughout Africa in recent years. A Central African country with a massive shortage of electric generating and distribution capabilities, hired Solutions based on a successful project The Company performed in the Middle East.

One of TC's best and brightest developed a simple non-technical solution modeled after a manual wristwatch. Jack Thompson possessed a triple doctorate from some of the most prestigious universities in the country. Bud often kidded him for having more letters *after* his name than he had *in* his name. Jack signed on with Solutions, LLC three months after Max and Bud's grand opening. Max assigned the entire Solutions team to the African project. Following months of dead-end suggestions and concepts, Jack designed a manually-powered electric generator that could be located anywhere. The team dubbed Jack's idea the "Jackson", combining Jack and Thompson.

The Jackson was the size of a small outdoor utility barn, the kind found in many suburban backyards throughout America. It could be delivered to any site by truck or plane or sling-loaded by helicopter. Once on site, the Jackson could become operational immediately. All that was needed to produce and distribute electricity was one individual employing a hand crank to wind a mainspring which, when fully wound, would turn a gear train just like a manual wristwatch, only on a much larger scale. The equivalent to the shaft that turns the hands on a wristwatch would be the shaft that turned the generator on the Jackson. The generator produced electricity that charged a series of eight NiCad batteries housed in the base of the Jackson.

The operator could simply plug a pump or any other electrical powered appliance or motor into the Jackson's numerous standard electrical outlets. Whenever he desired to supply electric power to a remote water pump for crop irrigation, pump clean drinking water, or provide lighting, he could simply turn on the switch. Jack's idea was manufactured and sold by the thousands to the Central African nation and other countries where electric power was not readily available.

Solutions, LLC's reputation for limitless problem solving was unsurpassed. The Company was loaded with extraordinarily gifted people. Bud recruited the architect of the corporate jet sharing business. Mike Kurtz believed that too many private and corporately-owned aircraft were parked in expensive hangers wasting tons of money on insurance, idle crew members, and requiring higher maintenance costs resulting from their lack of use.

Kurtz coined the term, "combined utilization." It was a simple concept. His idea led to the formation of a company that leased airplanes and helicopters, large and small, from both private and corporate owners. The fleet of aircraft would be offered to charter customers, but would continue to be available to the lessors. His solution allowed clients to schedule any available aircraft in the company's inventory. The solution provided greater safety, since pilots flew more often, which lessened the chance of their becoming "rusty." Insurance, crew, maintenance, and other operational costs were consolidated, lowering the overall operating costs substantially.

Kurtz struggled with finding a way to apply his combined utilization principle to the pleasure boat universe. He complained about the overwhelming percentage of boats, large and small, resting idle in marinas or slips in every body of water throughout the globe. "There's got to be a way," he whined, at least once a day. He claimed that he was close to a solution.

From bunker busting and smart bombs, to radar capable of seeing through walls, to winery irrigation systems using GPS, to the development of tamper-proof containers, The Company had the experience and skill to find solutions. Its finest days were yet to come.

Chapter 2

The Company

Max Quinn was raised in a classic Irish Catholic neighborhood on the eastside of Indianapolis, Indiana. He completed grades one through eight at St. Timothy Catholic School and finished all four years at St. Thomas More High School. Neither school was more than a mile from his home where he and his three older brothers and sister lived with both parents. Even though Mrs. Joan Quinn was a licensed Pharmacist, there was no such thing as a working mother in the 50s, at least not in this traditional Catholic neighborhood. All the moms stayed at home while the dads worked. Max's father, Jack Quinn, was a lineman for the Indianapolis Power and Light Company.

Much like his pop, Max had a great sense of humor and a smile that would light up a room. An outstanding athlete, Max excelled in football. He learned how to be a tough and skilled player from his older brothers, all who were state gridiron champions several times over.

In the '60s, Catholic high schools in large cities throughout America were frequently either city or state champs in team sports. This happened because most of the teams' rosters started playing the sport as early as the age of nine on squads sanctioned by the Catholic Youth Organization, better known as CYO. CYO football and basketball leagues served as "farm" teams for Catholic schools. By the time these young players started their high school playing careers, most already had received terrific coaching from talented men who also grew up in the CYO system.

A "big man on campus", Max had tons of friends and plenty of girlfriends. His natural good looks didn't hurt his chances for dating the most popular and attractive classmates.

Max's best friend, Sean Curran, was a star wide receiver on the high school's state championship team. The two were next door neighbors and almost always seen together telling jokes, practicing football or studying; the young men stood inseparable.

Unlike most popular jocks, Max and Sean excelled in math and science. Both carried a near perfect grade point average and, together, they were on a fast track to be offered full scholarships to prestigious universities.

Another CYO veteran and All-City Running Back for St. Thomas More became Max and Sean's good friend and inspirational leader: Bob Dugan. Dugan had a wonderfully wry sense of humor but also exuded an aura of holiness. He, like many young boys who grew up Catholic, believed he would one day become a priest. This sentiment wore off most guys after the first or second grade, but Dugan never lost his calling. Everyone who knew Bob knew that he would someday become a priest.

Bob not only inspired Max and Sean, but also throughout their high school years succeeded in steering them away from making poor choices.

During their junior year, the two broke into the high school chemistry lab to steal ingredients for making firecrackers, while another student was blamed for the robbery. Knowing the truth, Bob convinced the two pilfers to make known their wrongdoing and apologize to the student who was punished for their offense.

Bob was delighted when he witnessed Max and Sean enter the confessional box at St. Timothy's before Mass one Sunday. They owned up to their robbery the day before and apologized to the kid who was wrongly accused.

Afterwards, the three young men spoke about the penance dispensed by the priest. In addition to the obligatory Our Fathers' and Hail Marys', the two were instructed by the priest to apologize to the person affected by their lie, as Bob already advised they do. This experience left an indelible impression on both Max and Sean. It was also an event Bob would never forget.

The three would remain best of friends. After graduation, they all went their separate ways. Max was recruited by the California Institute of Technology in Pasadena and Sean received a full scholarship to the Massachusetts Institute of Technology in Boston. Bob went off to the seminary and, eventually, Rome, where he would be ordained a Roman Catholic priest by Pope Paul VI. He remained in Europe to complete his studies, receiving a Ph.D. in Philosophy before returning to America. Father Robert Dugan insisted his dear friends Max and Sean continue to call him Bob. Sometimes they did, but more often they addressed him as Father Bob.

Even though the two best friends were separated by almost three thousand miles, that didn't stop Max and Sean from continuing to be the greatest of pals. They always got together in Indianapolis when home for holidays and made it a point to celebrate spring break together whenever possible.

Their non-negotiable annual tradition was going to the Indy 500. Since the time their dads' thought they were old enough to appreciate the long day at the track, neither missed even one of The Greatest Spectacles in Racing.

* * *

At sixty years old, Max stands six feet, one inch tall and weighs 180 pounds with slightly thinning blond hair. He is an avid golfer and passionate toward exercise. Max and his wife Abby reside in Lakeway, Texas, a suburb of Austin near The Company's corporate headquarters. The couple met in Europe and married shortly after Max began working back in the States.

The empty nesters live in a modest home situated next to the runway at the Lakeway Airpark. Airparks are small, one-runway airports that are privately owned and managed by residents residing on the airpark property. Max can walk out his back door to the plane parked in his hangar next to their house and depart, in a matter of minutes.

Max maintains a Second Class Medical which enables him to keep his Commercial Pilot rating current. Doing so allows him and Abby to steal away to their favorite places at a moment's notice in his Socata TBM 850. The TBM 850 is the world's fastest single-engine turboprop. With an average cruise speed of three hundred knots, Max has the advantages of the cruising speeds typical of light jets.

His daughter Alex is the youngest of two and is an outstanding professional athlete-turned-coach. Max's son

Max Jr. married a lovely and competent emergency room doctor. Jr. is a gifted fighter pilot in the Air Force as well as an accomplished engineer in his own right, having received his degree in Engineering from the Air Force Academy and his Masters from the University of North Carolina. Max Jr's skill as an F-15E Strike Eagle pilot provides Max Sr. a great sense of pride and satisfaction. He introduced Junior to general aviation as a young boy. Also known as “Cyclops”, a U. S. Air Force pilot's given tactical nickname, Max Jr. earned his Private Pilot Certificate before he received his driver’s license at age fifteen.

Max, like so many Catholics of his generation, had fallen away from the Church. Sometime after high school, he stopped going to Sunday Mass and receiving the Sacraments. Abby wasn’t a Catholic, so after their wedding, neither of the newlyweds attended any denomination’s services until Max Jr. was born. Max knew it was important to give his son a foundation in faith. The couple chose the local Methodist Church because of its superior Sunday School program.

Then, metaphorically, a nuclear bomb exploded in Max’s world when he was deceived by trusted associates. Not knowing where to go or what to do, Max called his old friend Father Bob Dugan who had been recently assigned Pastor of St. Timothy’s in the Indianapolis neighborhood where they grew up. Max not only recovered from the blast, but recognized it for what it was: God’s way of giving him a wakeup call. Father Bob called it a conversion. Max and his Catholic Priest buddy were now closer than ever.

All his adult life had been dedicated to problem solving in one way or another. His education, upbringing and experience served him well. He knew he was at exactly the right place, at exactly the right time, for exactly the right reason. That combination he learned from his mom.

Little did Max know that he would need to draw on all of his expertise and much more for the challenge to come.

Max earned a Rhodes Scholarship where he met Bud Parker. Bud arrived at Oxford University in Oxford, England, by way of Tulane University. For more than a century, Rhodes Scholars have graduated with virtually any job for the taking.

Both Max and Bud were gifted thinkers and each pursued studies in chemical engineering and logic. In his last year at Oxford, Bud successfully obtained a patent on his "Hydrocean Electric Power" model.

He had designed a process which allows evaporated sea water to be collected inside what resembled a colossal mushroom growing on the surface of the ocean. High ammonia content in seawater causes rapid evaporation when restricted from open air. As the water vapor rises up through the mushroom's enormous stem, it quickly cools back into liquid form. Then a volume of water the size of a small lake settles in the lower half of the mushroom's gigantic cap. This continuously supplied reservoir of water rushes through pipes leading down the stem, spinning a turbine; similar to water pouring down a dam, driving a turbine which generates hydroelectric power.

"What the hell were you smoking when you came up with that contraption?" Max remembered asking Bud, believing it impossible until he saw a working model.

"I have an over-active imagination thanks to my superior mind."

"Don't you mean a confused mind?" Max replied.

"Max, there is profit in confusion. You and I could open a business and make a killing with your good looks and my superior brain," Bud countered. "Do you like apples? How about them apples?"

"You and me—in business together?" Max asked sarcastically.

"We can call the business The Problem Solvers." Bud's quick response provided the spark for the idea which eventually became Solutions, LLC.

"Yeah, well, we'll see." Max vividly recalled that moment; a moment that would change the direction of both of their lives.

At six feet, four inches, 210 pounds, with thinning brown hair, Bud, like Max, enjoyed good health and a good upbringing. Bud was raised in New Jersey so he believed he was worldlier than Max. His father was the captain of a large tug boat operated in New York Harbor. Bud got a lot of his street smarts growing up in his hometown of Bayonne with his four older brothers. He also spent a lot of time running around in New York City with his street-tough pals.

Bud was known for his clever platitudes. He didn't use them to impress, they were just part of his persona. He met his wife Jan in the States after completing his studies in Great Britain. He and Jan had four grown daughters which kept both of them busy.

Bud was a consummate professional with a reputation for being among the best and brightest in his profession.

Little did he know that he would need to draw on all of his expertise and much more for the challenges to come.

After leaving England, the two took similar positions at different American defense contractors. They often met each other when traveling since their job descriptions were nearly identical. Their companies were fiercely competitive, therefore Max and Bud were assigned to attend the same meetings where competing companies were bidding on projects the Department of Defense was procuring; and both always packed their golf clubs just in case. When asked if he enjoyed playing golf, Bud instantly answered back, "Only on days that end in 'y'."

While traveling for their respective companies, they enjoyed single malt scotch, expensive wine, prime porterhouse steak, staying at expensive resorts, playing lots of golf followed by a few games of gin, riding in the company jet, and hard work—just as long as all their expenses could be charged to the company. Working for giant defense contractors had advantages; living like rock stars on the company's dime was one of them.

Occasionally they reminisced about a nanotechnology symposium that took place in San Francisco. Max and Bud were well known experts in this discipline and quite certain there would be very little, if anything, to gain by attending the scheduled seminars.

While enjoying a couple fingers of Johnnie Walker Blue in the lobby bar of the Stanford Court Hotel, they decided to pack up and head for the Inn at Spanish Bay in Carmel, which was about a two hour drive from San Francisco. They chose the Spanish Bay resort because guests have playing privileges at most of the great golf courses on the Monterey peninsula, including Pebble Beach, Spy Glass Hill, and their favorite, The Links at Spanish Bay.

Max and Bud enjoyed their favorite vices for four glorious days, all on the company's tab. But what made this company paid road trip so special was not only getting to play the Cypress Point Club, but Max watching Bud score a hole-in-one on the famous par three sixteenth hole.

The Cypress Point Club is a private golf club well known around the world for its series of three holes that play along the Pacific Ocean, the 15th, 16th and 17th, which are regularly rated among the best golf holes on earth. The 16th is a long par three that actually plays over the ocean. It takes an Act of Congress to be able to play the course, but Max's classmate from Cal Tech was a member and invited the two to join him and a friend. It turned out to be a most memorable day for Bud.

Max and Bud worked hard and played hard. Bud enjoyed telling the story about the night Johnny Carson interviewed a guy who just turned one hundred years old. Carson asked the old man what he attributed his longevity to. The old man answered, "Johnny, I never smoked, drank, used the name of the Lord in vain, or chased women. I just worked hard all my life." Carson looked the man in the face and told him in Carson's own eloquent, unmatched style, "Hell, you're only fifty, it just seems like you're a hundred."

* * *

Sean Curran looked like he just made a Dom Pérignon commercial. Because of his size, the MIT football and basketball coaches pressured him to join their teams, but, instead, he chose to become active in school politics and developed a strong desire to pursue a political career.

He spent two sessions as a part time intern for a state Senator in the Massachusetts General Court. This was enough time for Sean to decide that members of

State Legislatures are generally made up of three different and distinct groups. He determined most were "hacks" that began their political careers volunteering to do grunt work for their local political organization, working their way up the ladder, hanging around, until eventually being drafted by their chosen party to run for office. Inept or lazy lawyers make up the second group. Sean was convinced these political hacks and dull normal attorneys sought office claiming they wanted to do *good*, but their chief motivation was to do *well.*

He determined that the last and smallest group was made up of bright men and women dedicated to solving problems in order to make their cities and states better places to live and work for all citizens. He saw these as virtuous people who understood the government's role. Since the "cream rises to the top", members of this group were often selected by their peers to fill leadership positions and therefore make the important decisions, leaving the rest to be "whipped" into line.

Sean argued that there are no angels in politics and that, absent accountability; a nation's people are at permanent risk. He lectured that democracy's greatest value may well be the average politician's cynical compulsion to survive the next election.

Immediately after receiving his Masters degree in Chemical Engineering a giant Indianapolis-based firm recruited him. There he met and married co-worker Karen Castelman. The couple would go on to have two healthy and happy girls. His new employer encouraged him to pursue his political passion. Sean knew this was the main reason his company had engaged him in the first place. He successfully gained a seat in the Indiana House of Representatives. His reputation preceded him. The

Speaker of the House made an unusual and controversial move by appointing Sean chairman of the powerful House Ways and Means Committee his freshman year in the General Assembly.

"It didn't take long for his contemporaries to discover that if Sean Curran told you a chicken dips snuff, you can look under its wing and find a can." The Governor of Indiana used this local expression when asked if he trusted Chairman Curran to help him move his tax reform bill.

But after serving three two year terms in the House and one four year term in the Indiana Senate, Sean failed in his attempt to become Governor of the Hoosier State. His defeat turned out to be a blessing.

Sean grew weary of what he referred to as, "all the low IQ stuff going on in the Statehouse." *Democracy must be something more than two wolves and a sheep voting on what to have for dinner,* he thought. He characterized the Legislature as a ''bad fraternity'' made up of guys who couldn't hold down a job at a fast food joint. He remarked how easily power and money affected so many of his colleagues. Way too often he observed legislators prideful behavior and their need for adoration manifest themselves when a young attractive lobbyist, hired for that reason, addressed them as ''Representative'' or ''Honorable." Sean watched this same dance take place at nightly fund raisers when the General Assembly was in session in Indianapolis. *Giving money and power to government is like giving whiskey and car keys to teenage boys,* he thought. Sean observed that most law makers acted as if it were a frat house kegger every night of the week. *Secrets? Seriously? Someone would be crazy to tell any one of these guys anything. The life expectancy of a secret is less than the time it takes them to down another free vodka rocks.*

But now he could devote more time to his family and to his position as Executive Vice President of Lilly's Corporate Research and Development Department. Eli Lilly and Company is the largest and only Fortune 500 Company headquartered in Indiana. Sean's job was a real job with real challenges, but he knew Lilly assigned him this prestigious position more because of his status as a high profile member of the Indiana Legislature rather than his impressive degrees from one of the world's foremost technical institutions.

Nevertheless, he and his capable staff succeeded in solving hundreds of problems the company faced during his tenure. Most solutions involved finding creative technologies, but not always. Sean was known for his ability to think quickly. One of the more noteworthy solutions he and his team were given credit for involved Lilly's worldwide distribution of scheduled drugs.

Lilly lost hundreds of millions of dollars annually due to theft. The giant pharmaceutical company shipped controlled drugs through insured carriers, but thieves would commandeer the shipments before they arrived at the customer's location. After studying the problem for less than an hour, Sean recommended that Lilly purchase a Boeing 707 cargo jet to be used exclusively to deliver products to the customer's door step. This solution alone saved the company millions in losses and insurance premiums while it gained Sean a reputation as not only a quick thinker, but it also proved his position was much more than a political accommodation.

Sean stayed active in both state and national politics. His name was on a short list for a U.S. Senate seat and even the Vice Presidency. His experience as a leading policy maker, accomplished engineer, and honest hardworking politician made Sean a desirable recruit for high office.

Little did Sean know, but he would need to draw on all of his expertise and much more for the challenge to come.

* * *

John J. "Jack" Thompson of the "Jackson" fame might have been the most valuable player on the wildly talented Solutions, LLC team. Jack was four years younger than Max and Bud. He hailed from Anaheim, California. His father was one of Walt Disney's famous "Imagineers" and was partially responsible for the creation and construction of Disney theme parks worldwide.

Max and Bud both agreed Jack was a little strange. Jack's childhood dream was to become a star of stage and screen. Unlike Max and Bud, Jack was five feet six inches, slight of build, bald as a cue ball, and not at all athletic. He never married and hardly ever interacted with the opposite sex.

For sure, Jack was a bleeding heart liberal. Bud and Max were the polar opposite of Jack when it came to everything except problem solving. The differences between the three men were stark, but complemented The Company's work product especially since Jack's worldview was that all life is simply a cosmic accident, a product of primordial slime; time plus matter plus chance.

Jack was a professed atheist, but Bud and Max held he was really a closet skeptic. Jack's studies in microbiology had forced him to acknowledge that all cosmological principles are not accidental, but are intelligently designed in order to support life. He was clearly struggling with his atheistic contemporaries' Darwinian position, "ex nihilo nihil fit" or "nothing comes from nothing."

Because of his father's vocation, Jack became inspired to not only dream of new ways to look at things, but he also developed an uncanny knack for solving problems. His father explained his own job was to combine new technology with storytelling. At The Company, Jack often reminded his colleagues to "plus it." His dad told him that was Walt Disney's way of asking his Imagineers to always do their best to make it better. Jack's position at Solutions was that of a go-to guy. He seemed to inexplicably find an answer to the toughest questions.

A year earlier Jack became furious and even threatened to quit after Bud recruited an extremely bright Ph.D. from Harvard. John Henn was easily the most peculiar person on staff. He was also downright butt ugly. He had a filthy mouth and reeked of cigarette smoke, not at all a typical Solution's problem solver. Nicknamed "Brain" by Bud, the same moniker the famous Greek philosopher Plato gave to his star pupil Aristotle. Brain, and his equally disagreeable looking wife, rarely joined in on company events.

Jack Thompson and Brain were like water meeting oil. Jack was a strict evolutionist and Brain made it a point to oppose anything Jack advocated. The two behaved like a couple of five year olds. Bud got his kicks telling about the time he had to break the two apart when Brain got in Jack's face about the age of the earth.

"Brain had said to Jack, 'Jack, the Stone Age did not end due to the lack of stones. It is impossible for

Planet Earth to be any more than hundreds of thousands of years old. Why is the earth's inner core still boiling? If this planet were billions of years old, the core would have burned itself out long ago, and don't give me that pressure or half-life bullshit.'" Unable to stop laughing, Bud did his best to continue.

"Jack was acutely aware he wasn't as smart as Brain, even though his credentials were far superior. That didn't stop Brain from piling on. I remember like it was yesterday." Bud was barely able to be understood because he was laughing so hard, but continued his recollection of the events.

"'You see much better than you think. Surely, Doctor Thompson, it is not necessary for me to remind you that the Piltdown Man was a total fraud and the Nebraska Man turned out to be a pig, not an ape man! Neanderthal Man was simply a man with rickets and arthritis. Need I go on, Jack?' Brain had finished with a devilish smirk on his face. Jack went postal when Brain accused him of being a fool." Fingers pointing to the sky, Bud looked up as he began to describe Brain's rant.

"'The truth is that only a fool says evolution is a fact. Science means 'to know' and 'systematized knowledge' derived from observation and study, Jack. It is based on reflection and experimentation. Evolutionists don't know anything about man's origins. They guess, they suppose, but they don't know. Honest scientists like me have become weary and embarrassed at the confusing, convoluted, and contradictory claptrap that dudes like you often pass off as science.' I could see Jack's face turning bright red." Bud's laugh was contagious. Everyone was now laughing hysterically and holding on to his every word. He proceeded by describing Brain's final blow: a direct hit.

"Chen was right when he said, 'In China we can criticize Darwin, but not the government. In America you can criticize the government, but not Darwin.' I've watched your type rushing to protect Darwin rather than putting him to minimal, let alone, required tests. If you can so easily believe in Darwin, then surely, Jack, you can believe that a creator of the universe could have been capable of making the earth *appear* as if it were billions of years old? Only an uninformed fanatic says that evolution *or* creation can be proven scientifically. Jack, you believe nothing times nobody equals everything. Evolution is a fairytale for adults. It's a guess, a speculation, an hypothesis, a theory, a faith. You're like a blind man in a dark basement looking for a black cat that isn't there." Bud paused and described how Brain had then chuckled in Jack's face.

"Even though Brain was much younger, stouter, bigger, smarter—you name it—Jack attacked him like a pit bull on a poodle. It took weeks before the two could be in the same room together, but somehow they managed to make up." With his hand flailing and belly shaking, Bud finished his tale.

Jack accused Brain of wasting too much time on "that meaningless and stupid idea." Brain insisted the fertile ground in the median of most Interstate Highways could be altered to grow cash crops instead of grass. He designed plans to standardize hundreds of thousands of acres enclosed within Interstate medians in order to efficiently plant and harvest feed grain or bio-fuel producing plants such as switch grass. Instead of paying enormous sums to keep grass mowed, the money raised from the sale of the crops would be dedicated to maintain and modernize America's Interstate Highway system.

Brain claimed to have overcome all the safety and

logistic problems. His idea included a custom made unmanned combine capable of being operated from a remote location similar to unmanned aerial vehicles operated by the Air Force; therefore eliminating most costs associated with planting or harvesting. He even got Jack to accept a bet for twenty thousand dollars that he could pull it off.

Unfortunately, Max reluctantly had to fire Brain. Bud thought they should have seen it coming. Every day at some point he would blurt out, "Evil spelled backwards is live, and sin spelled backwards is nice [nis]." At first everyone thought he was just being witty, but Max and Bud concluded this was more than a catchy phrase; it was truly Brain's worldview.

John Henn's brief stint at The Company seemed to change Jack in ways neither Max nor Bud could describe; little did Jack know, but he would need to draw on all of his expertise and much more for the challenge to come.

* * *

The Company's founders didn't form Solutions, LLC in order for the two of them or the company to make tons of money. Both men were dedicated to recruiting the finest problem solvers on the planet in order to be a superior source for developing creative technologies. Max later learned that this was the same philosophy employed by the "winingest" college coach of all time: the University of Tennessee's Women's Basketball Coach, Pat Summit.

Max met Coach Summit when his daughter Alex was being recruited to play for the Lady Vols soccer team in Knoxville. When Max asked Summit why she was assisting the head soccer coach recruit his daughter she replied, "All of us at Tennessee believe if we recruit the best athletes, we give ourselves the best chance to win."

Both Max and Bud's experience working for giant corporations taught them to know where to look and what to do when they saw something. They also learned the value of employee benefits. The toughest decision each had to make when deciding to start Solutions, LLC was giving up their many company perks. They managed to solve the problem by incorporating even more benefits into The Company.

All but a few part-time and entry-level clerical workers were provided company vehicles of their choice, along with insurance coverage and a monthly gas allowance. Whenever overnight travel was necessary, the employee's spouse was allowed to accompany the staff member. Max made sure The Company purchased the very best group health insurance policy available and provided each employee life, disability, dread disease, and long-term care insurance policies. TC's 401K plan was the most generous permitted by law. But the employee's favorite perks weren't the company vehicles or liberal benefits. Solution's Annual Retreat took the prize.

Max and Bud realized their work was their life. Maybe they devoted too much of their time working instead of relaxing, but neither succeeded in changing his modus operandi. They also believed the engineers and scientists they were searching for would need this same work ethic. To "force" the employees to "stop and smell the roses", the company suspended operations each year during the third week of January. TC's travel agency arranged for all employees and their spouses or guests to relax at a resort located south of the Tropic of Cancer, all expenses paid.

The "Retreat" could barely pass an IRS smell test. TC's published itinerary called for meetings each day, but for some strange reason the sessions ended up being cancelled, except for the social events, cocktail parties and banquet dinners. Solutions, LLC's Retreat always went first cabin. Sites selected for the annual meeting featured at least one championship golf course nearby and the property was always five stars and situated on a fabulous beach.

"They're going to have to carry me kicking and screaming out of this job," was a comment made by staff members and often overheard by the two owners. The employees even got to select the site. Hawaii always placed first, but Cabo San Lucas followed close behind with the Caribbean finishing in third place. St. Martin and the Cayman Islands were included in the rotation. Max and Bud didn't lose their beloved perks; they raised them to new levels making Solutions, LLC a fabulous place to earn a living.

Max learned it was counterproductive to take on too many projects at the same time. It was better to concentrate all of TC's extremely gifted resources on a single assignment and avoid spreading the talent too thin. Besides, Integra's smartphone solution clearly illustrated The Company needed only a small number of successful projects to assure its continued success. Plus, there was no lack of demand for their services, since TC's track record was well known and unsurpassed.

The Company grew but never exceeded one hundred engineers. All but a small number of its employees consisted of highly paid egg heads. Most of The Company's recent assignments employed nanotechnology. Both Max and Bud were leaders in this new and highly specialized area of research and development.

Nanotechnology entails the application of fields of science as diverse as surface science, organic chemistry, molecular biology, semiconductor physics, microfabrication; all areas where The Company's exceptionally gifted employees excelled. The discipline could create many new materials and devices with a vast range of applications, such as in medicine, electronics, biomaterials and energy production.

Finding solutions to difficult problems was similar to playing whack-a-mole. You pushed one thing down and something else popped up. But the blueprint used by The Company provided these uber- bright people with a dependable road map. Max developed a six-step outline which he put in place after The Company's first assignment. It wasn't magic, just logic. The blueprint contained many of the lessons he and Bud had learned the hard way.

> There were only a hundred pennies in a dollar.
>
> Ignoring the facts does not change the facts.
>
> Never depend on second hand information when firsthand information is available.
>
> The farther backwards you can look the farther forward you are likely to see.
>
> Good judgment comes from experience and experience comes from bad judgment.
>
> Use addition when solving a problem, not subtraction.
>
> A bad plan that is less bad is still not a very good plan.
>
> Keep changing. When you're through changing, you're through.

When you discover that you are riding a dead horse, the best strategy is to dismount.
If you don't measure it, you can't manage it.
Knowledge is knowing a tomato is a fruit; wisdom is not putting it in a fruit salad.
Do what is right, because it is right to do what is right.
Greed and patience don't live well together.
Whenever you consider removing a fence, make sure you know why it was put there to begin with.
The optimist sees opportunity in every danger; the pessimist sees danger in every opportunity.
As long as you keep your focus on the desired results and honesty and integrity are your North Star, you will find the solution.

These were the best of times for Solutions, LLC's founders. The highly talented and extremely valuable company employees were enjoying the fruits of TC's successes. The Company's main lobby had a collection of honors and citations which nearly covered all the wall space. Max and Bud were pictured with Fortune 500 CEOs, U.S. Senators, and high-ranking officers in the U.S. armed forces and in the armed forces of other friendly nations. Many of the framed photographs were of Solution's founders pictured with U.S. Presidents.

Solutions, LLC may not be a hugely profitable, publically traded company, but you couldn't convince a single employee there was a better chance to earn more or be challenged to a greater degree elsewhere.

The Company was unique and uniquely American. "If your problem is difficult, we can solve it immediately; if it's impossible, it might take a little longer," was TC's slogan. The best and brightest were gathered in one place in order to search for and develop creative new and sophisticated technologies to make the world a better and safer place for all. That is The Company's mission, and that's what TC does better than anybody else on the planet.

Chapter 3

Best Friends

The alarm clock sounded at the usual time. Max and Abby spoke for several minutes before hugging each other and rose to start their day. Max began his morning routine by switching on the TV.

"Good morning Austin. It's Tuesday, April 27, 2014." Max's favorite TV personality was reporting the day's news as Max listened to her while shaving. "When people are arrested on felony drug charges, they are usually dragged from their homes or places of business and booked into filthy, dangerously overcrowded county jails awaiting bonding proceedings. Physical and sexual assault is commonplace. The arrested person generally will forfeit his job or career, long before any conviction or acquittal of charges. These people are instantly transformed from taxpayer to tax burden. Statistics bear this out, of over fifty percent of men employed before a prison—," Max changed channels thinking, *now there's a problem Solutions ought to be working on.*

"—this seventeen year old woman holding the baby lived in the house with the dead man. Police believe the young man was a drug dealer." Another attractive female was reporting from the scene of an Austin police shooting.

"Depressing," Max said out loud, as he switched the TV off. *I should stop watching this crap first thing in the morning. Every time I listen to this stuff I get depressed. We're witnessing the burning of Rome; it's only taking a little longer*, he thought.

"All my love and enjoy your day. Be careful, I'll see you this evening," Max kissed Abby as he left the house for his forty minute commute. As usual, he immediately turned on his car radio after backing out of the garage.

"Gang members are thought to be responsible for the death of a rival"—he changed the station.

"Methamphetamines are now the drug of choice among college"—he changed stations again.

"Mexico's drug cartels have captured"—once more he changed to a different station.

"Experts believe they have discovered why angry men treat women"*—it's true, no one has ever gone broke underestimating the stupidity of the American public, especially when most them derive a good part of their knowledge about the world from whatever they witness on a movie screen. America is the only country where a significant proportion of the population believes that professional wrestling is real but the moon landing was faked,* he thought, as he jabbed at the off button.

"Good morning Mr. Q," Therese "Tess" Puglielli shouted. She sounded like a cartoon character whose name Max couldn't recall. Tess was Solution's youngest employee. She was the receptionist who greeted employees and visitors entering The Company's headquarters located just south of The University of Texas campus in downtown Austin.

"How's your morning so far boss?" Tess asked in that sweet sounding voice.

"Thank you for asking, Tess. I made the mistake of turning on the TV this morning. I compounded the mistake by listening to my car radio on the way here. Will you please do me a huge favor and change the channel on the lobby TV?" Max asked, answering her question with a question.

"ESPN," Dom said, moving toward the remote control almost by instinct. Dominic Kelly was TC's Employee of the Month and the only person inside The Company permitted to carry a weapon. He was the security guard and his post was in the reception lobby along with Tess.

"Anything except a steady stream of bad news please," Max replied.

"What did I miss?" Tess decided long ago it was her job to know everything that was going on in the lobby regardless the subject.

"I agree." Dom approved of Max's idea.

Both Dominic and Tess knew he was serious. Max wasn't a trickster like Bud. Everyone at TC knew there wasn't an unkind bone in his body. Whatever his reason, Tess and Dom were sure Max's request would help TC become an even a better place to work.

"The 'View'?" Tess kidded.

"No way," chided Dom.

"It doesn't matter to me, but, please, no more talking heads predicting doom and gloom or showing kids wallowing in drugs and poverty." Max answered their inquiries while taking two steps at a time as he climbed up the spiral staircase leading to the Executive Suite.

Two floors up Max's partner sat behind his desk with his feet propped up on his credenza. He was reading the Wall Street Journal while enjoying a cup of coffee.

"What's up Bud?" Max called out to his good friend. "You okay?"

"Red hot and still heat'n," Bud quipped. "Guess who's going to the Masters next April 'ol buddy? No don't, I'll tell you. We are! You and me! We got invited to the Masters!"

"You're kidding me? You lie like a rug. You're kidding me right?" Shaking his head in disbelief, Max snatched the invitation from Bud's hand.

"Integra is sending us six clubhouse passes good for all days, keys to a party pad just off the course and, get a load of this, they're sending the company jet. Read it yourself. It's addressed to both of us. Hey, we made them millions, plus Cookie's our host. I bet it was his idea to begin with, what you think?" Bud asked, grinning from ear to ear.

"You'd win that bet, I'm sure of it. I've always wanted to see Augusta in real life instead of on TV. I hear it's a lot hillier than what you see on the tube." Practicing a golf swing, Max was grinning as he continued describing his vision of Augusta National.

"Well you're about to find out first hand. They have a new Grumman 650 you know, going first cabin partner!" Bud said with a fist pump.

The Gulfstream G650 ultra-large-cabin, ultra-high speed business jet is the gold standard in business aviation. Most corporate owners had the interior designed for unmatched comfort and luxury. The G650 was considered not the Cadillac, but the Bentley of corporate aircraft.

"You New Orleans boys sure know how to live." Max remembered Cookie and Bud were fraternity brothers at Tulane. "I better wait until our annual family reunion to tell my brothers; they'll be green with envy.

What a coincidence. I had this on my list of things for you and me to do. I finally get to watch the tournament in person."

"Cookie's a good dude. He told me there are reserved seats for major sponsors on every green too. Works for me," Bud noted.

"Hey, do you think we would be pushing our luck to ask him if he can get us on the course Monday morning?" Max knew he was looking a gift horse in the mouth. "I have a buddy who got to play the day after championship. The course is set up the same way it was for Sunday's round. He's a Cadillac dealer. He told me all the major sponsors get invited to enter a foursome."

"I'm pretty sure Integra is a major sponsor. I say let's use 'em 'til we use 'em up." Since the tournament was almost a year away, Bud's answer was more of a confirmation.

"Bud, I know you're the ops manager, but I asked Tess to change the channel on the TV in the lobby. No more CNN or any of those twenty-four-seven news programs reporting nothing but horrific news. I'm sick of hearing all the stupid, hopeless and never ending reports of kids killing each other for drugs or money or gangs wreaking havoc or drug dealers—," Max stopped.

"Woe, slow down—did I tell you we got invited to the Masters?" Bud interrupted.

"Sorry, must be the caffeine." Max smiled, but shook his head in disgust.

"No problem, sounds like a good idea to me. I stopped watching and listening to all that bullshit a long time ago. I found myself getting pissed off at the television set every time I watched these talking heads discuss any subject, but especially politics. Sunday mornings were the worst. Then one afternoon I was listening to talk radio while sitting in my car at the blood bank parking lot getting ready to go in to make a donation. I go every eight weeks and you should too. It's really good for you. Each time you give blood you have some iron removed, which is a good thing. Plus it's a mini check-up. You can get your cholesterol count, blood pressure and temperature. And if there is something seriously wrong you can be sure someone will contact you so you can make the necessary burial arrangements before—" Bud stopped.

"Hold on—what? Did you change the subject or are you ranting?" a confused Max asked, because Bud had a tendency to go off on tangents.

"Sorry. Let me finish though. This time when the technician took my blood pressure he told me it was too high. It was too high because I was all stoked up listening to assholes pontificate about shit that wouldn't interest an idiot moron."

"So you did change the subject?" Max asked, knowing the answer.

"Yep, guess so. It's been less than eight years and more than five, but I can tell you this, I'm not only much calmer, but I learned it is the job of the talking heads to get you all wound up. That way you keep tuning in," Bud said, pointing his finger at Max.

"That sounds like something I ought to do. I'm sick of being pissed off all the time." Bud held up his coffee cup signaling for a refill as Max was talking and pouring himself a cup.

"Try it; you'll be a lot better off. Probably lower your blood pressure too. I get all my news from the Journal. That way I can pick the stories I am interested in and ignore the rest of the garbage. Remember this pal; it's the media's job to report about houses that burn, not houses that don't burn. Back to your stupid people comment, I had this great idea several years ago." Max guessed Bud was now starting a rant.

"I was going to start a web site called 'Choose to not be poor'. I wanted men's and women's clubs, country clubs, churches, you name it, to rent billboards situated close to schools. The billboards would contain the message, 'finish high school; don't have kids until you're married; don't get married in your teens.' It was an idea I got from a George Will column in the Sunday paper. Will wrote that if kids followed these three steps the likelihood of them being poor when they got older went way down. So I figure if kids saw this every day then maybe it would sink in. I'm damn sure even the stupidest kid knows he doesn't want to be poor." Bud was indeed off on a rant.

"Great idea, Mr. Altruistic, I didn't know you had it in you. Why didn't you go through with it?" Max was surprised his tightwad buddy would do anything in his spare time that didn't involve golf.

"Too busy chasing a buck. You know how it is? Or maybe too busy playing pasture pool. Do you ever think about how much time and money we blow chasing the ball?" Bud kept speaking while he got up from his desk.

"Golf is a curse and a cult. But it keeps us off the streets and out of trouble, right?" Max answered, knowing he'd guessed right. "Maybe you should give your billboard idea a shot now; I'd be willing to go halvies with you?"

"Yep, maybe you're right, but first things first. Let's call Cookie and tell him we're in for Augusta. We can save the culture some other time. It's not every day we get this kind of invitation. He is giving us six passes. I say we give your pal Father Bob a call. He'd love it, right?" Bud was sure Max would enjoy being with his old friend since he talked about him all the time.

"You're right! Good thinking," Max said, reaching up to give Bud a high five.

"Hey, it's what we get paid for around here." Bud replied, smiling and smacking Max on the shoulder.

"It will be great to see him and you'll finally get a chance to meet. Knowing Bob, he's probably not only been to Augusta already, but probably played the course. When I grow up I want to be a priest. You can't believe all the places this guy's been. And Catholic Priests don't stay at the Sleep Cheap Inn either. Wait 'til you hear some of his stories, you'll want to join the priesthood too." Bud could tell Max was grateful for the suggestion.

"We should ask Jack too. Even though he doesn't play, I know he still loves to watch. We can tell Cookie it was Jack who finally connected all the dots so Alf's smartphone voice could work its magic. Man that guy comes through in a crunch. How does he pull it off I wonder?" Max asked.

"Maybe one of these days he'll tell us his secret. For now, I'll get back to Cookie, you line up Bob and check with Jack," Bud instructed.

"Okay, I'm out of here; got important stuff to do at Dell this afternoon. See you at the airport Thursday. I told Sean to make sure to cross his legs and hang onto his wallet. You're so tight, you squeak." Knowing how much Bud enjoys spending other people's money, Max couldn't resist reminding Bud he was a world-class cheapskate.

"Sounds like a plan! We're on the company's dime, so let's make it to that great steakhouse you talk about all the time. Expensive food taste better when someone else is paying for it my friend. That's not being cheap. You say tightwad; I say thrifty." Hopping out of his chair, Bud finished his defense and prepared to leave for an appointment of his own.

The two were flying a scheduled airline to Indianapolis. Max made it a rule not to fly his plane when there might be drinking, staying up late and getting up early involved. This would be Bud's first Indy 500. Even though he never met Max's boyhood friend Sean, Max told so many stories about the two of them growing up, Bud felt as though he knew him already. This was race weekend in Indy; drinking, staying up late and getting up early were the rule, not the exception.

"I'll have Maggie arrange an airport limo." Maggie Ehrgott was Max's gatekeeper. She was much more than his Executive Assistant. Everyone at The Company knew if they wanted to get to Max, they had to go through Maggie.

"Okay, good luck!" Bud held both thumbs up on his way out the door.

* * *

It's been over three years since Max and Sean saw each other in person. Both Max and Bud would be visiting Eli Lilly's corporate headquarters in Indianapolis. Sean arranged an invitation for the two to pitch Lilly on Solutions, LLC's services the Thursday before race day.

On the day of the race, Sean had a police escort and suite passes for Max, Bud, Father Bob and himself. The weather was perfect and the race exciting. Bud remarked how much more violent the crashes were when seen live. Max shared the story his grandmother told about the 500. She was an avid fan and claimed she didn't go to the race to see a crash, but if there was one, she wanted it to happen in front of her.

Race weekend was nearly over. A great time was had by all. Bud was impressed with Max's friends, but a little envious. He wished he had a friend he was that close to. But then he realized he did. It was Max.

"Liz Taylor wants to get some work done on a certain body part to make it look much younger. She hires a plastic surgeon under the condition he tells no one about her adjustment." Sean began telling his joke. "After successful surgery, three bouquets of flowers were delivered to the recovery room, much to the dismay of the now conscious patient. Oh, Ms. Taylor, please calm down, I can explain. The doctor begged Liz for forgiveness. One of the bouquets' is from me and the other is from the anesthesiologist. We're big fans and no one will know. Well who's that third one from, Liz demanded? I can explain Ms. Taylor. That's from Bob down in the burn unit. He wanted to thank you for his new ears." Sean delivered the punch line perfectly and at the same instant, Max and Bud let out a belly laugh so loud they could be heard in the restaurant's bar which was two rooms away.

The three men enjoyed a twenty-four ounce prime porterhouse steak, served medium rare at St. Elmo's Steak House in downtown Indianapolis. Of course their meal began with Indianapolis' well known landmark restaurant's famous shrimp cocktail. The waiter served a bottle of 2004 Silver Oak Cabernet Sauvignon with dinner. Max and Sean got caught up and Sean and Bud got better acquainted. As the conversation was tapering off, Sean dropped the bomb.

"Wait, say that again!" Max asked in a near state of shock.

"I thought I heard him say he was going to run for President. Is that what I just heard you say?" Bud repeated Max's question.

"Okay sorry, I'll talk slower so you two masterminds can understand. After losing the Governor's race, I was approached by the party's leadership. They convinced me I could win. So I've been quietly exploring my options for months. Karen and the girls are on board. I even got Father Bob's approval. So all I need now is for you to give me the thumbs up, old buddy." Sean's explanation caused Max and Bud to appear like deer in the headlights.

"So you're asking me if I think its okay for you to throw your hat in the ring to be President of the United States?" Max asked. "How come nobody in the press knows about this? I just talked to Bob. He didn't mention a word. Why didn't you tell me?"

"Max, may I please run for President? Are you kidding me? No! I already made up my mind. But what do you think? Besides, I asked Bob to keep it a secret. I learned the hard way, if you don't tell anyone who you don't trust, a secret will remain just that; a secret," Sean lectured. "I didn't tell you because the less you know, the less they can beat out of you."

"Waiter, bring us the Cognac menu," Bud demanded. "Max, I know our Austin flight leaves early tomorrow morning, but this calls for a special toast." Bud was speaking as he signaled the cocktail waitress by swinging his hand in a circle.

After the three men left the restaurant they drove straight for St. Timothy's to pay Father Bob a surprise visit. Since Bud met Father Bob at the racetrack the day before all four men were comfortable talking about Sean's announcement.

"You guys may have a role to play if I get elected," Sean said, trying to be serious.

"Ambassador to Ireland, Oh thank you Sean," Father Bob spoke first.

"I think I'd make a good Secretary of the Interior, oversee all the parkland, you know golf courses, those kinds of places," Bud weighed in.

"Could I be pilot-in-command of Air Force One? Thanks Mr. Might-Be-President," Max said smiling.

"Yup, whatever," Sean replied. "Man you guys are lucky you're good engineers, 'cause you would starve to death as comedians. Bob, or I mean, Mr. Ambassador, consider your request granted."

The late evening turned into early morning. But after all the wise cracks, Sean talked seriously about his desire to find technological solutions to political problems. He said over and over that he believed employing creative technology was a better way to deal with many of the troubles the country has struggled with for years, sometimes generations.

"Think of all the problems GPS solved. Trucks carrying hazardous materials can now be tracked real time. Consider the millions of gallons of gas wasted by the airlines and the military because planes had to follow indirect routes rather than fly direct. I'm going to tell you guys something. I've learned that in politics there are two choices; do something or do nothing. Doing nothing is safer. Most politicians I've known do nothing."

"Sean, you give us a list of the biggest problems you believe you would be faced with as President. I guarantee The Company will find a solution for you," Bud claimed.

"You got a deal, Bud. But I have yet to hear any of you say you think I would be any good at this." Sean made the remark figuring he would get some smartass reply.

"Sean, what they know, you can learn. What you know, they will never understand," Father Bob said with a sly smile. "Just remember though, if you're going to be dumb, you better be tough. And keep in mind, there's a massive difference between the use of fine words, and the fine use of words."

"Sean, I believe our country is in the middle of a revolution, and revolutions don't end in a tie. You sound to me like a guy who knows how to get things done. Any good at this—how about the best I've ever heard." Bud's affirmation eliminated any chance of this late night conversation ending anytime soon.

Max and Bud missed their 8:20 a.m. flight to Austin by minutes because they arrived at the gate too late. Father Bob was droopy eyed at the 8 a.m. daily Mass, while Sean was home sleeping comfortably in his own bed.

* * *

Sean launched his campaign in a bid to win the 2016 presidential election. His candidacy was formally announced on March 2, 2015 on Monument Circle in downtown Indianapolis.

"Days go by slow, years go by fast." Sean was speaking to Max from his campaign headquarters in Indianapolis. "It's already April. What happened to January, February and March? Maybe you can muster up some support for me down there. I already know how it feels to lose. No fun at all."

"Count on it partner. I'll call in the heavy artillery as soon as we get back next Tuesday," Max told Sean, before leaving for Georgia. "Between Bud and Cookie, we have most of the city covered. Bud might even get

Jack to convert some of his tree hugging leftist pals. He told me the other day all you have to do with these socialists is fill them full of feeling until they feel they're full of thought; then they think they're really thinking."

"Tell Bud thanks. With help like that, how can I lose?" Sean hung up the phone after wishing his best friend good luck at the Masters.

Chapter 4

Masters Road Trip

Integra's G650 sat waiting at the general aviation terminal at Bergstrom International in Austin where the five Masters bound passengers began boarding. It turned out the sixth guest was Integra's CEO. He would be meeting the others at the course later in the week. The crew stowed the luggage while the passengers checked out the cabin of the luxury jet before departing on the two-and-a-half hour flight to Augusta, Georgia.

On board the men discussed their favorite pro golfers. Father Bob was a Rory McIlroy fan. Max and Bud were Tiger Woods supporters, but Jack followed Phil Mickelson.

"There's only one thing worse than losing and that's not having action," Cookie announced. "I'll give each of you your favorite and I'll take the field for $250 a man. Who's in?"

All four accepted Cookie's wager. It wouldn't be the last bet made during the junket either.

The weather forecast called for a chance of thunderstorms on Saturday morning, but the rest of the tournament was supposed to be pleasant and dry.

Max sat next to Father Bob in one of the two oversized captain chairs in the rear of the large and luxurious cabin. While enjoying a glass of Johnnie Walker Red on the rocks, the two began their usual philosophical discussion, a ritual they started during Max's conversion.

"Hey Bob, it seems like all I constantly see on TV are young people dying from drug abuse and crime. How worried should I be about my future grandchildren growing up in this culture of death? And how could a grandfather teach them how to go against the flow in a culture that's moving away from God?"

"Is this an official announcement," Father Bob asked, wondering why he hadn't been told one of the kids was expecting a baby.

"No, not yet, but hopefully Doctor Marie may be sooner than later," Max replied.

"Max, to answer your question, the Catholic tradition teaches that human dignity can be protected and a healthy community can be achieved only if human rights are secure and responsibilities are met. Therefore, every person has a fundamental right to life and a right to those things required for human decency. The foundational principle of all Catholic social teachings is the sanctity of human life. Catholics believe in an inherent dignity of the human person starting from conception through to natural death. They believe that human life must be valued infinitely above material possessions. If your future grandchildren are taught this at a young age, it will serve them well throughout their lives," Father Bob paused.

I asked you what time it was, I didn't want you to build me a clock, Max thought. "So you're not concerned with the cultural decay going on all around us?" Max asked, trying to get a shorter answer and one that didn't require at least a minor degree in Philosophy to understand.

"Max, I think you are being naive. The kind of behavior you're worried about has been going on for five thousand years. I agree, today's youth listen with their eyes and think with their feelings, but just think back to when *we* were in high school. Most mornings the daily newspaper published the number of Americans killed in action compared to the number of North Vietnamese. I recall that the number was always something like fifty-seven Americans to four hundred- seventy-six Viet Cong. I remember being pleased because of the disparity." Father Bob noticed Max shaking his head while he was talking.

"Most likely there was also a story about race riots or students protesting the war on some campus somewhere in the country. You wouldn't even be surprised if someone else got assassinated after both Kennedys and Martin Luther King were killed. Remember Bowen? He and a bunch of other people we knew down at IU believed the revolution was starting. So things could be a lot worse." Father Bob finished and turned to look out the window of the fabulous airplane cruising at Flight Level 450 at .91 Mach.

"Yep, I remember that. Bowen and Oberfeld were ready to march on Washington. My brother Terry was stationed in Quang Tri. Mom cried herself to sleep every night for the entire year he was in Vietnam. Maybe you're right, but I still think we're witnessing the burning of Rome; only it's taking a little longer." Max stuck to his hyperbole.

"You may be interested hearing about a plan I'm testing with our eighth graders. I got the idea after I married a young couple about four months ago. I don't keep track, but I guess I've presided over at least a thousand weddings. I'll bet probably ninety percent made the same vows, you know, I, Max, take you, Abby. I started thinking about the words and wondered if any one of those thousand couples really thought about what they were saying, let alone what the words mean. I call the project Marriage 101." Max was now interested in Father Bob's comments.

"Each student will be assigned a word in the Marriage Vow and asked to describe what they believe it means. For example, 'I', did you know what 'I' meant when you told Abby I, Max, take you, Abby?" Father Bob probed, pausing to take a sip of his Red Rocks.

"And what about 'take'? I'll bet most people would bolt off the altar and run for the door if they realized what *taking* a person really means. Then there's 'sickness'; I see a lot of marriages end simply because the sun goes behind a cloud, much less when things get really stormy. Now what if one of the partners is responsible for taking care of the other's bodily functions for *the rest of their lives?*" Father Bob noticed Max moving his head up and down in agreement while puckering his lips.

"I'm going to compile all the answers and organize them into a manuscript. I want the book to be assigned reading in either a Health or Religion class at St. Thomas More. If I can pull it off, I figure at least the kids who read the outcomes will have a miniscule idea of what many of them will most likely be reciting for real in less than eight years, likely to someone they probably don't know very well," Father Bob hesitated. He looked at Max, waiting for his reply.

"That's good stuff, Bob. You're right; I didn't look at the words before I said them. I figured I'd just repeat what the minister told me to say. But I see your point, especially when it comes to the 'better or worse' part." Smiling and appreciating Father's comments and feeling better about his grandchildren's future, Max finished by saying, "Thanks buddy, I knew I could count on you."

* * *

The guest house near the golf course was a man cave on steroids. There were six private guest rooms each with its own bathroom, king bed, and Jacuzzi. The newly remodeled ranch style home featured a giant kitchen and a massive great room with a full bar, two deluxe card tables, a professional black jack table, and three sixty inch flat screen TVs. But the best part was six brand new Lazy Boy recliners. The cave had only one rule: there were no rules.

After dinner, Max and Cookie took on Father Bob and Bud in a game of Hollywood Gin for a dime a point.

"Three." Father Bob placed the three of Diamonds on the stock pile after declaring he was going down.

"What the hell, Bobby," Max said in disbelief. "Is this all you priests do in your spare time? Play cards and gamble?"

"The name of the game is not necessarily the aim of the game." Needling Max had always been fun sport for Father Bob.

"We got our clock cleaned," Cookie protested. "Nice game, Bob. This should help with the new addition to the school at St. Timothy's, huh?"

"The way I figure, Bud and I just won a little seed money to help us from getting slaughtered the rest of the weekend." Father Bob wanted to take some of the sting out of the six hundred dollars each opponent just lost.

"If you think it will help me get to heaven, I'm

going to donate all my winnings to your school project," Bud told Father Bob.

"I can't promise, but I'm sure it won't hurt your chances. You may be that miracle I've been praying for. The project's much more costly than I thought, but God protects drunks and fools." Father Bob was smiling at and continuing to poke fun at Max. "Maybe you're an angel in disguise, Bud."

Max, Bud, Cookie, Father Bob, Jack and Integra's CEO Robby Drew moved from the heart of the cave to an equally comfortable open-air porch overlooking a tranquil pond reflecting a full moon. The butler served each guest two fingers of Johnnie Walker Blue poured in Riedel Vinum Single Malt Scotch glasses, and then offered each of the men a Vitola de Salida Cuban cigar.

The fifth of Blue was half empty when the atheist in Jack reared its ugly head. He decided to pick a fight with Father Bob by starting a verbal confrontation insisting there is so much evil in this world; therefore God does not exist.

Father Bob paused for a moment before asking Jack if he would answer a few questions for him. *Jack, do you think he came in on the noon balloon? You may possess multiple degrees, but Father Bob forgot more on this subject than you'll ever know*, Max told himself, knowing what was next to come.

"In Seminary I was taught that I must be willing to listen, and if I am willing to listen, I must be willing to change. Jack, are you willing to listen, and if so, are you willing to change?" Father Bob asked Jack in a gentle fashion.

"I like that a lot, Bob. Max, we should hang that on the wall at The Company. Bud, are you paying attention?" Jack replied.

"Leave me out of this, you pain-in-the-ass shit-disturber!" Bud complained.

"Yes, I agree to your stipulation. Now, convince me why I should believe God exists," Jack granted.

"Jack, if there is such a thing as evil, aren't you assuming there is such a thing as good?" Father Bob again asked in a kind, but inquisitive tone.

"I guess so." Jack paused and reflected before he answered.

"If there is such a thing as good, you must affirm a moral law on the basis of which to differentiate between good and evil. When you say there is evil, aren't you admitting there is good?" Father Bob answered his own question just in case Jack wasn't keeping up.

"Okay," Jack said, looking genuinely interested now. "I agree. If there is such a thing as evil, then there must be such a thing as good."

"Of course, when you accept the existence of goodness, you must affirm a *moral law* exists. This moral law tells you it is wrong to chop an infant to pieces or rape or murder, but it also prompts you to jump into a raging stream to save a complete stranger's life, even though you may be risking your own life. Do you agree?" Father Bob again asked Jack to respond.

"Yes, that's logical." Jack replied in a considerably less confident, almost humble tone.

"But when you admit to a moral law, you must conclude there is a moral lawgiver; *God* if you will. For if there is no moral lawgiver, there is no moral law. If there is no moral law, there is no good. If there is no good, there is no evil. Your question becomes self-defeating." Father Bob was looking directly into Jack's eyes. His stare was much less gentle. Max knew exactly what was coming next.

"Now Jack, just a few more questions, okay?" Father Bob asked, still peering into Jack's eyes. "Is there such a thing as cold? What is freezing if it is not cold? Is cold the opposite of heat?"

"Of course cold is the opposite of heat." Jack answered in a challenging but docile tone.

"Cold is not something, it is the *absence* of something. You can have lots of heat, even more heat, super-heat, mega-heat, unlimited heat, white heat and a little heat, but if you have no heat constantly you have cold. That is the meaning used to define the word cold. In reality, cold isn't. If it were, you would be able to make cold colder. Temperatures can reach minus 458 degrees below zero, which is no heat, but we cannot go any further after that. Absolute Zero is the total absence of heat. There is no such thing as cold, otherwise we would be able to go colder than Absolute Zero," Father Bob paused. "Are you following my logic Jack?"

"Fascinating, Bob!" *This is one sharp philosopher*, he thought

"Each body or object is susceptible to study when it has or transmits energy, and heat is what makes a body or matter have or transmit energy. Cold is only a word used to describe the *absence* of heat. Cold cannot be measured. Heat can be measured in thermal units because heat is energy. Cold is not the opposite of heat, just the *absence* of it. Do you agree, Jack?"

"It's impossible to argue against that principle, although I've never heard cold described in such a manner." The others could see that Jack appeared to be reaching for his thinking cap.

"Is there such a thing as darkness? What is night if it isn't darkness? Is darkness the opposite of light?" Father Bob continued, making sure Jack wanted him to keep going.

"Please go on, Bob." Jack answered in a much meeker tone.

"Darkness is not something; it is the *absence* of something. You can have low light, normal light, bright light and flashing light, but if you have no light constantly you have darkness. That is the meaning used to define the word darkness. In reality, darkness isn't. If it were, you would be able to make darkness darker. Darkness is only a word used to describe the *absence* of light. Light can be measured in intensity because it is energy. There is no speed of dark. Darkness is not the opposite of light, just the *absence* of it. The smallest amount of light always overcomes darkness. Darkness can never overcome light.

Now Jack, you began our discussion by stating you don't believe there is a God because there is so much evil in the world. We've established the existence of evil. Now, what is sin if it isn't evil? Jack, evil is not something; it is the *absence* of something. God is love and evil is simply the *absence* of God's love. It is just like darkness and cold, a word man created to describe the *absence* of God. God did not create evil. Evil is the result of what happens when man does not have God's love present in his heart. It's like the cold that comes when there is no heat or the darkness that comes when there is no light."

* * *

The golf tournament got off to a great start. Tiger Woods fired an opening round sixty-five, getting all thirty thousand plus patrons pumped up.

"Nice way to kill a Thursday, huh Bud?" Max

asked. Most of the guys returned to the guest house and were once again enjoying the best the giant smartphone manufacturer could offer.

"You bet. It only costs ten thousand percent more to go first class," Bud answered, smiling like the cat that ate the canary.

"You got that right. Poverty sucks!" Max countered.

"Max, you're supposed to learn a trade between the ages of eighteen and twenty-five. Between the ages of twenty-five and thirty, you're supposed to learn the tricks of the trade. Between the ages of thirty and fifty-five, you're supposed to practice the trade. From fifty-five on, you're supposed to practice the tricks." Bud was puffing on a Cuban and sipping on a cold beer while pontificating.

"Where do you come up with this stuff?" Max asked, shaking his head in disbelief. "Are you as pumped up as I am about Monday?" Max was referring to being allowed to play Augusta National on the day after the Masters.

"I think it will make Spanish Bay look like we were slumming. And hey, it's on their dime too. That was funny last night. Poor Jack took a knife to a gun fight. Bob took him to the woodshed." Bud didn't admit how much of an impact Father's comments had on him.

"Yup, but I think Jack really ended up appreciating the can of whoopass Bobby opened up on him." Max could tell Bud got a lot out of Father's victory over Jack as well. "What's your take on Sean?"

"You know him a lot better than I do, but I think the guy is a winner. I've never heard anyone, let alone a candidate for President, suggest the things he talked about. Like I told him that crazy night in Indy, he's got the gonads to get things done."

* * *

Saturday's forecasted rain came instead on Friday morning. It was just as well because the guest house, with all its creature comforts, was more than conducive for the guests to stay up way too late. Sleeping in because of the rain made for a great excuse. Even Father Bob slept late since he wasn't scheduled to celebrate Mass publically until he returned to his parish on Tuesday. Cookie was enjoying acting as the host so he managed to get up a little earlier than the others. The chef was preparing individual orders for breakfast. The smell of fresh brewed coffee and frying bacon filled the cave. Max and Jack met on the porch for coffee around mid-morning.

"Max, I was considering taking some time off. Call it a sabbatical. I want to ruthlessly eliminate hurry from my life. Downgrade my expectations. Learn to say no. I was thinking maybe volunteering some time with Green Peace." Jack was trying to start a serious conversation with Max; one he'd wanted to have for some time. "I love my work, but I've been feeling this tug for a long time. I think now would be the right time. What did you think about your friend Bob's answer last night?"

"Jack, none of us can know what the future holds. It could be next week you'll be making shampoo commercials."

"Very funny, asshole. I'm trying to be serious."

"Lighten up. We're on vacation. You're not supposed to be serious. I'm not sure what the hell you're talking about, but sorry, no way you can leave Solutions now. Besides, you might have a much better chance to save the whole damn planet instead of a few whales, or seals, or whatever. And to answer your other question, I think Father Bob took your atheist ass to the woodshed." Max repeated Bud's account. He was trying to act upbeat, hoping to somehow change Jack's mind.

"What are you talking about?" Jack asked. Max thought his question was made in a surprisingly optimistic tone.

"If you don't think you were schooled by Father Bob last night, you were the only one there who didn't."

"No, I know that. Actually I didn't mind. I thoroughly enjoyed and greatly appreciated his answer, but I'm asking about your saving the whole damn planet comment." Jack's question took Max by surprise.

Max told Jack about the conversation he and Bud had with Sean the evening he shocked them with his announcement that he decided to run for the presidency. Max explained that Sean wanted The Company to search for technological solutions to help him solve the country's greatest challenges if he gets elected.

"It's a big if. He's got a tough row to hoe, but if he wins, we're going to need you, Jack," Max said, staring at him.

"Well I guess that changes everything." Max detected a new enthusiasm in his voice. "Maybe after we find a way for the Palestinians and the Israelis to get along I'll take that sabbatical. But no, Bob didn't embarrass me; it may have been the best night of my life. By the way, I ran into Brain the other day. I found him through an old friend of mine. I called him to see if he had the twenty grand he owes me from the bet he made me about growing corn in the median of interstate highways."

"I'm going to go out on a limb and guess he

didn't pay up," Max replied sarcastically.

"You're clairvoyant, of course he didn't! Too bad he's such an asshole. The guy is as smart as they come. We could sure use someone like him around here." Jack knew how Max would reply.

"The Company needs Brain like we need a case of the clap. The guy is an accident waiting to happen, Jack." Max's rebuke came by shaking his head no.

"Good morning, Robby." Both Max and Jack greeted Integra's CEO.

"Max, I'm headed over to the course. See you over there. Sorry Robby, don't mean to blow you off, but I'm walking over to the driving range to watch Mickelson hit balls before he tees off."

"Are we good to go, Jack?" Max asked.

"I'm all in!" Jack answered.

"I didn't interrupt anything, did I Max?" Robby asked.

"No, of course not, please join me. Besides, I've been meaning to talk to you. Robby, we can't thank you enough. This is beyond fabulous!"

"Max, it's my pleasure and I sincerely mean that, and not just because of all you have done for Integra. I've got to say, you guys sure know how to enjoy yourselves. I've not had this much fun and relaxed at the same time since I can't remember when."

"Thanks, Robby, that's kind of you. You may change your mind after you get back and have to begin dialysis treatments." They both laughed at Max's characterization. "If you can't have a great time doing what we're doing, you're most likely on the wrong side of the dirt."

"Max, I came up with a fabulous idea yesterday while walking the course. I want you, Bud and Father

Dugan to join me, Cookie and three other guys this August. We're going to play one of my favorite courses in the world. It's called Old Head and it is situated on a tiny peninsula on the southern coast of Ireland."

"We know about Old Head. Bud and I played Ballybunion a couple of years ago when we were in Ireland for a nanotech meeting. We tried to get a tee time, but Old Head was booked solid, worse than St. Andrews. Every place we played the pro suggested we get down there."

"Well that settles it, you're in! I'm confident when you see the place, you'll fall in love with it just as I did; there's nothing like it anywhere on the planet." Robby finished by reaching to shake Max's hand.

"Well, like Rick told Louie at the Casablanca airport: Robby, I think this is the beginning of a beautiful friendship." Max answered and returned Robby's sturdy handshake.

* * *

The rain ended in time for the second round of the Masters Tournament to begin around 1 p.m. Max could see this session wasn't going to finish before dark, so he decided to head back to the guest house to relax. He was on the lakeside balcony thinking about Sean's upcoming race when Cookie strolled in. The two decided it must be five o'clock somewhere, so they summoned the butler for two ice cold Heinekens.

"Remember, Al, we're bottle babies." Cookie reminded the server to hold the glasses and just bring bottles only.

Steven A. Keebler, a.k.a. 'Cookie' was Bud's fraternity brother at Tulane University in New Orleans,

Louisiana. Steve was smooth as silk and had a world class gift of gab. Max guessed when the two were in college they must have done everything short of murder and he wasn't sure they hadn't done that. Cookie was a thirty-five year Integra guy. He started with the company right out of Tulane. It was Cookie who got Solutions, LLC its first assignment just a couple of months after Max and Bud opened for business.

Cookie knew where all the bodies were buried and could personally meet whenever he wished with the highest ranking executives in his company. This came in handy when there was a need for anything from money for a new R&D project to a charitable donation that would help secure the company's enviable position atop corporate America. "If I liked it, they love it," was Cookie's characterization of his relationship with the Integra hierarchy.

He did have one personality flaw; getting married was his hobby. Steve was on his fourth wife. Thankfully his two grown children were from his first, so he didn't have to deal with that dynamic. He sarcastically told his friends that all three of his former spouses were great housekeepers; they kept the house. But he had his hands full with his current true love. His new bride was much younger than he. Cookie didn't marry her for her beautiful mind. Bud poked fun at her saying, "The porch lights on, but nobody's home." Bud knew it didn't bother Cookie; nothing ever seemed to bother Cookie.

Nevertheless Max and Bud were close friends with Cookie and completely overlooked his shortcomings. In their eyes he was most dependable, completely honest and a good and trusted friend. Plus he enjoyed just about everything Max and Bud enjoyed. Cookie had the best golf game among the three and also a most liberal expense account.

* * *

Monday's foursome at the Augusta National Golf Club included Max, Father Bob, Bud and Cookie. The pins had not been moved from Sunday's final round, just as Max's car dealer buddy described. The course was in tournament condition except where the gallery moved through the course during the week-long event. The three men were so grateful to Cookie for pulling off this miracle that Father Bob and Bud cancelled the entire gin debt, which Max and Cookie had built up to twenty-five hundred dollars each over the past four evenings.

"Bob, I still intend on sending you a donation for your new building. When I die, if I die, I'll need all the help I can get." Not making magnanimous deeds a habit, Bud had to take a deep breath before continuing. "I've been called a lot of things, but an angel isn't one of them. But coming from you Bob, I consider it a compliment."

"Thanks Bud, the kids at St. Timothy's will appreciate your kindness."

"I never believed I'd live long enough to see this. I'm going to have Maggie watch your expense report to see when, not if, that twenty-five hundred dollars shows up." Max knew how much of a skinflint Bud could be.

"Hey, you know me; I don't mind spending other people's money, especially when it was yours to begin with." Bud couldn't resist getting in the last word.

They completed their round, but none of the group played as well as they hoped to. Cookie was the only one to break eighty.

"You've got no business being on a golf course if you can't break eighty; if you can, you've got no business." Max used one of the oldest saying in golf, while shaking Cookie's hand. "It's a good thing Robby left early. Had he played, you probably would have shot a hundred, right?"

"Robby had a load in his drawers when I started at Integra. He knows who keeps the smokestacks smoking. If you ever see me tanking in a golf game, it will be because they have pictures," Cookie replied.

"When I grow up, I want to be just like you Cookie; great round!" Bud's lowest score ever was a seventy-four, so he was being genuine in his praise.

Before walking off the eighteenth green, they all tried to make the thirty-three foot putt that won the Masters in a sudden death playoff, just seventeen hours earlier on that very spot. Tiger Woods won his sixth Masters by holing a thirty-three foot birdie putt on the eighteenth green after defeating Rory McIlroy, Phil Mickelson, Jordan Speith, and Adam Scott in a five man playoff.

All five pros finished regulation play at thirteen under par. Each parred the first playoff hole. Scott was the first to be eliminated when he bogied the second playoff hole. Speith was the next to go, followed by Mickelson. With only Woods and McIlroy remaining, for the third time in less than two hours, the two were playing the eighteenth hole. McIlroy missed his birdie putt by centimeters, leaving the door open for yet another astonishing finish by the world's number one ranked player, Tiger Woods.

None of Monday's foursome made the putt, but getting to play Augusta National was a rare treat even for the elite of America's corporate executives; especially the day after the Masters. The G650 roared off Augusta's runway at 9 p.m. Monday. Only four of the original five passengers were returning to Austin. Integra's CEO left Sunday after the tournament. Father Bob caught a commercial flight back to Indy where he was scheduled to return to his pastoral duties early the next morning. Max, Jack and Bud had a new project to pursue. Not the usual assignment. The three men were going to be working on Sean's campaign to be President of the United States.

Chapter 5

The Campaign

In recent decades, the presidential nominees of the Democratic and Republican parties have been either incumbent presidents, sitting or former vice presidents, sitting or former U.S. Senators, sitting or former state Governors. Sean Curran was none of the above. His strength in the race was proving to be his character. All along the campaign trail people from both parties could tell that Sean Curran wasn't the typical candidate the public had grown accustomed to.

Character is far from a cliché or a matter of hollow civic piety. Nor is it a purely private matter, as many claimed in the scandal over President Clinton's affair with Monica Lewinski. History shows character in leaders is crucially important.

Externally, character is the bridge that provides the point of trust linking leaders with followers. Internally, character is the part-gyroscope, part-brake providing the leader's deepest source of bearings and strongest source of restraint when the dizzy heights of leadership mean there are no other limitations.

The party leadership's confidence in Sean's ability to win the election exceeded their expectations. Defeating the recognized candidates, Sean easily earned the nomination by beating all four of his Primary opponents.

Taking place every four years, presidential campaigns and elections have evolved into a series of fiercely fought and sometimes controversial contests, now played out in the twenty-four hour news cycle. The stories behind each election, some ending in landslide victories, others decided by the narrowest of margins, provide a roadmap to the events of U.S. history.

"The idea that you can merchandise candidates for high office like breakfast cereal is the ultimate indignity to the democratic process," said democratic candidate Adlai Stevenson in 1956.

"Television is no gimmick, and nobody will ever be elected to major office again without presenting themselves well on it." This was spoken by television producer and Nixon campaign consultant Roger Ailes only twelve years later.

In a media-saturated environment in which news, opinions, and entertainment surround us all day on our television sets, computers, and cell phones, the television commercial remains the one area where presidential candidates have complete control over their images. Television commercials use all the tools of fiction filmmaking, including script, visuals, editing, and performance, to distill a candidate's major campaign themes into a few powerful images. Ads elicit emotional reactions, inspiring support for a candidate or raising doubts about his opponent.

Sean wasn't campaigning like someone who didn't have the right to win because history wasn't on his side. He was already winning the hearts and minds of Americans in both parties. He looked and sounded great on TV. Unlike his opponent, he appeared alone both in his commercials and on the campaign trail. Sean had an attractive wife and two stunningly beautiful daughters. His opponent persistently made public appearances with his family by his side. Sean would have none of that. He knew his wife and daughters would be subjected to the best and worst that public life had to offer, but he would do all he could to limit both.

Candidate Sean Curran's image was superior to his opponent. The country's mood was clearly moving toward the conservative. Polling showed not only the Curran/Bly ticket ahead in all but the bluest of States, but House and Senate races were trending conservative as well.

The candidates for President of the United States made the usual promises during the campaign. Lower taxes, balanced budget, maintain a strong defense, strengthen the safety net, create more jobs, stop global warming; the same promises every candidate and eventual winner has been making for the last eight presidential elections at least, if not every election since John Adams back in 1796.

Sean was different. He told the voters he intended to find solutions to daunting problems by employing creative technologies. On the campaign stump, Sean often referred to his background in the pharmaceutical industry as an example of how discoveries can bring an end to problems once thought too difficult to resolve.

Election Day was less than two months away. Max flew his TBM to Indianapolis to meet with Father Bob and Sean. The three wanted to spend some time together before their relationships would be forever altered. Unless the polls were completely wrong, Sean would become the nation's forty-fifth President. The three best friends were going to have dinner in the

Rectory at St. Timothy's Catholic Church on the Eastside of Indianapolis; the very neighborhood where they spent their youth.

A Mass in Sean's honor was scheduled for four o'clock. The parish faithful turned out in large numbers to wish him well. The Secret Service was also there in force along with a cadre of press and paparazzi.

The three enjoyed a fabulous dinner featuring Father Bob's housekeeper's specialty, roasted rack of lamb.

"Do you guys know how many sleazy attorney jokes there are?" Sean asked, as soon as the three men were finally left alone.

"Thousands!" Both Max and Father Bob answered at the same time.

"There are only two, the rest are true." Sean ended his joke, but Max and Father Bob were all too familiar with Sean's disdain for most lawyers. Sean frequently quipped that most attorneys have all the attributes of a dog except one: loyalty. His favorite mocking was lawyers believe a man is innocent until proven broke.

"Max, I hope your dance card isn't full. I've been refining the idea I talked to you and Bud about last year at Indy. If things go well I want to move quickly." Sean made his appeal to Max while finishing up his desert.

"Bud and I already have the structure in place. Jack is pumped up. The Company's locked and loaded," Max assured Sean. He was speaking somewhat in code so Father Bob wouldn't be placed in the loop.

* * *

President Curran's inaugural address lasted less

than thirty minutes. His message to the American public was clear and concise. His aim is to find and apply solutions to lingering problems, and once and for all, lead the country in overcoming the fear it has been gripped with throughout his predecessor's administration.

"Worry is wasting today's time to clutter up tomorrow's opportunities with yesterday's troubles," Sean began his inaugural speech, telling the American public it's time to stop wasting time and energy agonizing over problems and start solving them. "Worry is interest paid on trouble before it's due," Sean said, looking presidential. He'd just started his new job ten minutes earlier.

"Today, too many people tolerate everything but the truth. I believe you can have your own opinion, but you cannot have your own truth! Tolerance leads to indifference and indifference leads to apathy. Truth by definition cannot include everything. If it includes everything, there is no such thing as falsehood. If there is no such thing as falsehood, there is no such thing as truth." Sean had to pause because the applause was boisterous.

"Winston Churchill once said of the truth, 'It is the most valuable thing in the world. Truth is so valuable it is often protected by a bodyguard of lies." The new President spoke plainly; not fearing repercussions.

"People must again learn to work, instead of living on public assistance. Thomas Jefferson said, 'Our democracy will cease to exist when you take away from those who are willing to work and give to those who would not. It is incumbent on every generation to pay its own debts as it goes'. He was right then and he is right today. What have we learned in two hundred and forty years? The budget should be balanced, the Treasury should be refilled, public debt should be reduced and the arrogance of officialdom should be tempered and controlled lest America become bankrupt. People must again learn—." Sean was stopped by the deafening and harmonic chant of Sean, Sean, Sean.

"What we need today is more smart-idea incubators, less government tinkering with the economy and choke collars for Robber Barons. Let the bankrupt fail, the brilliant flourish, and the corrupt serve long sentences in dark cells." Sean paused once again for a roaring applause.

"A lot of people die fighting tyranny. The least I can do is vote against it. The roads we take are more important than the goals we announce. Decisions determine destiny." Again the President was interrupted, but this time with a standing ovation.

"Please listen to a lesson in irony. The Food Stamp Program, administered by the U.S. Department of Agriculture, is actually proud of the fact it is distributing the greatest amount of free meals and food stamps ever. Meanwhile, the National Park Service, administered by the U.S. Department of the Interior, asks us to 'Please Do Not Feed the Animals'. Their stated reason for the policy is because the animals will grow dependent on handouts and will not learn to take care of themselves.'' The crowd, judged to be at least six hundred thousand, erupted in praise for his observations.

"Whatever you are overflowing with will spill out when you are bumped. Be kind. Remember that everyone you meet is fighting a hard battle. I believe nothing is politically right which is morally wrong." Once more an enthusiastic cheer filled the air.

"Aristotle said, 'As in the Olympic Games, it is not the most beautiful and strongest who receive the crown, but those who actually enter the combat. For from those come the victors, so it is those who act that win rightly what is noble and good in life." President Sean Curran finished to a standing ovation.

* * *

Balanced budget, global warming, terrorism, illegal drugs, failing public schools, depleting supplies of fossil fuels, nuclear proliferation, federal deficits, national debt, organized labor, special interest, the Middle East, AIDS—the list went on. The country was suffering not only from fear brought on as a result of the previous administration's reckless spending, but also from the constant confrontations his predecessor engaged in throughout his two terms in office. Sean talked a good game during the campaign about finding new ways to deal with the nation's problems, but could he deliver? To even give himself a chance he must begin immediately. The President knew he needed to narrow his items down to problems having a possible solution using new technology, but instead decided to rely on The Company to choose.

Certain problems are inherently difficult for the normal human mind to solve. Yet paradoxically they can be effortless for one with an unusual mind. Sean wasn't just giving lip service. His extensive background gave him faith and confidence that The Company employed these unusual minds.

The human species use of technology began with the conversion of natural resources into simple tools. The pre-historic discovery of the ability to control fire increased the available sources of food and the invention of the wheel helped humans travelling in and controlling their environment. Recent technological developments, including the printing press, the telephone, and the Internet, have lessened physical barriers to communication and allowed humans to interact freely on a global scale.

Could Solutions, LLC find answers "using tomorrow's technology today" as their brochure implied? It was true, new inventions solved many of our world's scourges, from fighting diseases to fighting wars. Technology brings health and wealth. It eliminates other options because the other options cease to be options. Because of technology, polio no longer cripples. A populated area can be evacuated when a hurricane is approaching. Milk can be safely drunk because of pasteurization and books can be read at night thanks to eye glasses and electricity. An American can produce one hundred times more food with the help of his mechanized combine than one poor Columbian farmer can with his wooden tools.

"Good morning, General."

"Good morning, Mr. President," General Malcolm "Mac" Wright answered.

Major General Mac Wright was considered by many to be the smartest, yet toughest two star in the Army. Wright was picked by the President because of his behind-the-scene leadership in Iraq.

General Wright operated secretly with the Marine Commandant during the second battle of Fallujah. The fight was a joint U.S., Iraqi and British offensive in November and December 2004, considered the highest point of conflict during the Iraq War. It was led by the U.S. Marine Corps against the Iraqi insurgency stronghold in the city of Fallujah and was authorized by the U.S. appointed Iraqi Interim Government. The U.S.

military called it "some of the heaviest urban combat U.S. Marines have been involved in since the Battle of Hue City in Vietnam in 1968."

When coalition forces fought into the center of the city, the Iraqi government requested that the city's control be transferred to an Iraqi-run local security force secretly commanded by then Colonel Mac Wright. Wright directed the forces to begin stockpiling weapons and building complex defenses across the city in mid 2004. It was the bloodiest battle of the entire Iraq War, noted for being the first major engagement of the Iraq War fought solely against insurgents rather than the forces of the former Ba'athist Iraqi government, except for Colonel Wright's covert participation.

"I have complete faith in these men. I grew up with one of the founders. General, these guys can put round pegs through square holes." The President told General Wright about his connection with Max and confidently handed him a dossier on The Company.

"Sir, do you have a timetable?" Wright asked, believing the President desired results as soon as possible.

"I'm up for re-election in forty-five months, thirteen days, nine hours and, let's see, maybe twenty-seven minutes give or take a few—but who's counting," the President replied, smiling at the General.

"I understand sir; I'll begin immediately," Wright said, moving toward the door.

* * *

Sean and Max discussed the need to create a buffer between them. Unless it was absolutely necessary, TC must coordinate everything through proper channels.

That meant no face to face contact with the President.

The law does not prohibit the President from engaging in unilateral or secret discussions. Indeed, many former executives have done so. Camp David was the location of choice for plotting, planning and scheming. But there was a huge downside if a plan failed or was uncovered prematurely. Any President who acted independently would be severely criticized unless the initiative had already been successfully implemented.

The government's vast secrecy bureaucracy does two things with great frequency. The first, of course, is keeping secrets. The second is devising elaborate reasons why you can't know what those secrets are. What often gets overlooked is the absurdity of the reasons cited. Sometimes they're craven cover-ups learned years after the fact. Sometimes they're ironic or cynical invocations that disclosure would aggravate the very problem it's supposed to solve. Sometimes they're bald contradictions of established policy or routine procedure. Either way, the government has left a long, twisted trail of pretzel logic when it comes to all of the reasons you can't know what its doing.

Regardless of how or if The Company recommended that a problem be solved, the project must be kept secret. Too much political capital would be lost if the news got out that the President was secretly involved in anything without at least consulting his own Cabinet.

* * *

As Max stood staring out his office window at the Austin skyline, he knew he had a tiger by the tail. Having the U. S. government for a client was his least favorite assignment. He enjoyed the most complicated initiatives, because his staff always did better when seriously challenged. At least this project had that factor.

He also tried to avoid choosing assignments requiring too much new or undiscovered technology and projects that might take years to develop and complete. The President's challenge potentially had all his objectionable factors except one; Sean was his best friend and President of the United States.

"General Wright on your secure line," Maggie buzzed in.

"Thanks boss," Max told Maggie. He occasionally called her boss as a way to acknowledge the way she shielded him.

"Good morning, General Wright."

"Good morning, Mr. Quinn."

"Please, call me Max, General Wright."

"Will do Max, thank you, and call me Mac."

"General, I appreciate that, but my father would be disappointed in me."

"I'm grateful for you and your father's respect for our armed forces. Max, have you ever heard the expression, when you're up to your ass in alligators, it's difficult to remember your original task was to drain the swamp?"

"That's good, General; I'll have to remember that one."

"Maybe I should have said 'we', when *we* are up to our ass."

"General, the President told me he explained our relationship to you. He also instructed me to check all of that at the door. He wants to play this by the book. In other words, I am not only absolutely committed to this project, but I am completely subordinate to you. My team will in no way shape or form deviate from your directives." Max statement was made in a stern and convincing tone.

"Max, I've been a part of all kinds of operations both on and off the battlefield. Nearly all of them began with all parties involved desiring the same outcome. I'm here to tell you that's rarely the result. I'd make a lot of money if I could place a bet on it failing. Most of the trouble in the world is caused by people wanting to be important. The good news is, if something bad happens, eighty percent of the people don't give a damn and the other twenty percent are glad. But I do like the sound of your commitment. I too assure you I will do everything in my power to serve the President well."

"General, our company has the best minds in America working on this project. I'm confident, but at the same time a little apprehensive. My team's been involved in a number of projects requiring secrecy, but none as high profile as the assignment we're about to embark on." Max's comment was made in hopes of getting his hand held by the general.

"That's why you're getting the big bucks, Max. If it were easy, the Marines could do it. I've read a lot about The Company. You guys solve problems with technical tools. It's what you do and you're damn good at it. Just keep your eye on the ball. I'll do the same. I fully expect spooks from every agency and country will be snooping around. It's impossible to keep any undercover presidential initiative totally secret. My hope is to avoid having any 'gates' attached to this project." General Wright's reply was made in an almost groaning tone.

Twenty-five years after Washington Post reporters Bob Woodward and Carl Bernstein changed investigative journalism forever by bringing down a President with their coverage of the Watergate scandal, their legacy remains in the knee-jerk attachment of the "gate" suffix. These days a boy scout can't scam a can of peanuts without triggering a flurry of "Peanutgate" coverage. Scandals, semi-scandals and pseudo-scandals that hardly register on the Richter scale of corruption, it doesn't matter; they all get the "gate."

"General, you're right; we are good at what we do. I'll follow your orders regarding security and keep a tight noose around the people in the know. I don't see how anyone other than the three of us will ever have all the necessary details." Max knew the General was aware he was referring to Jack, Bud and himself.

"Very well, Max, but remember, don't chance throwing the ball when you can run it. I'm a huge Woody Hayes fan. When he was asked why he didn't want his quarterback to throw the ball, the long-time Ohio State football coach answered, 'because three things can happen and two of them are bad.' That's my philosophy too."

Chapter 6

Got It, Mr. President

The more Max went over the President's wish list the more he became comfortable with how TC should approach the challenge. He knew Sean so well he was able to "sense" what his best friend was trying to accomplish; notwithstanding security.

Technology certainly had limits. *But why put limits on yourself,* he thought. His team didn't just need to think outside the box, it needed to jettison the box altogether. The basic idea is that to be creative you need to challenge your own assumptions and look at things from a fresh angle. You need to break out of conventional thinking and take off the blinders formed by past experience.

Max recalled that Dr. Wernher von Braun's original idea of using a heavy rocket for moon travel would not have succeeded. Von Braun was the lead scientist in charge of the Apollo Moon Landing project. It wasn't until one of the support engineers became so discontented that he sent a letter to NASA's Director stating there was only one way to get to, and return safely, from the moon. Von Braun reluctantly revisited this approach. He then became convinced his subordinate's plan was indeed the only option. Max was determined to avoid these problems and simply treat Sean's assignment as all the other successes achieved by his organization.

Sean gave Max some of General Wright's background in order for TC's team to have complete confidence in his security plan. Max learned Wright was a young Lieutenant during the evacuation of South Vietnam, served in the Pentagon, and commanded a Special Forces team during Operation Desert Storm. Most impressive was the fact that Wright acted as a liaison with the CIA; something Max knew was likely against the law. The General's curriculum vitae proved he knew firsthand not only how spy agencies operate, but also how to keep the President's initiative secret.

General Wright instructed The Company to keep all results locked away and reiterated that only Max, Bud and Jack should have the combination to the safe. Max and Bud had yet to decide how they were going to keep findings known only to them, but this was the plan he and General Wright agreed to in order to protect the President. He vividly recalled General Wright's final instructions, "*Avoid being fast and loose and stay in your own lane.*"

* * *

In the past, TC's clients presented the problem and The Company discovered a solution. President Curran's initiative required the team to not only find a solution, but *also* identify the problem.

"If you're looking for sympathy, look between shit and syphilis in the dictionary," Bud told Max. Max was complaining about Global Warming being one of the problems on the President's list.

"To argue Global Warming is a fact, that questions have already been answered with a consensual *yes*, and that there is an unchallenged scientific consensus about this is fricken unjustified and pure bullshit. It is also morally and intellectually deceptive." Max was adamant about his position and would claim Global Warming was a hoax whenever and wherever he had the chance.

"So I'm not the only one with a case of the ass, huh? That's the Max we know and love," Bud said, grinning at Max.

"Did you know when Mt. Pinatubo erupted in the Philippines, the volcano spewed out more chlorofluorocarbons into the atmosphere in less than a day, than all the cars, trucks, and coal fired power plants *combined* have ever released; in the whole damn world? I need to tell Sean to get his head out of his ass. This is navel-gazing in the extreme." Max not only realized he was frustrated, but recognized it was time to grab the reins and widen the teams focus.

"You've got that right! I'm dying a death of a thousand qualifications. Take drug abuse; are you telling me these people aren't aware of the danger of abusing drugs after all these years? I say we figure out how to eradicate the behavior. You know, an end-justifies-the-means solution, even if the cure is worse than the disease. Let the politically correct police pull us over, so what? Stop with all the touchy, feely, empathetic, 'it's not your fault, it's the environment you live in' bullshit. Sure, these people causing all the problems suffer plenty of horrible consequences for their stupid choices, but what if it was impossible for them to make the choice in the first place? If you have a hammer, everything looks like a nail. We've got the hammer, so let's use it. I say if you're going to be a worm, you might as well be a snake." Bud had a most unique way of blowing off stream.

"Okay, let's settle down partner. We need to stick to the plan. I'm with you though. If he thinks we can find a solution to any one of these items—," Bud interrupted Max.

"If you're aunt had balls she'd be your uncle; whenever it's harder than it looks, look harder, right?" Bud's wisecracking was getting to Max.

"Bud, don't be surprised if one of these days I shoot you in the face."

Max learned the biggest obstacle to problem solving is a narrow focus. He stressed how strongly adversity needs to be viewed. He preached you can't allow yourself to become bogged down and unable to adjust. Those able to solve problems and move on to new challenges aren't necessarily smarter, better-educated, or more experienced. But they are more skilled in thinking about problems, not getting impatient. Successful problem-solvers aren't overwhelmed by the enormousness of the problem.

Many scientists get weighed down by minor things because they tend to view everything as a setback; they personalize difficulties. Successful problem-solvers however learn to reframe their thinking and look at things in an altered mode. They don't over-define things as problems. These same successful people find a time and place that permit their creative problem-solving abilities to formulate. A long weekend, a quiet time at a certain part of each day, a long walk, a drive in the country, or just a good night's sleep might enable a solution-seeker to separate the forest from the trees.

"We're out of here. Meet me at the club. I'll grab some beer. Eighteen holes should help get our head out of our ass," Max instructed Bud.

"You were reading my mind, partner. Make that twelve ice-cold Heinekens, just in case we go for twenty-seven," Bud agreed. The two would end up playing thirty-six holes of golf and consuming all the beer before the day was through.

* * *

Once the team finally returned to the blueprint that gained Solutions, LLC so much success in the past, the focus turned to a particularly difficult item on the President's list. Several other issues on the list might have qualified, but TC's problem solvers managed to choose the only one that was a perfect fit. The problem was easily identifiable. Its moving parts were well known. If a solution could be found, all parties would agree on the desired results. It was a giant problem for sure. Bud identified the item. But the solution was not going to come from a low tech discovery. There would be no Jack Thompson "Jackson" solution. No, this would require first and foremost an adaptation to an existing technology no one could have ever dreamed possible.

Bud was also the first to suggest the revolutionary approach. It would be controversial, but what plan wouldn't be? The solution was fair, attainable and so ground-breaking, both proponents and opponents might at least reflect on it; if it worked. And that was a big if. Nothing like this exists. That fact didn't cause any of the TC brain trust heartburn. This is what they do.

Max recalled a meeting years ago with a new client. Exxon/Mobil hired Solutions to find a way to free up millions of barrels of oil and natural gas trapped in wells thought to be exhausted. Everyone knew there was oil remaining in the wells, but how much and could it ever be economically recovered was the assignment. The solution seems easy today. But “slickwater fracking” wasn’t even a word before Max, Bud, Jack and two other Solutions super thinkers began searching for answers.

“Once again science and skill overcomes fear and superstition.” Bud bragged after nailing the answer. “Those that can, *do*—those that can’t, *teach*—those that won’t, *consult*.”

“Careful Bud, you’re going to throw your shoulder out trying to pat yourself on the back. Besides, I’d rather be lucky than good any day.” Even though Jack was delighted with Bud’s finding, he cringed the way Bud bragged sometime, and this was one of those times.

“Never trade luck for skill. Jack my boy, it’s not bragging, it’s confidence. It’s not bragging if you can back it up.”

“I’m calling the meat wagon. You’re about thirty seconds from dislocating your shoulder, but I’m not sure the EMTs will be able to get your sorry ass into the ambulance. That puffed-up head of yours won’t fit through the door.” All Jack could do is shake his head in disbelief.

Following Bud’s breakthrough, experience told the team the end game was already in sight. The most difficult projects required creating brand new technologies, not presently existing in any form. Bud’s proposal gave the team a readymade roadmap to follow. Re-engineering was easier than reverse engineering, and modifying existing technology was easier still. Bud’s plan called for the latter.

Max was the project lead. Jack and Bud would serve in their usual roles. The process was characterized as, “Max makes the snowballs; we throw 'em.” Secrecy was the rule of the day. The plan was to start with a skeleton crew then ramp up as needed. Bud, in his own one-dimensional style, frequently reminded all involved, "Remember boys and girls, loose lips sink ships."

Since secrecy was second only to finding a solution, TC had to set up a new lab in a remote location away from The Company's headquarters. Starting a lab is like launching a small business. Researchers are trained to work within a rational and methodical framework. Few scientists get to design their new laboratory from the ground up, but TC's new laboratory would be equipped with the latest and greatest research and development tools available anywhere and located anyplace Max, Jack and Bud desired.

The short list of scientists and engineers assigned to the project contained the names of the best and brightest on staff at TC. All project personnel were vetted in order to reduce a root cause of secrets being handed over to undesirables, moles or traitors. General Wright insisted on this procedure. Max and Bud knew it was unnecessary, but acquiesced to the General's demands.

The President was surprised and relieved at how quickly Max's team performed. He began to receive regular progress reports. Sean was delighted with the element The Company identified and was equally impressed with the preliminary findings. After all, Curran's background had been in research and development; he'd realized the potential immediately.

General Wright provided frequent status reports. Thankfully all was quiet so far, but the General instinctively knew this peace might not last. Progress was slow but steady. Slow because only a handful of team members were focused on the project in the interest of security; but steady because Bud once again successfully isolated an important key to success. Now it was just a matter of trial and error to arrive at the next stage.

* * *

"I'll be out-of-pocket for a week starting next Tuesday. Bud and I are headed to Ireland on business," Max explained. "I'll make sure you're kept advised if anything unusual comes up. I am allowed to leave the country aren't I, Master?"

"Sounds more like monkey business. I could have you arrested you know, but sure, have fun. Max, this may just work, huh?" Max was certain he and his team had exceeded Sean's expectations, so he knew Sean's "monkey business" remark was just for fun.

"What, didn't you read the brochure before you hired us? Of course it will work, but all work and no play. You know what can happen. I'll stay in touch."

"Maybe after this gig is over, I'll get to jet off somewhere and play golf for a week too," Sean said, knowing the nature of Max's trip to Europe.

"When you're through being the most powerful person on the globe, I'll treat you to a month you won't forget," Max added.

"You've got a deal. And hey, be careful. General Wright tells me it can get ugly if you guys don't check your six regularly," Sean said, before hanging up.

* * *

The Old Head of Kinsale is home to a world class golf course located in County Cork on the southwest coast of Ireland. The Club has developed into one of the most recognized and sought after golf experiences anywhere on earth and is a sanctuary for those seeking the finest in personalized service.

"We just went to heaven without having to die. Thanks Robby!" Bud made his declaration while seated next to Max in Integra's G650 returning to Austin from Ireland.

"I'm battin' a thousand with you guys. Every time I'm with you I'm having a great time." Robby instructed the flight attendant to serve each of his guests a glass of champagne while answering Bud. "What say we plan on spending a long weekend in Palm Springs? I have a home on LaQuinta. That's another great course."

"You were right Robby. Old Head is probably the most beautiful course I've ever seen. If you're telling us LaQuinta is a great place, I can't wait to see it!" Bud answered.

"You'll enjoy the Mountain Course, but when it warms up, we're headed to Pine Valley. We don't have to go all the way to Ireland to shoot a hundred when the wind decides to blow; we can do that in the calm Pennsylvania springtime." Robby didn't add that Pine Valley is rated the best and toughest course in America. "Thanks again men, I had a great time and am delighted you made the trip."

"We might want to think about asking Tony to join us. He'd fit in perfectly don't you agree?" Bud asked. Tony Clark was alone at the course. Robby invited him to join their group since one of their foursome had to cancel. Clark ended up playing all four days and became most friendly with Bud.

"Didn't he say he lived in California?" Robby asked.

"I think so, Sacramento area," Max added.

"He's right up the road. Good idea Bud. Why

don't you ask him?" Robby was looking in Bud's direction.

"I'll call him right away," Bud replied smiling. He had become fond of Clark. The two had been paired with each other all four days.

* * *

The Company's team continued to take positive steps toward perfecting the President's initiative. Although Max was still considered the lead, Bud and Jack were spending much more time probing the intricacies of the newly discovered technology. Max appeared to be distracted. Both Bud and Jack were moderately concerned, since the timeline set by the President was going to be difficult enough to meet with all hands on deck.

"Bud, I need you and Jack to meet me here tomorrow morning, it's important." Max made his urgent appeal from a phone at the lab.

"What's up?" Bud's curiosity stemmed from Max's tone. He wasn't used to Max being so excited.

"I know this sounds corny, but I think I discovered the Philosopher's Stone." The Philosopher's Stone is a legendary alchemic substance said to be capable of turning base metals into gold or silver. It was also sometimes believed to be an elixir of life, useful for rejuvenation and possibly for achieving immortality

"Now that *is* great news Max. You know I always wanted to sail to Tahiti with an all-girl crew. Should I reserve the boat?" Bud couldn't resist pulling anybody's chain, especially Max's.

"I'd tell you I'm serious, but that would only encourage you. See you at nine. And hold off on reserving the boat until you see what I found."

* * *

"Why have you nothing to report? You have been active for over six months and you can't tell me if they are building a new weapon or creating a new recipe for KFC," Chen Lee barked. He held the same position in China as America's National Security Advisor.

Spying can be done without fancy gadgets and guns, as long as you are informed on the rabbit (person being followed), know the surrounding area, and avoid attention at all costs.

"We know The Company guys are involved, but they could be working on anything and everything. I spent several days with the principals in Ireland. We believe their orders are coming from the highest places in their government, but I can't confirm that. It appears to be a homeland initiative since we have not detected any Central Intelligent Agency involvement that we know of." Tony Clark was desperately trying to give a coherent explanation. A Chinese national born to an American mother and Chinese father, Clark looked more Caucasian than Asian, allowing him to excel as a Chinese spy in America. He changed his name to Anthony Clark when he began working as an espionage agent for the Chinese government.

"Detected any CIA involvement that we know of—we believe their orders are coming from the highest places—what kind of report is this?" Lee screamed, throwing the report onto his desk as he stood up and walked toward his office window, turning his back on Clark.

"What I meant was—the people we know who are

working on the project, if it is a project, are all of The Company's regulars, and you know what that means." Clark looked like a child scared of the dark after answering his boss. "We're doing our best!"

"Try not doing your best, maybe then you'll be successful," Lee said sarcastically. "Keep me advised. They have been at this for some time now. They must either be close or are already in the development stages. No more amateur reports like the one you just gave me, or you may find yourself in a lower department."

Chapter 7

The "Accident"

Chance alone is not enough to make new discoveries. The scientist or inventor must have a prepared and open mind in order to detect and understand the importance of the unforeseen incident and to use it constructively. As the French scientist Louis Pasteur famously said, "In the field of observation, chance favors only the prepared mind."

That's the genius behind all accidental inventions. The scientists were prepared. There are many stories of accidentally invented food. The potato chip was born when cook George Crum tried to silence a persnickety customer who kept sending French Fries back to the kitchen for being soggy. Popsicles were invented when Frank Epperson left a drink outside in the cold overnight, and ice cream cones were invented at the 1904 World's Fair in St. Louis. But no food invention has had as much success as Coke. Atlanta pharmacist John Pemberton was trying to find a cure for headaches. He mixed a bunch of ingredients together. The recipe is still a closely guarded secret. It only took eight years of being sold in a drug store before the drink was popular enough to be sold commercially.

Bud and Jack arrived at the lab promptly at 9

a.m., just as Max had requested. The three men sat around a small table in the new lab's break room. A fresh pot of coffee filled the room with a pleasant aroma, making it feel like they were meeting at a Dunkin' Donuts store.

Little by little Max provided details of an unintentional finding he made while reviewing results on the President's project.

"Just as electronic circuits are made from resistors, capacitors and transistors, biological circuits can be made from genes and regulatory proteins," Max pointed out.

Bud was dumbfounded but Jack acted as if he just witnessed the birth of his own child.

"The circuit consists of four sensors for four different molecules that feed into three two-input gates. If all four molecules were present, all three gates turned on and the last one produced a reporter protein that fluoresced red, so that the operation of the circuit could be easily monitored—," Max continued explaining his finding.

"How—no, a better question is—why did you stumble across this *ACCIDENT*?" Bud asked, not realizing he just officially named Max's discovery. "So this is what you've been doing while Jack and I have been hard at work?"

"Listen, I intentionally waited until now to brief you two guys. I started seeing the potential right after you nailed Sean's initiative, Bud. Accident—yes—coincidence—no. For now let's keep it hush hush. We'll have plenty of time to talk about it next week in Kauai. I know a great place in Poipu where we can hang." Max figured he could smooth over any hard feelings at next week's Annual Retreat in Hawaii.

"At least you weren't gambling. Jack and I figured you picked up some bad habit since we rarely saw you in the lab," Bud complained.

"Sorry guys, when I get through, you'll see how important this discovery is." Looking like a kid in a candy store, Max smiled and gave each man a high five.

* * *

All but two of Solution's ninety-seven employees, along with their spouses and some family members, boarded a chartered Boeing 757. The plane was traveling to the Lihue Airport on the island of Kauai in the Hawaiian Islands. The Company's employees chose the Princeville Resort for their annual meeting. Princeville at Hanalei is recognized as one of the premier Ocean View Resort Communities in the world. The unbelievably beautiful resort was situated among the lush sea cliffs that tower over Kauai's picturesque Hanalei Bay. It was a perfect setting for The Company's well-traveled employees.

"Jack, Bud and I decided it's time for you to take up golf. You'll be able to tell your friends the first course you played was the famous Prince Course." Max knew the three could talk securely and uninterrupted. The timing proved to be perfect. Max had plenty of time to convince Bud and Jack how important his discovery could be. The three spent part of the nine days in Hawaii brainstorming. They agreed to dedicate the time necessary to develop the *ACCIDENT*. There was a significant roadblock though; funding.

"A vision without resources is a hallucination," Bud warned.

"I already solved that problem. Who do you know

that can come up with the kind of funding we need?" Max asked.

"Cookie? Of course!" Bud guessed. "Why didn't I think of that?"

"I can't remember ever being this pumped-up." Max noticed Jack was actually shaking as he talked. "Do you guys realize the potential? Philosopher's Stone hell; this is like finding the Holy Grail! Sure glad you talked me into sticking around, Max. We might become famous you know."

* * *

"Please have luggage outside your door by 1 p.m. tomorrow. Buses will depart from the side lobby at 3 p.m." Solutions, LLC's travel agent made this announcement at the Retreat's annual gala the last evening of the ten day "business meeting."

"Bud and I are delighted to report we exceeded last year's record earnings. Therefore, all of you can count on finding your specially marked envelopes when you return to your desks on Monday." Max was referring to generous bonus checks that would be awarded to all the employees. He made the announcement from the lectern on the Princeville's bandstand with Bud at his side. "Enjoy the rest of the evening everyone. And please, dancing 'til dawn is not only permissible, but encouraged."

The chartered 757 with Solution's two-hundred twenty-seven employees, spouses, children and guests arrived in Austin. During the flight home, the site selection chairperson announced that next year's Annual Retreat would take place at the Ritz Carlton, Grand Cayman.

* * *

The Company team applied its six step development process to the President's initiative. When it comes to developing new technologies, you need to take the best ideas and turn them into a viable solution. Skip a step, and you take a chance that your time, money and effort will be spent in vain.

The "idea generation" phase focused on framing ideas in terms of a solution to a problem. This step eliminated ideas that didn't solve the problem, and then focused on defining multiple concepts to providing that solution. At this point, these concepts should include as many different approaches as possible. Bud nailed this one after he and Max's thirty-six hole, beer drinking golf outing gave them a change in attitude.

Next, the "product definition" phase took the concepts from step one and evaluated them based on their merits; outlining the requirements in as much detail as possible, then perform tradeoffs, based on the requirements, to select the best concepts. This phase defined how the resulting technology would perform and generate schedules. At this point, proposals were generated for internal review. Max and Bud didn't skip this step, but since the solution was not being developed for competitive reasons, most of the factors were already completed.

Once phase two was completed, TC moved to "design and development." This step represented the go-ahead to develop hardware. Models, drawings and schematics were generated, software was written and analysis was performed. During this phase, TC held reviews to evaluate progress and guide the development process. Because only three people could know these details, the initial test plans were developed by Max, Bud and Jack.

"Prototype construction" was the next phase. This step was the culmination of the development. Initial samples were built for review, evaluation and testing.

The next step, "verification and testing" was used to determine whether the solution met the requirements. It included inspections to ensure the technology encompassed all of the specified functions and testing to verify performance requirements.

Finally came the "production" stage, but it would have to wait on the President's orders.

Max and Bud knew that if these six steps were followed, the chances of spending a large effort with either no results or the wrong results were minimized. The end of the design and development stage of the President's initiative was in sight. Jack Thompson once again singlehandedly overcame the final hurdle.

Jack regularly referred to himself as a disciple of William of Ockham. William of Ockham's fame as a great logician rested chiefly on the maxim attributed to him and known as "Ockham's Razor" which stated, "Other things being equal, a simpler explanation is better than a more complex one"— or, "The best and sturdiest solution to a problem is most often the least complicated."

Jack's eleventh hour discoveries were mostly straightforward answers. Max and Bud were happy he was on their side, but were at a loss as to how he repeatedly pulled simple answers to very difficult questions apparently out of midair.

Jack Thompson of "Jackson" fame might have been the swiftest thinker on the widely talented staff of The Company. But unbeknownst to every one of Jack's contemporaries, he didn't always come up with his extraordinary and mostly simple solutions on his own; or even with assistance from other Solutions employees. Jack had a wild card he affectionately referred to as his very own "idiot savant." Not in all cases, but when Jack was confronted with a problem he couldn't put his head around; he would pay a visit to Dennis Reinbold.

Reinbold was a card carrying genius. He had more degrees than a thermometer, but didn't have a lick of common sense. Jack and Dennis grew up together and went to the same grade school and high school. They were good pals and much alike, except Jack didn't consider himself to be a nerd. If you looked up geek in the dictionary, you would see a picture of Dennis; dark rimmed glasses, pocket protector and all.

Jack never forgot the night Reinbold accepted a bet he couldn't eat twenty White Castle hamburgers. Dennis won the bet, but paid a heavy price for victory. Reinbold kind of reminded Jack of Paul Newman, when he played a character named Lucas Jackson in the movie "Cool Hand Luke." Lucas ate fifty hard boiled eggs on a dare. Jack remembered Reinbold suffering the same reaction as Cool Hand Luke.

Vital elements of the Presidents gig, as it was sometimes referred to by TC's team, had everyone stumped. Jack knew the importance of General Wright's directive, but was confident his close friend would keep his secret safe. After all, Reinbold had been brought into the loop on many confidential projects in the past, and no one was ever the worse for it. That's how Jack kept his reputation as The Company's go-to-guy whenever there was a really tough problem. *This time should be no different,* he thought.

* * *

Solutions, LLC only made a modest profit. Most of TC's earnings were paid out to the employees in the form of high salaries, benefits, and generous bonuses. Max had complete trust in Cookie to deliver the necessary funding. But Max knew the *ACCIDENT* must be protected more so than even his best friend's project. *Was the ACCIDENT more important than the U.S. President's standing? Was it more important than keeping your word to General Wright? Was it more important*—Max struggled. *Yes, it's the most important thing I ever attempted, and Bud and Jack feel the same way.*

"So his wife smacks him with a frying pan and the guy asked why. She tells him, because I found a note in your pocket with the name Penny written on it! He explained that Penny was a horse he made a bet on and she apologized. A week later, she nails him with a bigger frying pan. After he regains consciousness, he again asked why. She said: your horse called."

Cookie finished telling his joke while he and Max were sitting at the bar where the two usually met when they talked business.

"Funny! Is that a joke or just one of your irreconcilable differences?" Max asked, wondering if maybe it actually happen to Cookie.

"It wasn't a frying pan," Cookie replied meekly.

"I need a favor; a huge favor," Max said. "We're working on this idea."

"Count me in, Max. Your ideas always end up making me lots of scrilla. If my wife keeps bellyaching, I'm going to need all the cash I can get my hands on," Cookie said, rolling his eyes.

"This one's different, really different. Cookie, this has to remain between you and me." Max knew he was about to betray General Wright's trust, but he and Cookie had a history of keeping secrets.

"Sounds serious." Cookie's discreet reply was out of character.

"It is serious, it's controversial and it's very bold, probably dangerous, classified, and has everything to do with National—." Max paused on Cookie's interruption.

"I get the picture. What is it?" Cookie insisted.

"Okay, but remember, it's just between us girls, right?" Max asked.

"Max, you remember the Trion initiative. I was the one who insisted no one could know. You kept your promise, so you can count on me to take it to the grave unless you personally tell me otherwise." Cookie smiled and nodded back at Max after promising to keep his secret.

"Cookie, I may need some seed money. I can pull together what I hope will be the necessary funds to complete the project, but I recall too many times when these types of cases required more resources to complete than we estimated." Max was expecting an energetic start, but a grueling finish to his 'accidental' discovery. "Any funds will be repaid with interest. We can call the loan anything you want."

"You keep saying us. May I ask who *us* is?"

Max gave Cookie the Readers Digest version—only it was the short version of the President's initiative; not the *ACCIDENT*.

* * *

General Wright supposed he had everything under

control. He received reports about chatter gathered by the CIA regarding a secret project being run by The Company. This didn't take him by surprise. He expected some snooping. After all, the intelligence community was a behemoth. It had to be fed. There were too many people working for these agencies around the world. Spies have managers the same way grocery clerks have managers. And managers don't want to pay the help to sit around and do nothing. So if there was as much as a peep about some clandestine activity ordered by an American President taking place, spooks were immediately put on the case.

By law, the CIA was specifically prohibited from collecting foreign intelligence concerning the domestic activities of U.S. citizens. Its mission was to collect information related to foreign intelligence and foreign counterintelligence. These restrictions on the CIA have been in effect since the 1970s, but General Wright's experience at the Farm taught him the CIA's motto was, "It was easier to ask for forgiveness than beg for permission."

Wright knew he couldn't beat them, so he might as well join them. He called his go-to guy at the agency to find out what, when, where, why, how and who was doing what to whom. Time was of the essence. According to the updates he was receiving from The Company, progress was now being made more rapidly. That meant the bad guys could have something significant to retrieve if his security plan was breached.

CHAPTER 8

Trouble Brewing

"Steve, this crap has to stop. I can't stand your being gone all the damn time. How come you don't take me with you anymore? And don't tell me it's because of that stupid project you told me about. I'll bet Abby gets to go when Max travels, the way it used to be with me and you. Remember?" Cookie's wife complained while Cookie looked on with an utterly bored expression.

Liz Keebler was fifteen years younger than her husband Steve. She met Cookie while vacationing in the Cayman Islands. He was there on business with his company's executive officers on what Integra characterized as an executive brainstorming session; a euphemism for blowing a lot of company money on fun, relaxation, golf and lots of great food, wine, and booze.

This was a lifestyle Cookie was accustomed to. He met Liz at one of the finest restaurants on the island. It seemed to be love at first sight when she laid eyes on Steve at TV personality Chef Tell Erhardt's Grand Old House. But after being married for three years, the passion she had in Georgetown so long ago seemed a distant memory.

Cookie traveled extensively. He and Liz had no plans to have children, not that Liz had motherly pangs anyway. She was attractive and knew it, but hated the fact that Cookie didn't tell her. She was a power shopper and enjoyed sipping fine champagne while visiting her favorite chic boutiques.

Cookie learned the hard way that most women turn out just like their mothers, but he enjoyed being around Liz's mom. He thought this was a good sign, since he recalled not being particularly fond of his first three mothers-in-law.

* * *

Jack paid Reinbold a visit in order to receive a progress report. This was Jack's customary move after assigning Dennis a task neither he nor any of the Solution's team could solve.

"Hand me that bottle of pills on my desk. I keep forgetting to take the damn things. The pills are supposed to help me remember where I put the pills."

"Hey Dennis, how does a nice guy like you end up knowing a creep like John Henn?" Jack asked Reinbold while he was fumbling with the pill bottle.

"Who?"

"The guy you told me you were working with on *our* project. Remember, I told you I knew him from work? Maybe you ought to take more of those than the doctor prescribed. I think you are suffering from a severe case of CRS, Dennis."

"What is CRS? And who did you say I was working with?" Reinbold asked, looking more confused than ever.

"CRS stands for 'can't remember shit', and forget it, it's not important. I hope you can remember why I'm here. Let's get to work, and remember, don't tell anyone anything about this project or our ass is grass. That especially means John Henn."

"Who?"

"Forget it!"

* * *

"Doc, I have to reschedule the Costa Rica trip. How does your February look?" Max asked, hoping he answered okay. "Besides, the fishing is supposed to be a lot better that time of year."

Max met Doctor Mike Glass at the Air Force Academy. Both men were attending their sons' graduation ceremony. The two dads decided to treat Max Jr. and Mike Jr. to a one-of-a-kind, once-in-a-lifetime Alaskan fishing trip. The experience cemented their friendship and the four now look forward to spending a week traveling to unique fishing destinations every other year.

"Works for me, Max. Both the boys said they're flexible and there aren't any buns in the oven that I know of. How about on your end?" Mike replied.

"None that I know of. I say we gear-up on the seventeenth. Come in the day before. Abby and I will put on the dog for you guys."

"It looks like a five hours flight in your bird. Do you want to sit that long?" Mike knew Max wouldn't want to spend that much time in an eight passenger airplane, nor would he.

"The bird holds enough fuel, but I'm for making a stop. Maybe we let the boys take turns flying there, and you and I share the return leg. We can figure it out later."

"Sounds good to me, Max. Looking forward to being with you."

"Same here Doc, see you then. Give your girlfriend a hug, and keep the pointy nose forward and greasy side down."

* * *

"I detected Steven Keebler meeting with Max Quinn and sense he may be part of TC's team. I've also been shadowing Keebler's wife, Elizabeth. I am convinced she is irritated with him. I've observed the two arguing every time they're together. I devised a plan. I'll be with TC's principals and Mr. Keebler at the LaQuinta Resort near Palm Springs in a few weeks. I've been invited to play golf with the same group I joined with in Ireland." Keeping his fingers crossed so his boss wouldn't jump down his throat, Tony Clark made his report over the phone to his superior. "I'll keep you advised."

"You do that, Mr. Clark. And don't screw it up!" Clark recognized he needed get this right after hearing that remark.

* * *

General Wright decided it was time to circle the wagons. CIA was reporting the Russians, Chinese and even the Brits were poking around. He didn't want this thing to take on a life of its own. He always put himself in his enemy's shoes in order to determine how he would deal with a situation. His security structure was so tight that no reports could be made to the spy's handlers. Wright was certain espionage was taking place, but he also knew if these spooks couldn't find out what the project was about, a worst case must be considered.

Wright knew that would only cause their efforts to intensify. To dismiss the notion that the Americans were plotting their destruction, Wright devised a plan to defuse the concerted effort being made by both friend and foe.

Many intelligence services collaborate. There may even be deniable interaction channels with presumably hostile nations. The role and functions of the CIA are roughly comparable to those of the United Kingdom's Secret Intelligence Service, the SIS or MI6; the Canadian Security Intelligence Service; the Australian Secret Intelligence Service; the Russian Foreign Intelligence Service; the Indian Research and Analysis Wing; the Pakistani Inter-Services Intelligence; the French Foreign Intelligence Service; and Israel's Mossad.

General Wright arranged to meet with Great Britton's MI6 to offer an explanation and allay their concerns. By doing so he would also make certain the same story would be captured by the rest of the intelligence gatherers. Of course he knew his disclosure would be questioned, but at least all parties would learn the United States was not involved in a concealed plan that could threaten their stability. Disseminating disinformation was an important part of international relations. It was a perverse way of communicating, but it often turned out to be a good way to turn the heat down. His plan looked good on paper, but so did General George Armstrong Custer's.

* * *

"Good afternoon Mrs. Keebler. My name is Tony Clark. I work for Neiman Marcus. I'm calling to give you some good news. You have been selected to receive an all-expense paid familiarization trip to our new store in

California. Please give me just a moment longer to assure you this is a legitimate call." The Chinese spy had captured Liz's full attention.

"And a good afternoon to you, Mr. Clark."

"You are a very good customer of ours and based on your purchases, you will be an excellent choice to provide us your opinion of our newest location in Newport Beach." Clark heard Liz taking deep breaths while he was speaking.

"This is very exciting, Mr. Clark," Liz said, her voice noticeably trembling.

"I will make arrangements for you and a companion to travel first class to the coast where you will be our guest for three nights at the Newport Beach Ritz Carlton Hotel. There is nothing to buy because you already purchased a Dolce & Gabbana handbag last week at the Domain Mall in Austin. Does this help you to confirm this call is legitimate?" Clark's skill in manipulating weak people was on display.

"Oh my God, I can't believe my ears. I never win anything."

"Mrs. Keebler, I'm afraid you still haven't won anything. Neiman Marcus's is inviting you because of your loyalty to our company and your impeccable taste. Your opinion of our new store will greatly assist us. If you accept our invitation, I will have all the contact information along with airline tickets sent by Fed Ex to you tomorrow."

"When can we go, when can we go?"

"At your earliest convenience, Mrs. Keebler."

"Oh my goodness, thank you, thank you so much!"

"Thank you, Mrs. Keebler, and good day. I will speak to you after you review the materials I am sending to you." Clark was pleased with his performance. He hoped his boss would be also.

* * *

Max started feeling like the *ACCIDENT* had created a lot more questions than answers. Now that a potential result was proving to be successful in concept, the road ahead became obscured with questions concerning morality, decency, rule of law, fairness, responsibility, accountability, all that small stuff.

Since day one, there had been an "ends justify the means" mentality, just as Bud prophesied about the President's project at the outset. Like all men who put their heart and soul into their work, Max was having a difficult time seeing the forest for the trees. He decided the best way to overcome his concerns was to fly up to Indy and visit Father Bob.

* * *

For Catholic Priests the confidentiality of all statements made by penitents during the course of the Sacrament of Reconciliation is absolute. This strict confidentiality is known as the Seal of the Confessional. Priests, and anyone who witnesses or overhears the confession (an interpreter, caregiver, or aide to a disabled person), may not reveal what they have learned during confession to anyone, even under the threat of their own death or that of others.

"Bless me Father, for I have sinned, my last confession was during Lent last spring." Max was kneeling in the confessional box at St. Timothy's behind a dark screen where Father Bob was seated on the other side.

"Max, lies are sins, but sometimes people don't deserve the truth." Father Bob was providing dutiful guidance to Max after he made his confession. "Go in peace and sin no more."

* * *

"So you think we need to discuss this with others?" Max met Father Bob later that evening to ask him his opinion about his accidental discovery.

"Max, pragmatic solutions always create new problems. Too many scientists and engineers believe *truth* is what works. Solve the problem, and worry about the consequences later. That's the nature of Pragmatism. I can hear Pandora's Box opening. Yes. I strongly believe you need to assemble a panel of devil's advocates. Not just politicians, but perhaps other clergy. Recruit medical and legal experts. Patience is not permission, Max. I think you might be disobeying the first rule of holes; if you dig yourself into a hole, stop digging."

"I get it Bob, you're right."

"If these trials you're describing are successful, it is possible Sean could persuade the public to fully embrace your idea. But what you have disclosed to me will have lasting consequences. Indeed, your discovery could greatly impact nations and cultures. Genies are fickle creatures, Max. You let them out of their bottle and it's impossible to either get them back in or tell them how to behave. But I must admit this is different, very different." Father Bob spoke like a professor lecturing to a class of future Ph. Ds.

"Go on Bob." Max persuaded his friend to keep digging deeper into his predicament.

"At first glance it must be immoral; although I can't compare it to anything I've studied or read about in the past. It's difficult to predict exactly how the Church will weigh in; although I'm pretty sure you won't be receiving invites to the Vatican any time soon. But it seems to me no one should be able to have this kind of power, regardless of how noble the outcome. It may even be a form of rejecting God."

"A difficult problem and a mystery for sure," Max guessed.

"Max, getting to Mars is a problem. Falling in love is a mystery."

"You do that to me all the time, Dr. Dugan. I swear I'm going to take a basic course in philosophy one of these days just to keep from walking into these traps."

"Seriously Max, I know you live, breathe, eat, drink, and sleep science, but you need to take a step back every now and then. You must pause and observe the *limitations* of science. It cannot even answer the questions of a child: why am I here; where do I come from; what is the purpose of life? I believe Einstein put it brilliantly, 'You can speak of the ethical foundations of science, but you cannot speak of the scientific foundations of ethics.'"

"This is exactly why I flew up here, Bob. I knew you could help."

"That's why you need to get more critical eyes examining possible adverse and unintended consequences. In reality Max, there is nothing so beautiful as the good; there is nothing so ugly as evil. Truth is not contradictory. When we have rejected God, we are alienated from him and we are alienated from ourselves." Father Bob was now reaching deep into Max's questions and the philosopher in him was approaching full speed.

"A man is looking for meaning and pictures himself on a mountain in the company of the spirit of the age. He is enjoying some tasty food and calls it by its right name, but the rationalist and existentialist of the day ridicule him and call it something cursed. Then he comments on how delicious the milk is and they tell him milk is just the secretion of a cow, no different than its urine. The man did not know how to respond. After a few moments go by, *Reason* comes riding in on a horse and rescues him. As he goes riding away from the mountain, *Reason* turns around and says to the spirit of the age, you lie because you don't know the difference between what nature has meant for good and what nature has meant for garbage. Again, in reality Max, there is nothing so beautiful as the good, there is nothing so ugly as evil. Truth is not contradictory. That's true, that's real, Max." Father Bob stopped and walked over to shut his office door.

"But in our imagination we have reversed it. We have made good to become ugly and boring and we have made evil to become intriguing, attractive and full of charm. Good and evil are like the positive and negative poles of an electric current. You transpose them and darkness falls. That's why man is a stranger to himself today." Father Bob paused to ask Max if he understood.

"Yes, please go on Father." Father Bob could sense he may be baffling Max.

"From rejection of God he moves to separation from God. From separation he moves to domination. Now he has become a slave. Think of the many ways in which we sought to be free. Technology has freed us; industry has freed us; science has freed us; chemistry has freed us; art has freed us; education has freed us; and somehow we believe drugs are freeing us. We supposedly have broken a thousand tyrannies, and yet we may be referred to as restless and intoxicated with a sense of freedom; and freedom is not the same thing as autonomy." Father Bob paused again to make sure Max was still listening.

"Science today has given us improved means in order to attain some of our damnable ends. Many of our technologies have only made us more sophisticated in our evil. And yet we run and run and run and keep telling each other that somewhere around the corner is this utopia, and yet we deny the reality, live in fantasy, and say someday we will find this peace we want on Earth. And you look around us, from violence on the football field, to violence in airplanes, to violence in committee meetings, to violence on the battlefields of war; we are still struggling, denying reality, refusing to come to grips with the fact that God has diagnosed the problem; we are too possessed by ourselves. When we have rejected God, we are alienated from him, and we are alienated from ourselves."

"I don't know what to say Bob! I mean, that was beautiful. That kind of reminds me of the old Jewish guy who owned Fritz' drugstore, remember? He taught us if it's a good idea today, it will be a good idea tomorrow."

"Yep, that's exactly what I meant." Father Bob knew he had just taken Max into the deep end of the philosophical pool, and he drowned.

* * *

Exactly two years, four months, three days and fourteen hours later, results were being reported to President Curran almost daily. *If the moral, legal, ethical, secrecy, politics, and decency questions need not be considered, then The Company's solution might just be available in time for my re-election campaign*, the President employed wishful thinking. Solving political problems with creative technology was foreign to most policy makers, but President Curran was not the usual policy maker.

Los Angeles used to have a terrible smog problem. Too many cars were driving too many miles. In the early 1970s, the catalytic converter and unleaded gasoline were phased in for new cars and by the year 2010, there were almost no pre-1972 vehicles still on the road. Vehicles built with the catalytic converter and modern computer systems emit ninety-nine percent less pollutants per mile than the 1960s models. Technology and the phasing out of old vehicles that lacked this technology had solved this problem.

Traffic congestion was another political problem. Time-of-day toll roads could now be implemented and this "Smart Grid" technology advance would go a long way in reducing traffic congestion, as would time of day parking rates, so that parking prices would be higher during peak times and fall off-peak.

The ubiquitous cell phone made everyone a roaming reporter who could call 911 if an attack takes place, greatly reducing urban crime. People made videos and took photos and this made streets safer. Potential criminals knew that, due to this technology, they were more likely to be caught red handed.

The Company's progress was impressive by any measure. The discovery was gaining desired results. TC's team had served the President well. The finding they developed would surely be heralded as great news to all Americans. General Wright's security plan had so far evaded attempts by undesirables to uncover the secret project. *Too bad I can't rely on a single member of Congress to keep a secret. Thank goodness for General Wright*, the President thought. Any leak at this point would surely doom the project. His initiative offered the country a new opportunity to deal with this problem once and for all.

Sean knew if you had knowledge, you had the luxury to act rather than react. This new discovery would provide an abundance of knowledge. It was so simple. It was fair. It was just. And it was merciful. If TC's trials were successful, then once again it would be shown that technology can change people's behavior for the better.

When technologies establish reliability, they tend to be adopted. This is because human enterprises generally seek to improve because nobody likes to get worse at anything. Sean believed even those persons or organizations preferring to remain static in their use of technology may be forced to adapt to market or other forces, thereby adopting new tools or processes. P*eople involved in competitive enterprises are always trying to do things just a little bit better,* Sean thought.

In-store cameras have had a dramatic effect on robberies. Cameras placed at intersections and on roads made drivers more aware of speed limits. Computers could track social security numbers, fingerprints and DNA. *It was amazing how much technology has been created to focus on law breakers*, Sean continued his effort to justify TC's findings.

Unfortunately, technology won't make a crook honest. It won't cure hatred. It can't cause a person to become more kind. But every now and then a discovery comes along that saves people from the consequences of their poor decisions and reckless and selfish behavior.

Webster's Dictionary defines "solution" as a means of solving a problem or dealing with a difficult situation. At least at this point, the President's initiative could easily have been added to Webster's as an excellent example of a solution.

The design and development stage of Sean's directive ended. It was time to begin testing The Company's new finding. Secrecy had been maintained. The new creation performed well in the lab and Max, Bud and Jack were the only people on Earth who knew how to replicate the finding. The trials were scheduled to last for at least eleven months.

TC required this amount of time in order to gain the greatest number of results possible, but the President also needed more time to explain this solution to a public adverse to change. The Solution offered a quick and effective end to a problem that had divided political parties and the nation's citizens for decades. Sean needed to come to a decision when and how to make known his initiative. Maybe his best friend could help.

* * *

The *ACCIDENT*'s design and development stage lasted almost a year and trials might take at least another year, probably longer. Initial testing was met with a great degree of success. Since there were no moving parts, the team correctly postulated the discovery was either going to work as planned or fail entirely. But the accidental discovery performed flawlessly. What surprised Max, Jack and Bud most was it worked the same in every scenario. It didn't matter if different factors or conditions were present; it still provided the desired results. But funds were being rapidly depleted; it was time to hit-up

Cookie. Max had not spoken to or seen him for months.

* * *

"The less I know, the less they can beat out of me," Cookie said, insisting Max need not disclose any details to him.

"Great, then all I need from you is a check. Make that a big check."

"That shouldn't be a problem. All I have to do is mention the funds are for The Company and Robby will give away the farm. Sales of the next generation smartphone keep sky rocketing. I should skim a little for myself. My wife is ready to drag up. She won't stop ragging me about being gone so much. If I throw her a bone maybe I can buy some peace and quiet. Put what you need together and I'll take care of the paperwork, okay?"

"You know Cookie, one of these days you and I are going to fly to Catalina, jump on-board a hundred fifty-five footer, cruise to Cabo, and golf 'till we drop. We'll use the chopper on board to take us to some of the best courses on the planet. When we get through playing we'll fly back to the boat and pour ourselves some Beefeater on the rocks with blue cheese stuffed olives. Then we'll have the ship's cook serve up a half dozen fresh stone crabs while we watch the humpbacks breach. Maybe we will have her grill us a juicy porterhouse topped off with a bottle of Silver Oak while enjoying the sunset. Sound like a good way to kill a month?" Max asked Cookie while licking his lips.

* * *

The verification and testing phase of The Company's Presidential initiative was underway. Security as usual was on everyone's mind. General Wright reminded Max, Jack and Bud to remain vigilant when leaving the confines of the lab. Wright believed the heat was turned down to low after his briefing with the Brits had gone so well. His CIA contact reported no worrisome activities.

Test platforms were being acquired during the first months of this vitally important step. The lab inventoried enough samples to last throughout the verification and testing stage.

General Wright had been a part of too many operations, both overt and covert, to ever feel completely comfortable even under the most benign of circumstances. There was no reason to believe anyone but The Company's principals had full knowledge of the project. If this was true, only those three men would be of interest to the enemy; the enemy he was referring to in this case would be anyone except Max, Bud and Jack.

Wright didn't know, nor did he want or need to know, any of the project's details. Certain that the President received briefings from Max, the General figured that would be the concern of the Secret Service, not his. Reports coming from his intelligence sources confirmed all the usual suspects were mobilized, but as of this moment, his security plan was functioning as intended. It was the next moment he was concerned about.

* * *

Abraham Lincoln was the first U.S. President to be assassinated; James Garfield, William McKinley and

John F. Kennedy were also assassinated while in office. Andrew Jackson, Harry Truman, Gerald Ford and Ronald Reagan all survived assassination attempts. For these and many other reasons, a President's visitor will not just be noticed, but will also be frisked and photographed prior to coming into contact with the nation's chief executive. The presidential press corps is on hand twenty-four/seven reporting on and observing everyone and everything moving in and out of the White House. The President's second residence at Camp David is less overwhelming, but still a presidential visitor is likely to be identified either immediately upon arrival, or shortly afterwards.

President Curran strictly avoided meeting face-to-face with Max. Any contact could send up a red flag. There were too many eyes watching Sean's every move. The President and his family are given round-the-clock protection by the Secret Service. If the President or any of his family members so much as cracked a window open to allow in a little fresh air, either a prying camera in the hands of the press or paparazzi or the Secret Service would be recording their every move.

"Stay close to me and don't speak to anyone," General Wright instructed Max. The two made their way into the White House through an entrance known only to a small number of people, mostly high ranking military officers.

"Good evening, your highness." Bowing at the waist and pretending he was tipping a medieval hat, Max greeted his best friend.

"Forty thousand professional comedians looking for work and I've got to listen to this? Okay, smartass cut the crap. I need your advice." Sean greeted Max by shaking hands with his best friend.

"You know Sean, John Kennedy proved you

didn't need to be a Protestant to be elected President. LBJ proved you didn't need to be from the North to be elected president. Nixon proved you didn't have to be honest to be President. Jerry Ford proved you didn't even need to be elected to be President, and Jimmy Carter proved we don't need a President."

"That's real funny. Is that all you got? Thanks for the horseshit. Max, I'm starting to feel like a dog that caught a fire truck. It sounds like your trials are going well. General Wright tells me the lid is still tightly on the project. But I'm racking my brain trying to figure out how to break the news when the time comes. I know my opponents are going to have a field day regardless. If I were introducing a cure for the common cold they would still excoriate me. I know that. It's my friends I'm worried about."

"Sean, you should get some other eyes on this now! Get your inner sanctum on board first. Then take the next step. Mr. President this is going to be controversial even if it works perfectly. If it doesn't, either way, you'll be up that proverbial creek without the proper means of locomotion. My guess is your Cabinet will be more pissed about not being told in advance, not because your initiative either worked or didn't. Time is still on our side. I can arrange for a tour of the facility."

"You sound like one of those drug commercials that air during Jeopardy. We're given two reasons to take the medicine and nineteen reasons how it may kill you.

"Max, you remember when we were flying back from Vegas in your old airplane, the Bonanza? You let me fly from the left seat. I remember this like it was yesterday." Sean stopped when Max interrupted.

"I remember, it was severe clear that day," Max added.

"Yup. We were coming up on the Rockies south of Grand Junction at fourteen thousand feet. I told you it looked like we weren't going to be able to make it across the mountain range. Like a smartass you asked—"

"You're not going to crash into them are you?" Both men asked the same question in unison.

"Yeah, well, I felt like slugging you in the mouth. I thought what an asshole. I'm serious and you're cracking wise. So maybe I should take your advice again."

"What a coincidence. I talked to Father Bob the other night. I asked his advice about a similar problem. He basically gave me the same answer I just gave you," Max replied.

"Tell me you didn't," Sean blurted out.

"Of course not, Sean!" Max knew he hadn't actually lied to his best friend, but was sure he was guilty of a serious sin of omission. After all, he told Cookie about Sean's initiative, not Father Bob; even though the funds were going to be used for the *ACCIDENT.* Max told Father Bob about the *ACCIDENT.*

"That's all I need is for this thing to leak out. Talk about up shit creek without a paddle; the next time you'd see me, I'd have a king size piece of my ass missing." Sean grabbed the back of his pants with both hands. "So when are you leaving?"

"I'm going to be gone the week of February 17th. Junior and I are headed bill fishing with Doc and Mike. We'll be in Costa Rica, but the lodge is on the Pacific coast and it looks to be pretty remote. I'm not sure cell phones will work." Max's delivered his answer in a way he hoped Sean would realize he didn't want to be interrupted while away with his son and friends.

"Not to worry, I'll get you a satellite phone just in

case my hair catches on fire." This wasn't the answer Max wanted to hear.

* * *

Liz Keebler scheduled her trip to California. She invited her friend Lois Austin to join her. The two women arrived at the Ritz Carlton Newport Beach. Their room overlooked the opulent Newport Beach Marina. A welcome bouquet of beautiful white roses and a luxurious fruit basket full of fresh California grown fruit and nuts greeted them in their fifteen hundred square foot two bedroom suite. The card attached to a chilled bottle of Salon 1995 read, "Welcome to Newport Beach, enjoy your Neiman Marcus experience and sunny southern California. Please meet me in the lobby at 5 p.m. for cocktails." It was signed Tony Clark, Development Manager.

Information Liz received from Clark before she left Texas instructed her to tell no one the reason she and Lois were in the area. Clark told Liz she would be a mystery shopper. Her assignment involved strolling through the store, visiting the departments she and Lois most enjoyed. Her responsibilities ended with providing Clark daily reports on how she was treated and how the new location compared to her other favorite department stores.

In return, Liz not only received all her expenses paid while in California, but she was also provided with a $1000 per day expenditure to purchase any items she desired. She had to agree to spend at least one hour each evening alone with Neiman Marcus representatives. Liz agreed to all the requirements before being provided first class round trip airline tickets for both her and Lois.

TELL NO ONE OF YOUR MISSION was her final order.

Clark met Liz and Lois shortly after they checked in per his instructions. *These two broads are exactly alike, narcissistic,self-centered bitches. This is going to be like drowning baby chickens*, Clark observed.

* * *

"General Wright, I demand you tell us what the hell you're up to. That song and dance we heard last year was just that. We know the Chinese have moved assets in and you can be sure the Russians are doing the same." The MI6 Assistant Director for North American Affairs lodged his complaint because of the considerable intelligence he was receiving pointing to increased troublesome activities.

"Sir, you must tell me from whom you are acquiring your intelligence. First of all, the briefing you received last September was accurate. Nothing has changed," General Wright began his reply, comfortable he was speaking with someone who clearly lacked experience in operational matters.

"General—." The Director was interrupted by Wright.

"Excuse me sir, allow me to finish. The project is a homeland initiative as I reported. I repeat; nothing has changed nor will it. Sir, please enlighten me. Why do you take the position a sovereign nation is required to divulge its secrets to you or anyone? If I were to demand classified information about your country's internal activities, I would expect you to tell me to kiss your ass," General Wright replied in a commanding voice.

"General, you're going to be blindsided if you cut

us out of the picture. I only called to warn you and express our desire to help."

"I sincerely appreciate your offer and will respectfully take it under advisement. In the meantime, our country will greatly appreciate any foreknowledge you can provide. I think we've all got what we need here." He hung up after the two bid farewell, but Wright knew he needed to call an audible.

* * *

Being Vice President is like the last cookie on the plate, nobody wants it, but it's always taken. President Curran decided to disclose his closely guarded initiative first to his Vice President. Dennis Bly hailed from Florida. He was elected to the Florida Legislature before successfully gaining a U. S. Senate seat from the state. After serving two terms in the Senate, Bly made a failed attempt for the Presidency. He finished fourth in a field of six candidates running in the primary election. He was popular among Hispanics, so choosing him for a running mate was a smart decision on Curran's part. The two men were not at all close. Like Sean, Bly was an experienced politician, but unlike Sean, Bly was extremely cautious. The President was certain his revelation would be met with great trepidation.

"Mr. President, I do wish you would have informed me about this at the outset. I don't see how I can help you now. I thought…" Sean interrupted him.

"Yes, I understand fully. But I'm sure you recall frequently listening to me speak about my background in creative technologies during the campaign. I have complete confidence in my colleagues at Solutions and, quite frankly, I believe my judgment now offers us an outstanding chance to solve this problem. I intend to brief the Cabinet and members of the House and Senate Intelligence Committees, but at this point secrecy is still vital. This will remain between the two of us, okay Dennis?" He purposely showed his respect for the office of the Vice President, but Sean also knew it was Bly's sworn duty not to divulge state secrets. *I hope this former legislator can keep a secret*, he thought.

* * *

Mrs. Keebler met Tony Clark and his associate Paula Sims in the lobby bar at the Ritz Carlton after she finished her first day's duties as a mystery shopper. Tony and Paula acted happy to hear she had not only expended the entire $1000 provided by Neiman Marcus, but also informed them she spent at least another $1000 of her own money. Liz bragged to the two spies that her husband made lots of money and she was sure he wouldn't mind. Her remark provided the perfect opening for the two experienced professionals.

"So what kind of work does your husband do that allows us to count you among our best customers?" Sims' question was intended to allow her partner a follow-up question in order to make Liz as comfortable as possible with their interrogation; an interrogation Liz had no idea was taking place.

"He travels way too much for one thing, but he's worked for Integra Corporation for over thirty years. He's one of the big shots there." Both Clark and Sims could clearly see she was bragging.

"I talk to Alf dozens of times each day," Clark exclaimed.

"Does he have anything to do with my new best

friend Alf," Paula asked in a playful tone.

"I don't think so. He spends most of his time traveling. That's how I met him. After we got married he took me everywhere, but now he travels alone. I wouldn't mind if his trip were to Peoria or Atlanta, but he goes to some great places. We met in the Cayman Islands." Liz was still bragging.

The briefing continued. Clark and Sims knew they had accomplished their first day's goal of bonding with her. Getting the information they desired would likely be easier than they thought possible.

Chapter 9

Can This Work?

The Cabinet Room is the meeting place for the cabinet secretaries and advisors serving the President of the United States. It is located in the West Wing of the White House Complex, adjoining the Oval Office and looks out upon the White House Rose Garden. White House police sealed off the room and only those invited to the briefing were welcomed.

The President provided details of The Company's discovery and why he kept his initiative secret. Shocked and stunned faces listen intently. Never before had any of these seasoned politicians and policy makers heard such a bizarre tale. Yes, they all recalled Curran the candidate calling for technological solutions to difficult problems and yes, they were familiar with his background in research and development, but this was not just off the reservation stuff; this bordered on science fiction.

President Curran continued his copious report. Before he began, he asked the panel to hold their questions until he finished, but that didn't stop some of the loyal opposition from interrupting his presentation.

"You can't, you must not," complained the House Minority Leader. "If it looks like a duck and quacks like a duck. It's big brother. It's 1935 Nazi Germany being replayed. Don't tell us this is good for America."

"Mr. President, even though the trials are performing brilliantly as you suggest, have you considered unforeseen and unintended consequences?" Sean had invited the Chairman of the Joint Chiefs of Staff so he could ask tough questions. So far Sean wasn't disappointed in him. "Have you considered how our enemies might react? Have you considered how our *friends* might react?"

"Mr. President, have we not learned anything from recent history. It's the cover-up, not the crime. Kennedy's Bay of Pigs; Johnson's Vietnam secrets; Nixon of course; Reagan's Iran Contra and Clinton's scandal—won't we ever learn?" The Senate Minority Leader asked Sean this rhetorical question while pointing his finger at him.

Sean began thinking he may have severely screwed up by not lining up the needed support before moving forward with his initiative. Glancing at his Vice President didn't offer him any solace. He knew Dennis opposed the idea the night he disclosed the plan to him.

My plan is dead, he thought. Many of Sean's favorite truisms flashed in his mind.

Courage is fear that has said its prayers. A man without courage is like a knife without an edge. Think what you think, not what they think. Everyone is trying to push; don't be pushed. Don't let your critics determine your agenda. It's better to shun the bait than struggle in the snare. Never take a hostage you're not prepared to shoot. The bitterest tears shed over graves are for words left unsaid and deeds left undone. And then it hit him. *A good leader is not the person who does things right, but the one who finds the right things to do!*

Just then a voice beckoned from the far end of the

massive conference table.

"Listen please. I know of no jurisdiction issuing driving permits to the blind. Nor do alcoholics make good bartenders, and we for sure don't let our enemies dictate how we should act. Nothing is being taken away from a single citizen," cried the Speaker of the House. "The definition of insane is when you continue doing the same thing over and over while expecting different results. That has been our policy since this problem first surfaced."

"Medically speaking, I have no objection. I am not going to weigh in on the morality though." The Surgeon General put in his two cents worth.

"Do we continue wasting billions and billions of dollars? This harms nobody. This helps everybody. This is the solution. If you don't like change, you are going to like irrelevance even less." The Senate Pro Tem directed his comment at the Minority Leader.

"It's not often I agree with my esteemed colleague, especially on matters of morality, but I believe we should seriously examine this idea." The President sat still trying not to appear utterly surprised and pleased when the Minority Whip made this comment.

"What's a more moral choice, do nothing or take advantage of this technology to address a problem that will benefit many more people than the affected?" Vice President Bly began asking political questions. "If we don't act when we could have, we will have to answer to the American people and explain why we chose to do nothing."

The President could not hold back a smile. *I was wrong about Dennis. I was wrong about the way I approached this initiative; well maybe not*, Sean thought, and finally spoke up.

"This technology may offer us a solution to a problem my four predecessors have been trying to solve with zero success. Tomorrow is the devil's favorite word. We all know the crisis will only grow. Let's not be afraid to go out on a limb; isn't that where the fruit is? If trials succeed, and it appears at this point they will, I intend to announce the discovery to the American people and ask Congress to enact enabling legislation. In the meantime, it is vitally important the program remain top secret. Your oath requires you to comply with my order, but I ask you sincerely to please honor my request. We can all see this plan will not be without its detractors. Indeed, we may all learn it is not a suitable solution. In any moment of decision the best thing you can do is the right thing, the second best thing is the wrong thing, and the worst thing you can do is nothing. For the sake of our beloved country, may we all proceed forward with the best interest of the United States of America? We must make our decisions, and then our decisions turn around and make us."

* * *

"I ordered both men to stop. One of them ran toward the door, but the other turned toward Tess. I spotted the weapon then fired immediately." Dom calmly and succinctly described events to the investigating officer.

"I don't know, I don't know. I thought he was going to kill me." Tess was unable to stop crying.

"I've never seen either of the men here before. We rarely have strangers coming into the building. That's what caught my attention. I spotted the two as they were walking out of the stairway door, right over there."

Pointing at the main entryway, Dom moved to the spot where he was illustrating the events that took place less than twenty minutes earlier.

"When did they enter the lobby?" One of the detectives asked.

"I have no idea how they got into the building. I know they didn't sign the register. When I asked one of them for identification, both men clearly became nervous. I instructed Tess to contact the police. That's when they both started running and one of them made the move toward Tess and drew a concealed weapon." Dom continued to confidently explain everything he had observed to the two investigators assigned to the case.

The dead man had been shot once in the heart. Dom fired off one round from his Arcus 98DA, a double action semi-automatic pistol. Police found nothing which could identify the body, and there was no sign of his accomplice's whereabouts, but the investigation had just begun.

Bud immediately contacted General Wright. The Company was crawling with Austin police. The dead man was taken to an undisclosed site. Maggie called Father Bob to tell him about the incident since her boss was still airborne on his way to Indianapolis. Father Bob picked up Max at Mount Comfort Airport, the nearest airport to St. Timothy's. He immediately reported the episode. Max spent the rest of the afternoon getting more details and trying to comfort his employees, especially Tess.

Max was flying to Indy to meet with a group of distinguished men in order to get their reaction to the *ACCIDENT*, just as Father Bob had suggested earlier. He and Father Bob were going to have dinner at the Rectory with The Reverend Daniel Young, Archbishop of

Indianapolis; Reverend Michael Leep, former President of Notre Dame University; the former Governor of Indiana Marc Lockhart; and Ed Martin, a successful Indianapolis businessman turned Deacon in the Catholic Church.

After the chef and servers completed their duties and departed the Rectory, Father Bob asked Max to begin. Each man agreed beforehand to keep the discussion confidential. Since Father Bob had hand-picked the panel, there was no chance of the *ACCIDENT* being compromised.

“I must say, I don’t know how I feel. I need time to allow this to sink in.” Archbishop Young began speaking first after Max completed his report.

“You say you have tested this so-called accident and the results were successful?” Ed Martin, the businessman turned deacon, seemed to be intensely intrigued when he questioned Max.

“Is it just me, or does this scream of men playing God?” Father Leep protested in an aggressive tone.

“Father, please enlighten me. On what grounds do you think this immoral?” Governor Lockhart respectfully asked Father Leep to further explain his objections.

“Max, you keep calling it the accident; please tell us more about this characterization.” Hoping to bring calm to the room, Father Bob interrupted the two men who were getting a little too antagonistic.

It was after 2 a.m. when the session ended. The men were thoroughly exhausted; their minds still racing as they departed the Rectory. Max and Father Bob stayed up most of the night discussing the comments, questions and criticisms made by the invited devil’s advocates.

Surprisingly, the prestigious panel agreed in principle; Max should continue development. There were of course still moral, ethical and operational questions to address. Max assured the attendees that the plan was in its adolescence stages. But he was pleased and relieved he had taken Father Bob's sage advice.

"Thanks again, Bob. I'm leaving for Costa Rica, but when I return, if you don't mind, I'll be back to pick your brain some more, okay?"

"Be safe on your journey, but remember, Max, your prejudices will distort your perception. After the game, the King and the Pawn go into the same box."

"I didn't get enough sleep last night to even begin to grasp what the hell you mean by that philosophical nugget, Bob."

"It means I want you, Max Jr., and your friends to have a safe and fun fishing trip."

"Real funny! I'm glad my confessor is also a comedian."

Max, your *ACCIDENT* may indeed be a solution to this horrible problem, but be certain your goal is to make the world a better place; not just a better place to be in the world. Because when it's over, we will all receive the same perfect justice."

* * *

With the *ACCIDENT*'s trials nearly completed, only one hurdle remained. None of the team succeeded in uncovering an answer to this nagging problem. It was a deal killer. Unless an answer was found, the vitally important accidental discovery could die a natural death.

Jack gravitated to his geeky friend's house hoping he could once again obtain an eleventh hour solution. He saw Dennis was at home and figured he was most likely involved in his usual strange activities, which always included torturing some species of insect. Reinbold had been working for years to find a cure for prostate cancer. *Why he experimented with bugs was anyone's guess*, Jack thought. It didn't matter to Jack what Dennis was trying to accomplish. He knew one day he would likely succeed because Reinbold's mind was the most potent Jack ever had the pleasure of taking advantage of. After all, that's why he was here, to once again call on his old friend to make him a hero.

Jack parked his car at the curb in front of Reinbold's house. *Strange, most homeless people in Austin hang out at busy intersections. This guy is working in the middle of a residential neighborhood*, he thought, as he crossed the street to throw a dollar into a panhandler's hat.

* * *

Bud inspected several properties that could serve as a suitable site for a lab to begin testing the *ACCIDENT*. He chose an innocuous looking building in a neighborhood business center, located at Steiner Ranch in the Texas Hill Country. Since there would be considerable activity at the site, Max suggested the operation take on the appearance of a for-profit learning center. A sign advertising "technical training now in session" would be posted outside the seven thousand square foot storefront at the suburban Austin strip mall.

Max was thankful he escaped the site selection process, but it was his responsibility to set up security. After completing this unpleasant task he noticed a panhandler loitering near the entry of the business next door. *If I didn't know better, I'd think that bum is casing our new office*, Max mused.

"If only I were king." As he eyeballed the vagrant, Max couldn't help express his sardonic feelings out loud.

Chapter 10

Unintended Consequences

Crocodile Bay Resort is located on Costa Rica's South Pacific Coast, which has been referred to by National Geographic Magazine as "The Most Ecologically Intense Place on Earth." It is also where the edge of Costa Rica's largest coastal rainforest meets the pacific. Maximum landing weight for an F-15E Strike Eagle is forty-four thousand pounds. The max landing weight for a TBM 850 is seven thousand, twenty-four pounds. Cyclops had no difficulty painting the TBM onto the centerline of the narrow, twenty-seven hundred foot runway at Puerto Jimenez Airport. The airport was cut out of the jungle adjacent to the Crocodile Bay fishing lodge. The flight took almost five hours as Max had flight planned. The airstrip was deserted. A small building with a fuel pump was the only sign of civilization after the plane descended below the tree tops.

"Way to keep the score even, boys. Same amount of landings as takeoffs." Cyclops and Shot split flying duties on the way down to their destination, so Doc tactfully congratulated the two fighter pilots.

"Look at all the monkeys," Mike Jr. said, pointing to a troop of spider monkeys in the jungle surrounding the runway.

"They taste like chicken," his dad replied.

"This is a good sign; here comes the cavalry right on time. Let's get this stuff off the bird and start having some F U N." Already grabbing the luggage, Max spelled the word fun out loud when he saw the hotel's transport approaching.

* * *

"Mr. President, we have a problem." The President's secure phone line rang in with news General Wright hoped he'd never have to report. Wright proceeded to provide an up-to-date briefing on events.

President Curran realized the toothpaste was out of the tube. The Israelis claimed they were not attempting to blackmail the United States in order to obtain the information, but it didn't matter. His initiative was no longer a secret.

Sean was acutely aware that in politics, especially presidential politics, as the Senate Minority leader correctly affirmed in the Cabinet Room just days earlier, the cover-up was always worse than the crime. Curran must now go to the American people with his plan. The trials were not complete, but data was proving The Company's discovery could be an acceptable solution to the daunting problem.

* * *

General Wright waited in the Oval Office. The President entered the room accompanied by Bill Clemens, U. S. Ambassador to Israel. Clemens and the President just conducted a secure call with the Israeli Defense Minister. Noticeably upset, Sean sat down at his desk and instructed the Ambassador to brief General Wright.

"Mr. President, over the years I've learned quite a lot from these people. We all know how capably their military operates. I'm upset with myself more than I'm upset with them. I would have recommended the same coarse had our roles been reversed." Keeping in character, General Wright offered his standard reply if someone, anyone, acted the same way he would have.

"They made a good case for obtaining the formula. I agree our situation pales in comparison to theirs. I'm inclined to take them up on their offer. But Bill, I want you to let them know how utterly pissed off I am and that their actions will not be without consequences." Sean already developed a strategy, even though his comments sounded as if he was seeking advice.

"I understand, Mr. President. I don't think I'm going out on a limb here to say I'm sure the Defense Minister is painfully aware of your dissatisfaction. I've met with him on many occasions, but never have I seen him at a loss for words," Clemens replied.

"General, between you and me, I hope we get a chance to pull off the same move they did. I'd get a great deal of pleasure watching them squirm as much as I had to. But, we need to move on. I'll brief the Vice President. General, you handle the detour, okay?" Standing up, shaking his head, Sean moved toward the door confident his orders would be carried out.

"Roger that Mr. President," General Wright replied.

"Bill, stay on top of things okay?"

"Count on it, Mr. President," Clemens replied.

* * *

"But how?" Max snapped, as he interrupted Bud.

"The Israelis; they know about the President's project. General Wright said they are threatening to go public unless the information is shared with them. You better sit down. We should have seen this coming. In hindsight it stuck out like a sore thumb."

"What are you talking about?" Wondering if his betrayal had anything to do with it, Max asked Bud, hoping he was wrong.

"Cookie's wife Liz, the Israelis somehow got the secret from her. Cookie must have told her about the project, but how in the hell did Cookie know?"

"Unbelievable!" Realizing he guessed correctly, Max mumbled.

"According to a briefing I just received from General Wright, the Israeli's were successful, but the Chinese failed. Evidently Cookie told her about the initiative and then used the project as his excuse for being gone so often. The Chinese shuttled Liz off to California so they could wine and dine her and a friend. According—," Bud was interrupted when he heard Max f-bombing.

"Is the narcissistic bitch okay? I feel sorry for the poor bastard that had to deal with her." Max's question was rhetorical. He was seething from Bud's revelation.

"According to the CIA, both countries were trying to obtain the same information. The Chinese weren't successful, but the Jews are a determined bunch. Even though they were asked to back off months ago, Mossad agents were able to get enough information from her to threaten going public unless details were provided. Wright is working on how to take this detour now. But how in God's name did Cookie know?"

"Unfortunately I can answer that. I told him."

"What the fuck! I thought we agreed…." Bud began asking, but Max stopped him in mid-sentence.

"I know. I know. I'm sorry, but you'll have to trust me for now. I'll explain everything later. Remember what happened on the Saudi project? It's sort of like that."

"Wow! Okay, I understand. It never fails. Murphy's Law, if it can go wrong it will." Bud recalled his reason for divulging sensitive information while working on a secret project in Saudi Arabia years earlier. "I get it." *Max must have a really good reason to make the Saudi comparison*, Bud thought. "They can't possibly know can they?"

"No way! But we need to do some damage control. Can we confirm only the three of us still have the information? Let's not tell Jack about this yet. He's way too emotionally involved in the project." Max was determined to keep the *ACCIDENT* known only to the three of them.

"We'll be back on Tuesday. Hold down the fort, partner." Speaking from his cell phone in Costa Rica, Max continued swearing out loud.

"Expect a call from Wright. He's got a severe case of the ass, so be careful," Bud warned.

"Roger that. I wouldn't want to be in the same room with him right about now."

"That makes two of us. Try and enjoy the rest of your trip."

* * *

"Do we know how they intend to use the

technology?" Speaking from Crocodile Bay over the secure satellite phone provided to him by the President, Max questioned General Wright about the breach he knew he was responsible for.

"The Israelis obtained enough information to determine that it would provide their country with a much needed weapon to combat a similar situation in America. Their problem presents even greater challenges. That's why the President believes we should make the actual blueprints available, and allow them to begin deployment at their discretion." Max could tell Bud was right. The General sounded thoroughly pissed off about the breach in his security plan. *There is no way I'm fessing up to this right now*, Max thought.

"Look, if the solution is truly a viable option to combat this problem in the United States, surely it will provide the same results anywhere. Besides, once we have announced the discovery, why not take advantage of the opportunity to have them help us to verify that it works?" Max understood Sean's strategy and was confident General Wright agreed.

"The President needs to move on this soon. He believes the only way to avoid a damaging diplomatic crisis is to acquiesce to their wishes. They were careful not to issue an ultimatum. But if the President believes there are good reasons to share the new technology—if the Israelis agree to keep the project secret for now— that suits me just fine," General Wright was relieved his role was nearly complete as he wrapped up his briefing.

"Jack is the best man for the job. He understands all facets of the project and can spend the necessary time with the Israelis to safeguard they have all the essential procedures in place." Max hoped Wright would agree so he could try to enjoy his fishing trip with his son and the

Glass'; uninterrupted.

"Very well. Let's make it happen." The General's answer was a relief.

* * *

Both juniors caught their limit each day while Doc and Max, as usual, did more relaxing than fishing. Max Jr. pulled in the largest, a four hundred and sixty-seven pound Blue Marlin. The four arrived back at the lodge near sunset on the fifth day of their excursion. The front desk attendant informed Max he needed to go to the airstrip because of a report he received about an airplane that may have been vandalized. It would take Max less than a ten minute ride in a golf cart to arrive at the parked and tied down TBM.

"You guys sit tight. I'll be back in a few. It's probably local kids being curious, and hopefully it's not our plane anyway," Max told the three men.

"We're coming with you." Mike Jr. stood up at the same time Max Jr. was telling his dad the two were going to accompany him.

"There's only one golf cart. One of you would have to hang on the back. The cart might not make it there and back with all that weight. Just hang in here, I'll be right back. Have a cold Heineken waiting, okay?" Max barked his order while walking out the door. He noticed there were two golf carts, but one was the groundskeeper's stocked with tools, so he didn't bother telling the boys.

Max jumped on the hotel's transport cart and made his way through the moonlit darkness. When he arrived at the airstrip he could see the silhouette of the TBM parked next to two smaller planes. The entire airstrip was deserted, quiet, and dark.

Max parked the vehicle about thirty feet from the flight line in order to be certain he wouldn't accidently run it into the any of the parked planes. He made his way to the passenger side of the TBM with the help of a small but powerful flash light. Just as he was about to stick the key into the plane's door lock, a pair of lights shone directly at him.

For reasons Max would never figure out, he instantly started running back toward the golf cart. He could hear footsteps chasing after him at the same pace. Believing he would be caught if he tried to board the cart, he continued running, too frightened to yell for help. Suddenly he heard a man cry out in pain, then another cry, clearly coming from a different man. The next sound he heard caused him to halt instantly.

"It's okay pop." Max Jr. shouted out while he and Mike Jr. ran to catch up with Max. Max was already on his golf cart heading toward them, pointing his light on the two fighter pilots.

"Let's get out of here," Max shouted, instructing the two boys to climb on the cart.

"You go, our cart's right behind you," Mike Jr. jumped on their cart and began following Max as Max Jr. directed him to keep his eyes peeled for more trouble.

The three made it back to the lodge safely. Max instructed the hotel manager to immediately contact the police. Mike Sr. was in the bar waiting for their return.

"Mike and I thought we should make sure nothing funny was going on, so we followed you. The groundskeeper's cart was available, so we just hopped on. We tried to catch up with you, but ours was too slow. As soon as we pulled up we noticed lights come on and saw two men walking toward you. When you started running we both grabbed whatever we could get our hands on and took off toward you." Max Jr.'s voice sounded strained since his heart was still racing.

"Remind me to never mess with you, badass." Doc was still trying to figure what happened in the span of less than twenty-five minutes when Mike Jr. ribbed his best friend.

"Mess with me hell. I just tripped my guy with a rake and kicked him in the head, but you may have broken your dude's fricken neck. I clearly heard bones cracking. Mike smacked the guy on his head with a garden shovel." He was laughing, but Max Jr.'s belly wasn't shaking as he described his version of events. All three were still noticeably shaken from the ordeal.

"What, do I have stupid written on my forehead?" Doc asked. "If you two were Marines, I might buy into this bullshit, but come on; you're Air Force fighter pilots. You drop bombs and fly your hundred million dollar jets back to the Officers Club to brag about it. Bartender, you need to get us another round. I've been shit by experts, and you guys are no experts."

The local police arrived in less than fifteen minutes, but found no traces of the two would-be attackers or the vehicle which alerted both Jr.s of the situation. Max provided as much information as he could recall. He omitted describing the two fierce fighter pilots' involvement. Cyclops and Shot were all too familiar with how things were done differently out of the United States, since both were deployed to Afghanistan with their respective fighter squadrons. Max also thought it important to report the incident to General Wright.

The four fishermen decided to cut their stay short by one day. Doc didn't need much more convincing after Max's police report. They had all the happiness they could take. But this fishing trip would be one they never forget. Max didn't say a word about his suspicions. He was certain the men were not at all interested in the plane; they were after him. But since they failed, was anyone close to Max safe? The Quinn family reunion was only a month away. He needed to disclose his fears to all his loved ones.

Max and Doc split the return leg to Austin. The fishing was tremendous and the Crocodile Bay Resort exceeded their expectations, but all four were relieved to be home. Abby served up another of her specialties and both Mikes departed the airpark early the next morning. The four decided they would return to Alaska for their next fishing adventure two years from now.

* * *

Dennis Reinbold took a plastic grocery bag filled with garbage to a trash can in his back yard. Immediately after daily Mass, Father Bob headed to his car holding the Blessed Sacrament, which he would be distributing to several of his parishioners living in a senior citizen center near the Church.

As Reinbold was putting the lid on his outdoor trash can that was sitting next to his unattached garage, two men snuck up behind him. One man slipped a sackcloth bag over Reinbold's head while the other grabbed him by the legs, causing him to knock the trash can over when he kicked it with one of his feet. A third man pulled a cargo van up to the garage door. The two men lifted Reinbold into the back of the van where a fourth man was waiting to inject him with Propofol. The abduction took less than fifteen seconds.

Father Bob opened the garage door only to

discover two masked men with weapons pointed at him. A third man followed him into the garage and immediately covered the priest's head before he could make any appeal for help. A cargo van backed up to the garage. As soon as Father Bob was lifted into the back of the van, another kidnapper injected him with Propofol, immediately rendering him unconscious.

MOIS, The Ministry of Intelligence and National Security of the Islamic Republic of Iran's Secret Police was responsible for the abductions of Father Bob and Dennis Reinbold.

The two men were taken to a remote location outside of St Louis, Missouri. Each of them remained blindfolded and sedated while being transported by van to the Iranian safe-house. The spies kept their nationality and location of the hideout unknown to either victim.

The Iranian's first interrogation session of the two men yielded nothing. Reinbold insisted he could not recall anything he and Jack discussed at their meetings. Reinbold was not purposely trying to withhold any information. He hadn't taken his meds for over three days. Father Bob however was steadfast in his refusal to violate his vow of silence. The spies believed he possessed the information they needed. There was a problem though, the information Father Bob possessed was not the information they were seeking.

When the next interrogation session began, Father Bob watched the man he just met a day earlier being injected with a needle containing a drug meant to get him to divulge information to his captors. Father Bob knew he would be next.

Iranian intelligence's infrastructure was not at all sophisticated. A truth drug or truth serum is a psychoactive medication used to obtain information from subjects who are unable or unwilling to provide it, and is classified as a form of torture according to international law.

* * *

"Father Bob may be in trouble," Max told the President. "I've been trying to reach him for the last two days. I spoke with the grade school principal. He told me they have searched everywhere, but when he couldn't be found they finally called the police and reported him missing. The police were required to wait at least twenty-four hours before a missing person case could be officially opened. Once the police finally got involved they discovered signs of foul play around the Rectory's garage. We can't ignore your initiative as a reason for his disappearance." *What have I done*? Max thought.

Sean was shaken by the news. He immediately ordered his Chief of Staff to notify the FBI Director and summoned General Wright. *Why would anyone want to harm Father Bob,* the President thought?

* * *

"I don't understand General, are you telling me people's lives may be in danger?"

"Mr. President, I have to consider that possibility. Max may be right. Your friend's company is responsible for the discovery of extremely sensitive munitions. America's enemies, as well as our friends, will go to great lengths to obtain any information they believe might provide greater security against a new weapon. I would act the same under similar conditions."

"I still don't get it. Solutions is a small company

made up of a bunch of overachieving scientists and engineers. Who could possibly want to bring harm to any of them?" Scratching his head in disbelief, Sean thought to himself, *all I wanted to do is keep this a secret so some Congressman wouldn't shoot his mouth off trying to impress a good looking lobbyist.*

"Mr. President, this is my fault. The Company discovered the bunker busting bomb and several other highly effective weapons. I didn't consider the degree Solution's reputation as a purveyor of new weapons technology would have on this project. I simply discounted their record of achievements, even though they were clearly described in the dossier."

"General, I doubt the result would have been different. You had an almost impenetrable shield over the project from the outset. We can fix this. Let's get back to work." Sean believed the General was being too critical of himself.

* * *

Max, Bud, and Jack sat in a state of confusion; the break-in and shooting at The Company, the incident in Costa Rica, and now this. Max confessed he asked Father Bob his opinion about the *ACCIDENT.* Both Bud and Jack understood after he explained his motive. In an odd way, they were gratified the panel of "devil's advocates" weighed-in. But now they had to deal with a missing Father Bob and the possibility the *ACCIDENT* may be in jeopardy of being compromised.

Jack rushed over to Reinbold's house after he was unable to reach him by phone. He pounded on the door hoping his friend was just preoccupied experimenting with his bugs. But there was no answer. This was the third time in as many days Jack tried to make contact with Dennis. He decided to walk to the back of the house where he discovered the trash can upended, with its cover laying several feet away. He knew something was amiss. An uncovered trashcan would have driven his ultra-sequential friend crazy.

Frightened and convinced Reinbold may be suffering the same fate as Father Bob, Jack knew that he should get word to the authorities immediately. But how can he explain this to his contemporaries? He began worrying—w*hy was my friend Dennis Reinbold connected with a project being carried out by The Company? Will I have to confess to my colleagues that it was Dennis who really solved all those problems I took credit for discovering?* Right now that didn't matter. He needed to alert Max and Bud immediately.

* * *

The President and Vice President would be discussing routine matters over their weekly working breakfast. The session began promptly at 6 a.m. each Wednesday when both their schedules permitted. Vice President Bly knew the President was grateful to him for pulling his initiative out of the fire. But now the President told him about the possible kidnapping of two men, one of them his high school friend, and that they are likely linked to the project.

I didn't hire on to receive this kind of abuse, the Vice President thought. They both knew that if the Israeli accommodation was uncovered a huge scandal would ensue. But if two men, one of them a Catholic Priest, had become collateral damage, well they both could likely kiss their chances for a second term goodbye. President

Curran could go on to write books and give speeches, but Bly's desire to succeed Curran would go up in smoke. Dennis had ample experience in politics, especially Washington, D.C. politics, and was acutely aware he and the President were going to sink or swim together.

* * *

Eight men were involved in the abductions of Father Bob and Dennis Reinbold, but only two were staying at the safe-house with their captives. Father Bob made it a habit of staying in good physical shape ever since his all-star running-back days in high school. Reinbold on the other hand was frail and even more so now because of the effects of the barbiturates his captors kept injecting into him.

The two had their hands tied together in front of them and were being held in a locked bedroom with bars on the only window. It was the middle of the night when Reinbold awoke complaining loudly from stomach pains. One of the captors entered the room when he heard the cries coming from one of his prisoners.

Father Bob struck the man a tremendous blow to the back of the neck with a small wooden chair. The man fell unconscious to the floor. Dennis sat up and screamed "watch out." Father Bob looked up just in time to see the other kidnapper race into the room armed with an AK-47.

Father managed to squeeze past the armed man while rushing out the bedroom door. The Iranian chased after the priest who was trying to escape through the unlocked back door. The trained spy ordered Father Bob to stop or he would fire his weapon. He did as he was told; knowing any further movement might mean certain death.

Reinbold was trying desperately to pull himself out of his bed without success. He let out a shriekish cry, causing the captor holding Father Bob at gunpoint to flinch and look back toward the bedroom. This momentary lapse was enough time for Father Bob to shove the substantial kitchen table that stood between the two men into his captor's legs. The kidnapper fell backward, firing off several rounds into the ceiling from his automatic weapon. Father Bob then forcefully kicked the table onto the spy and escaped through the unlocked kitchen door.

The man knocked unconscious by Father Bob's blow with the chair was now starting to come to. His companion freed himself form the table that pinned him down momentarily and rushed into the bedroom to help him up, scolding him and explaining that his inattention to details was the cause of their failure.

Meanwhile, Father Bob was running as fast as he could on the road leading from the safe-house toward a cluster of lights in the distance. The two Iranians quickly dragged Reinbold from the bed and tossed him into the van. Then one of the men retrieved everything that could identify them and dumped all of it into the van with Dennis.

This action turned out to be the only correct move either had made in the previous four minutes, a move that had been drilled into them during their extensive training.

Father Bob came off the road he had been awkwardly running on since his hands were still tied-up. He got as far away as he possibly could without causing attention. He lay down in some tall grass holding his breath, trying not to make a sound. Darkness was his friend. He was able to see some of the activity at the safe house and was certain his captors would be pursuing him.

Moments later he saw a van speed by. Still too frozen with fear he lay there for another hour trying to decide his next move. *Were more people on the way? Was his fellow captive still in the house? Was he okay?* He wondered, remembering his awful cries of pain. He lay there, praying.

Father Bob could see the first hint of sunrise from his hiding place. Nothing had moved since he first lay down in the tall grass. The van had gone, but didn't return. The safe house was completely dark. He didn't know if his captors left Reinbold behind or if they were searching for him.

In reality, the Iranians were now following the procedure for when an operation in enemy territory was compromised. They were getting rid of any and all evidence of their presence. Father Bob was safe to move about because the Iranians were long gone. Too bad he didn't know this. Making his way back to the safe-house, Father Bob could feel his heart beating and recognized his breathing was rapid, too rapid. He paused to gather himself before continuing.

The safe-house was completely dark. Aided by the tiny amount of light from the early morning glow, he carefully and quietly walked around the entire building, looking for signs of his fellow captive.

Finally, after recognizing the house had been deserted, he slowly opened the same door he escaped through less than four hours earlier. The place was empty, no spies, no Reinbold, no anything. The kidnappers had completely stripped the hide-out of any sign of their presence. He managed to free his hands from the bindings.

Instead of returning to the road, Father Bob decided to make his escape cross country. The safe-house was situated on a country farm. He noticed lights off in the distance earlier that morning as he made his run while it was still pitch black. Now that it was dawn, all he could see was rolling farmland with stands of trees separating corn and soybean fields. By following the section lines he believed he would eventually come upon either a town or a friendly farmhouse that would have a phone; and save his fellow captive.

* * *

President Curran was once again seated in the White House Cabinet room with both political friends and foes. He'd only disclosed his initiative days earlier in the same room. The results of that session had not only surprised him, but he left the meeting with his sails full of wind because of the support he'd received from even his most belligerent opponents. He was certain the outcome of this session would be much different.

"You say acquiesce, I say capitulate," complained the House Minority Leader. "I say bring on a diplomatic crisis. Isn't anyone else in this room fed up with constantly being thrown under the bus by these people? This would never have been allowed in the last administration."

"Madam Minority Leader, the only thing worse than nostalgia is amnesia. You forget; we are staunch allies. If you yearn for the good old days, I suggest you review your history book. Believe me, it is not a time America should want to revisit. If events were reversed, we would be asking for the same thing, and please note that I stated 'asking', not demanding." The Speaker's clever response was a good sign for Sean.

For a second time, Sean was wrong about the

outcome of the session with America's leading policy makers. Vice President Bly carried the day. He skillfully articulated the President's plan. He made a bulletproof argument for allowing the Israelis to obtain the complete technology in order to either confirm that the solution will work, or provide the U. S. cover in the event the plan blew up in their face.

* * *

"An unidentified body of a man was found floating in a cove of the Mississippi River south of St. Louis. Police are following steps to identify the dead man." A local St. Louis news correspondent made this report from the scene of the crime.

It took little time for the FBI to identify the body found one day earlier as one Dennis Reinbold of Austin, Texas. Reinbold died of affixation brought on by a sackcloth bag which was found draped around his neck. An autopsy showed he suffered from acute heart trauma caused by an unusually high content of barbiturates.

"Jack went to claim the body to have it returned to Austin," Bud told Max.

"There is no one else. No family. No friends. Jack tried to tell me something when I spoke to him just before he left. He stopped, but said he would tell us when he returned. I've never seen him so distraught. You have any idea what it could be?" Max asked.

"Not a clue," Bud answered. "But why Dennis Reinbold? It's sad to see Jack so brokenhearted, but I'm surprised to hear he has a heart." Max wasn't shocked by Bud's insensitivity, not even when something this awful occurred.

"There's a special place in hell for you, Bud,"

Max replied.

* * *

"Father, which of these chairs is the one you used to escape from the bedroom?" An FBI field agent asked Father Bob at the place he and Reinbold were held captive. "If we're lucky we can retrieve DNA evidence from your kidnapper's blood left from the blow you delivered."

The FBI took over the investigation of the murder of Dennis Reinbold. The safe-house was located, and Father Bob was able to provide a great deal of information to assist in bringing the criminals to justice. The FBI's investigative authority is the broadest of all federal law enforcement agencies. The Bureau's investigative philosophy emphasizes close relations and information sharing with other federal, state, local, and international law enforcement and intelligence agencies. The FBI Director was highly aware of the President's interest in this case. That fact meant the case would be treated differently than other murder cases.

* * *

Father Bob was back in his parish recovering from his ordeal. The FBI continued questioning him regarding the safe-house, his captors, and any other information he could recall. Max flew to Indianapolis to provide comfort and to receive comfort from his friend and confessor.

* * *

"Bless me Father for I have sinned," Max said, making his confession to Father Bob at St. Timothy's.

"Sean asked me if I knew about the project you guys were working on for him. I of course told him no, but Max, you've got to tell Sean you deceived him." Father Bob was speaking as he and Max walked to the Rectory.

The two men stayed up late sharing their accounts of the kidnapping and the episode in Costa Rica. They came away feeling sorry for Sean, now knowing how it feels to be in danger for your life; a feeling every U.S. president experiences constantly. On the drive to the airport early the next morning Father Bob told Max he believed he was becoming obsessed with his finding. Not just because of the deception, but the way he omitted telling Sean the truth and the reason he lied.

"You're moving about like a skipper without a compass, be careful. Sean deserves the truth, Max. Not because he's President and not because he's your best friend. He deserves the truth because tomorrow, God isn't going to ask, what did you dream; what did you think; what did you plan; what did you preach? He's going to ask; *what did you do*!"

* * *

After his friend's murder at the hands of the Iranian kidnappers, Jack confessed his relationship with Reinbold and the likelihood that it was he who was responsible for Reinbold's death. He frequently broke down during his testimony. Bud and Max believed this was what Jack wanted to tell them before he went to claim the body.

Both men were completely taken aback with his

revelation. Max especially recalled the many times Jack seemed to accomplish the impossible when it came to finding answers to problems that were holding up the completion of assignments. Bud was still in disbelief when Jack revealed it was Reinbold who was responsible for many of the findings Jack bragged about. But men of science were all too familiar with colleagues taking credit for other's achievements.

Most people believed Galileo's greatest achievement was the invention of the telescope. But in 1608 Dutchman Hans Lippershey completed the first ever telescope and attempted to receive a patent for it, but was denied for no discernible reason. When Galileo heard about Lippershey's work he quickly built his own telescope in 1609. Thomas Edison was widely believed to have invented the light bulb, but Heinrich Goebel was likely the first person to have actually invented it back in 1854. He tried selling it to Edison who saw no practical use in Goebel's invention and refused. Shortly thereafter Goebel died and shortly after that Edison bought Goebel's patent.

"I wish we could have met him," Bud said, seeking Max's nod of agreement. "Jack, it's over. You're forgiven! We all have egos. The more I thought about it, the more I believe I may have done the same thing."

"That means a lot to me, you guys. I have to find a way to make amends, but I'm struggling with trying to discover if I'm sorry for what I've done because I did it, or because I got caught," Jack confessed. "I'm determined to change my life. Maybe I pay your priest friend a visit one of these days."

"It saved my ass," Max replied.

Dennis loved his alma mater more than anything else in the world; including science. I'm going to find a way to honor and remember him. Maybe then I can fine some solace." Jack's voice was cracking while he spoke.

"I say we put all this behind us for now and concentrate on bringing these two projects home. All three of us can put our thinking caps on to help you, Jack." Max offered Jack some relief while thinking Sean may be able to help.

"I'm with you on that. Jack, you and I need to focus on our modus operandi. It's kicking our ass," Bud announced. Both Jack and Max could tell from his tone that the discussion about Reinbold was over at least for the time being.

Chapter 11

BPI

Living in Israel posed a persistent threat from terrorist attacks. The first and most immediate effect of terrorism were psychological. Terrorist campaigns could be expected to psychologically affect a sizeable portion of the population of a targeted society, either directly, by harming a person or their family, or indirectly, through the extensive media coverage of the attacks.

The Israelis began immediately deploying the new technology. Positive results were nearly instantaneous. Unlike America, the Israeli government didn't have the strict laws preventing it from acting without the approval of Israel's elected parliament, the Knesset. The country's Prime Minister could in effect: fire, aim, ready! The Israeli government demonstrated no reluctance in deploying the new technology received from their American allies. Positive results were shown at every location. Not since the discovery of the computer has the government been so successful combating a problem.

The U.S. administration received steady reports. President Curran paid close attention to every line, as did Max and Bud. The Israelis developed a method of deploying the solution in ways The Company and the President never considered. Would or could the United

States attempt to use the same process?

* * *

"Max, that favorite expression of yours—if it ain't broke, don't fix it—well it's broken." Jack looked demoralized as he continued his assertion. "Our protocol is wide of the mark. If we don't change something we're going to run out of time and money, not necessarily in that order."

"We need to rethink how to expedite development, or this *ACCIDENT* will have to go on life support," Bud weighed in.

In the natural sciences, a protocol is a predefined written procedural method in the design and implementation of experiments. Protocols are written whenever it is desirable to standardize a laboratory method to ensure successful replication of results by others in the same laboratory, or by other laboratories. For the *ACCIDENT*, proper procedure was critical.

"Lab rats," Max declared. "We can follow the same protocol as other research shops. Either rats or fruit flies," Max shouted. "Do I have to do all the thinking around here?" Max asked sarcastically.

"Even a blind squirrel finds an acorn every now and then," Bud responded. "You sure pulled that one out of thin air."

"I got lucky. Some days you get the bear, some days the bear gets you," Max replied.

"Dennis Reinbold would be impressed, Max," Jack said, with noticeable sadness in his voice.

"Bud was right, Jack," Max replied. "Your friend would have made a great team member. I'll have Maggie pull together some contacts and begin working up a new protocol."

"There's plenty of info right here. Stanford has tons of data I can pluck immediately." Jack was pointing at his laptop. He was referring to the post graduate studies he had taken at Stanford University in California. "After I left there, I hoped I'd never have to work with those nasty creatures ever again," Jack complained, but he was delighted with the new direction the *ACCIDENT*'s development phase would be taking.

* * *

Radio-frequency identification (RFID) is the use of a wireless non-contact system using radio-frequency electromagnetic fields to transfer data from a tag attached to an object, for the purposes of automatic identification and tracking. Some RFID tags required no battery and are powered by the electromagnetic fields used to read them. Others use a local power source and emit radio waves. The tag contained electronically stored information and did not need to be within the line of sight of the reader. It may be embedded in any entity in order to track.

Bud was well versed in the technology. He had been introduced to it years earlier while working with his former employer. This experience led him to select the course of action for the President's initiative.

* * *

"Mr. Speaker, Vice President Bly, members of Congress, and fellow Americans." President Curran began his address to a joint session of Congress.

"Tonight I'm announcing a plan I believe will permit the United States to once and for all solve a problem that has divided our country for over three decades. My predecessors tried but failed on many occasions. During the campaign, I spoke of my desire to utilize creative technology to resolve some of our country's most pressing problems." *I believe hell*, he thought before continuing. *It better work!*

"Much of the social history of the Western world, over the past three decades, has been a history of replacing what worked with what sounded good," Sean paused, trying to sense the mood.

"I spoke often of my tenure as research director for a large American pharmaceutical company in my home state of Indiana. I experienced firsthand the benefits derived from discovering new technical methods to deal with heretofore unresolved problems." Sensing he may be about to leap into an abyss, Sean froze for a moment.

"Today there is an estimated thirteen million people living in our country unlawfully. Most immigrants who come to the United States do so seeking better opportunities for employment, avoidance of political oppression, the opportunity to rejoin their loved ones, the prospect of providing better lives for themselves and their children, and for the educational and medical services benefits." Taking a deep breath and feeling a little nervous, Sean paused to ponder his options.

"There are obviously those that come across our border looking for a better wage and a job. I don't know that most of us here in America really understand what true poverty is in this country. We know that poverty exists here and that people do go hungry, I'm not discounting it, but the vast majority of our country does not worry about putting food in our mouths. You only need to walk around the mall or check out the local buffet to see that. But in many countries it's not just about feeding themselves; it's about wanting to change their future and the future of their children. Money is not the only motivator. Many just wish to live in peace and give their kids a chance." Knowing it was now too late to turn back, Sean stopped and looked out at the standing room only House Chambers.

"Tonight I'm pleased to announce the discovery of a technology that can eradicate illegal immigration. Tomorrow I will propose comprehensive immigration reform legislation requiring federal agencies charged with homeland security, border protection, and immigration to physically implant a device into any person who is in the United States illegally." Sean stopped, not from applause, but from the sound of hundreds of confused voices with stern faces and eyes that were slit.

"My proposal contains a grace period allowing sufficient time for all unauthorized immigrants to come forward and identify themselves to authorities. My proposal will require all illegal aliens treated in American hospitals to be implanted with a device. All unlawful immigrants arrested or currently incarcerated in either federal or state prisons or jails will be required to have a device embedded. In other words, any and all persons who entered the United States illegally will be subjected to the law. Any person who is discovered to have arrived without fulfilling the same requirements all other *legal immigrants* have satisfied, will be subject to the law." Sean paused for a polite applause that was difficult to hear over the moaning.

"I'm holding in my hand a test tube containing the BPI device. The 'B' stands for border. The 'P' stands for patrol and the 'I' stands for implant." Sean looked up, fearing his shaking hand may be noticeable to the audience.

"Days after being elected your President, I called on trusted friends in the business of developing creative technologies to help me discover solutions to harsh problems. This BPI is a solution. The Border Patrol Implant is a relatively noninvasive procedure. As you can see—or I should clarify and say what you can't see— is the tiny size of the device. Test results have proven there will be absolutely no adverse effects on any implanted person, including infants and the elderly." Sean was stopped by more applause and fewer moans coming from the audience. He used this pause to put down the test tube that contained the nearly invisible article.

"The device enables illegal aliens' movements to be tracked. Therefore, law enforcement, border patrol, and other agencies of our government will be able to know the whereabouts of these people in order to assist them in their journey to become American citizens if they wish. That's right; they will be welcomed and encouraged to become American citizens, just like many of our grandparents were." Sean paused once more. This time the President was interrupted with a rousing applause.

"The grace period provided for in my proposal will be sufficient. After receiving the implant, he or she must begin their journey toward U. S. citizenship." More applause interrupted the President's speech. "After the grace period expires, any unlawful immigrant not taking advantage of the provisions offered them—when they are apprehended, and they will be apprehended eventually— will be immediately deported." Sean was forced to stop because of roars coming from the most right-wing legislators.

"My proposal stipulates any company found

guilty of hiring an illegal alien will be required to pay a substantial fine and also be responsible for all the costs associated with the deportation." Again the President stopped speaking because most of the members were standing while applauding, with a few notable exceptions.

So far it appeared his proposal was being met with enthusiasm by all but the loyal opposition. This was to be expected. But the most important audience was not in the House Chambers. Polling had already begun, even though the President's speech wasn't finished.

"After these immigrants have taken the oath of citizenship, the implanted device will be deactivated forever. Never again will these new citizens be subjected to BPI's reach. No, these men, women and children—" The deafening cheers coming from the House Chambers caused Sean to pause once again.

"No, these men, women and children will now be welcomed with open arms; the same way the twenty-two million immigrants who made their way through Ellis Island between 1892 and 1924 were." The President continued to receive cheers from the chamber.

"Economic benefits of comprehensive immigration reform employing the BPI, which includes a legalization program for unauthorized immigrants and enables a future flow of legal workers, would result in a large economic benefit and a cumulative $1.5 trillion in added U.S. gross domestic product over ten years. In stark contrast, a deportation-only policy would result in a loss of $2.6 trillion in GDP over ten years." *Thank you dear God*, Sean thought.

"Comprehensive immigration reform increases all workers' wages. Legalized workers invest more in their human capital, including education, job training, and

English-language skills; making them even more productive workers and higher earners. The price of cowardice will only be evil; we shall reap courage and victory only when we dare to make bold choices." Sean finished to yet another standing ovation.

* * *

The speech took thirty-three minutes seventeen seconds. He was interrupted fourteen times, three of which were standing ovations. Overnight polling showed Americans were generally in support, but most said they needed more details. Informal poles in México and other Central American nations showed the President's speech receiving a ninety-five percent negative rating.

Following the President's speech the night before, U.S. markets tanked in early trading. Not until mid-morning did traders move back into stocks they believed may benefit from tighter controls on illegal immigration.

The Border Patrol Implant was on everyone's lips. Now the heavy lifting would be done by the bill's sponsors and supporters in Congress. Of course the President would be using his bully pulpit to move the legislation along, but presidents don't pass laws; the Congress passes laws.

An American President gives a speech to a joint session of Congress, and immediately afterwards the opposing party picks a spokesperson to give a response to the President's remarks. This is uniquely American. Opposition Members in the House of Commons in the British Parliament are famous for giving fiery speeches in opposition to remarks made by the Speaker of the House or the Prime Minister, but nothing like the attention given to a response to an American President's speech. The

American media provide nearly as much coverage to a response as to the actual address to Congress by the President.

President Curran's speech to Congress prompted a range of reactions from liberal critics whose divergent responses mirrored the fractures on display brought about by the extraordinarily controversial Border Patrol Implant. The critics began early in the day when Democratic presidential hopeful Dan Gearin delivered an address billed as a "prebuttal" from a border crossing in California. It was followed by an official response from the Democratic Party by Rhode Island Gov. Mark DeMasie, who disappointed many Democratic establishment figures when he announced that he would not join the presidential race.

Dan Gearin was the senior Senator from Delaware running to unseat the President. Known as one of the deans of his party, Gearin was handsome, articulate and a familiar face to most Americans who paid attention to politics or current events. His speech reacted to the President's outrageous pronouncement given one day earlier. The reason for the delay in responding was simple; everyone was caught off guard except the Israelis.

"My fellow Americans," Senator Gearin began. "Last week featured a rare moment of encouragement in the nation's often tiresome and vindictive immigration debate. Thousands of young undocumented immigrants began applying for temporary permits allowing them to live and work legally in the United States. This is a small but significant step that could help more than a million immigrant students and military veterans who were brought to this country illegally as children and who have lived in fear of deportation since.

But leave it to this administration's anti-immigration zealots to find a cloud in this silver lining. In their Potemkin Village, any measure of relief for undocumented immigrants is too much, except to plant a needle in the neck of millions of hard working and dedicated immigrants."

Gearin's speech was vitriolic. Over and over he condemned the President's proposal, predicting it would divide the country further on the question of illegal immigration and even accused the President of committing crimes against humanity. At one point he demanded that the President resign. The speech went on for over an hour.

"The United States has a right and a duty to restrict immigration to this country. But people who are powerfully motivated to come here anyway will find themselves highly vulnerable to smugglers and to their abusive employers. The only practical answer is tougher enforcement of laws against illegal working conditions, overcrowded housing, and the smuggling of illegal immigrants, not this barbaric device. These people are not illegal aliens, they are undocumented immigrants!" The Senator's arms were flailing from rage.

"Frequent use of the phrases 'illegal immigrant' and 'illegal alien' by our mainstream media is wrong and is not being faithful to the principles of our U.S. Constitution. The Constitution states that someone is innocent until proven guilty. The use of the word illegal is prejudicial. Simply put, only a judge, not a journalist, can say that someone is an illegal. These human beings are undocumented immigrants, not criminals! The term *illegal alien* is pejorative, unlike undocumented immigrant, which purposefully removes a stigma that should rightly be done away with." Gearin finished what would become his new stump speech.

After Gearin's diatribe, most of the media's talking heads were bowled over. Never before had they witnessed the opposition party attacking a sitting President in such a vicious manner.

Chapter 12

Paradigm Shift

"Eight Israeli citizens were killed and more than forty wounded in a multi-pronged terrorist attack north of Eilat in southern Israel. Five civilians were killed when terrorists opened fire on a passenger bus and another civilian was killed in a separate attack on an empty bus. An Israeli combat soldier was killed when his jeep hit a roadside bomb, and a member of the Israeli police special SWAT unit was killed when his unit led heavy fighting against a group of retreating terrorists. A father of three was killed when terrorists infiltrated Israel from Sinai and led a coordinated attack against those constructing the fence on the Israel-Egypt border. The attacking terrorists used automatic rifles in addition to anti-tank missiles. Two coordinated bombings shook Tel Aviv last evening, causing officials to put into effect the country's highest alert. The Prime Minister will be addressing the nation shortly. This is Vicki Lynn reporting from Tel Aviv." The well recognized CNN reporter closed the segment with her trademark smile.

The alert came after the American President's speech. Officials in Israel determined that it was best to disclose the technology the President of the United States unveiled as already being deployed to combat terrorism in that country. The disclosure resulted in a backlash by Palestinians. However, by any measurement, the success of the device was unquestioned. The Israeli government now possessed a way to track down any foreign agent who had been detained by police or captured while in the country.

The violence taking place in Israel continued because of the decision to deploy the BPI in Muslims living and working in the country. Mostly isolated incidences, the Israeli government had no plans to halt its use. Even though there had been collateral damage, the results were changing the paradigm for the country's way of dealing with domestic terrorism.

"Racial profiling is a standard defense against illegal aliens over there. Hell, when I went back to Tel Aviv to check out their progress, everywhere I went someone was checking *me* out. They wrote the book on racial profiling." The Israelis not only implanted unauthorized immigrants living, working or imprisoned in the country, but Jack explained they also developed a hand-held device that detected the presence of the BPI anywhere.

"I'm not sure that would ever fly here," Max wondered.

"If things were different they wouldn't be the same," Bud replied.

"What?" Both Jack and Max asked Bud the same question at the same time.

"Unless the United States secures its border there will continue to be a stream of illegal aliens pouring into this country. Sure, you can tag everyone who wants to stay here, and keep tagging anyone who comes in illegally, but what about the people who sneak in and don't want to become citizens? It sounds like the Israelis found an effective solution." Bud's comment sounded judicious.

"I can tell you this; it works. I observed a border detail screening a large group of Palestinians crossing the border into Israel. Most of them were men and most were day laborers. Several of the soldiers were operating the portable tracking device screening the crowd. Next thing I see is about a dozen members of the detail, each grabbing one of the Palestinians and taking them into custody. A couple of weeks later I was asked to ride along and observe a sweep of a local shopping area." Jack's explanation of the effectiveness of the portable tracking devise was gaining Max and Bud's undivided attention.

"They pan the crowd looking for implant hits, right?" Bud asked.

"No! They search for Arab looking men or women to confirm they *have been* implanted with the BPI; racial profiling," Jack answered. "If an implant is not detected the detainees are asked for their papers."

"Their papers? Sounds like a cartoon. Your *papers* please; may I see your *papers?* That's funny." Jack's story reminded Max of a Saturday morning cartoon show he used to watch as a kid. "Rocky and Bullwinkle I think. Remember Boris and Natasha?"

"All I can say is that it works. We were discussing how to deal with the problem of continued illegal entry. I suggested they take a look at the device we came up with to identify contaminated water years ago, remember? It looks like they took my advice," Jack speculated.

"Hey, the end justifies the means. Bottom line: if you're going to visit another country to work or play, do it the right way or suffer the consequences." As usual,

Bud was being his predictable scornful self.

"Sean has all the necessary information. Maybe it was a blessing the Israelis had a chance to shake-down the BPI first. Those people have a much larger problem than we do for sure. I for one like the way they're proceeding," Max added. "Let's see if we can get a hold of one of those hand-held tracking units. If they used your idea, they should be more than willing to accommodate us."

* * *

Israel's Attorney General announced recently that he, several members of his staff, and some one hundred and sixty employees of a new thirty million dollar anticrime computer center in Tel Aviv had all been implanted with the BPI. The device would help control and track access to the new anticrime center which housed a centralized database intended to improve Israel's already superb record of solving crimes. In a country where terrorism was a problem, being able to track precisely who had access to the "delete" key in a criminal database could be quite useful.

The Israeli Army has considered implanting the BPI to forever end the anguish of Unknown Soldiers. The country's banks have entertained the idea of offering the implant to customers as a way to prevent thefts at ATM machines and retail stores. Nursing homes see some advantages in injecting implants in patients with Alzheimer's disease who might wander or be incoherent. Police have suggested that pairing implanted officers with implanted handguns would keep track of the weapons if they were stolen or misplaced. So far such applications remain mostly in the discussion stage.

* * *

"Good morning Mr. President." Sean's Chief of Staff greeting was met with a handshake as Sean walked into the Cabinet Room.

"Give me a reason," Sean fired back. "That no good son-of-a-bitch blackmailed me into giving up the device after his piece of shit agents exposed the plan by illegally spying on us. Then the prick announced his country possessed the technology and has already deployed it for months—immediately after *I* tell the American people it was *my friends* who made the fricken discovery. Now the bastards are suffering the consequences of employing the device in ways that are sure to stir up the pile." Very much out of character, President Curran complained to the two men in the closed door meeting. "And you're lucky you caught me in a good mood, or I would tell you exactly how I feel."

"He sure threw you under the bus," the Chief of Staff agreed.

"I wish I had it to do all over again. I sure wouldn't have been so accommodating to the asshole."

"Mr. President, I predict your decision will pay off in the end. If the device fails to provide an acceptable solution our country will have avoided making a big mistake." Vice President Bly pronouncement helped calm the mood. "If they're successful; heads we win, tails we win. Oh, and by the way Mr. President, nice guys have skinny kids."

"Thanks Dennis, I needed that. You know how much I appreciate your loyalty and support."

* * *

The BPI was so successful that several Western European countries were considering using the device for the same purposes, especially France.

Islam is seen as the religion of the poor people and many in France believe their country faces an Islamic future because Muslims are said to be more than ten percent of the French population. The French expected Islam to adapt to France, but many believe it is France that is adapting to Islam. Even if many government elites in France are in denial over Islam, the people in the streets increasingly are not. Some have become fed up with what they see as the growing Islamization of France. By implementing the use of the American's new BPI device, the French government can at least get better control over the problem of Muslims entering the country illegally.

* * *

President Curran's controversial bill was being debated in both the House and the Senate at the same time. Winston Churchill posited, "Democracy is a horrible form of government, but it is the best there is." Passage of the bill was going to be difficult at best. But to make the task even more complex the proposal contained an ex post facto provision.

A form of ex post facto law, commonly called an amnesty law, may decriminalize certain acts or alleviate possible punishments. An example would be replacing deportation of an illegal immigrant if they agreed to have the BPI implanted into them.

The Border Patrol Implant bill didn't offer amnesty, but it offered amnesty. The bill didn't mandate deportation, but it mandated deportation. The bill didn't add new criminal penalties, but it added new criminal penalties.

"Contradiction, I don't think so!" One of the bill's sponsors was being interviewed on a Sunday morning news program.

"But Congressman, current law requires illegal aliens to be deported. This bill allows anyone currently in the United States unlawfully to remain in the country. Isn't that amnesty?" The show's host asked the first of many questions prepared for this interview, knowing the ratings would be off the charts.

"No, it is not amnesty, not even close. You are not reading the complete text. The bill requires every single person now living in this country illegally to register with the government, be implanted with the BPI, begin their journey toward citizenship, *or* be deported back to their country of origin. That's a lot of things, but amnesty is not one of them," the Congressman answered.

"Oh really?" The host's rhetorical question was ripe with sarcasm.

"Listen, amnesty is defined as an undertaking by the authorities to take no action against specified offenses or offenders during a fixed period. There is *no* fixed period in the bill. Offenders do have a specific time in which they can come forward to be eligible for implantation, but that is not the same as *authorities taking no action*. To the contrary, that my friend is the authorities taking *plenty* of action." The guest paused, looking for his questioner's reaction.

"Fair enough Congressmen. What is your response to critics making the claim that this is just a different way of deporting undocumented workers, and that nothing will change to help these people?" This time his tone was much less sarcastic.

"Nonsense! Before these critics start firing their arrows, I suggest they read the bill. Everything will change. If these unlawful immigrants really want to stay in America, they now have the opportunity to do so without first being deported. If they truly want to become American citizens, under the new law, they would be allowed to take that step without being deported first. For the love of God, read the bill. I'm not saying this is the perfect solution, but for heaven's sake, if you're going to criticize the measure, do so after you have actually read what's in the bill."

"Why single out small business? The penalties are extreme. A fine and the cost associated with deportation?" The host's question was a softball.

"Com'on, if it looks like an apple, tastes like an apple, and smells like an apple, it's an apple. Any employer, big or small, knows if he is hiring an illegal alien. The current law is too lenient. Perhaps if there were more severe penalties in the existing statute we wouldn't have the problem in the first place." The Congressman was getting more comfortable supporting the measure.

"Are you saying it's all about jobs?"

"Look, if people knew there was *not* an opportunity to find work here, the biggest motivation to enter the country illegally would be removed. We all know why these unlawful immigrants are being hired; the owner of the business doesn't have to pay them the same as a citizen. That's wrong. That's why the penalty is written into the bill. Regardless if this Border Patrol Implant bill becomes law or not, I intend to introduce legislation making it much less advantageous for an employer to hire an illegal alien." The Congressman's face was flush from his passionate reply.

"Finally, Congressman, most of the criticism is

coming from people who firmly believe this is morally wrong; human beings should not be treated like animals. This notion of actually implanting a devise into their bodies in order to track their whereabouts, doesn't that at all bother you in the least?" The anchor's face appeared to grimace in pain with this question.

"You characterize the implant as morally wrong. Is entering a country *illegally* morally wrong? Is allowing millions of people to enter our country by not securing borders morally wrong? Is taking away the jobs of our citizens morally wrong? Is stretching the social safety net to the breaking point morally wrong? This problem is getting worse, not better. It's not going to go away on its own. It has divided our nation long enough." The guest had to stop for a drink of water.

"In the United States we require citizens to possess some sort of identification otherwise they can be arrested for vagrancy. Current law requires all citizens to obtain Social Security Numbers for their newborn children shortly after birth. Cars are licensed. Drivers are licensed. Cell phones can now be tracked. Is the proposal perfect? Show me a law on the books that's perfect. Like it or not, we're talking about people who intentionally broke the law—"

"But Congressman," the host interrupted.

"Please let me finish," the Congressman demanded.

"We can lock them up, but we don't. We can deport them, but we don't. We can make their lives unbearable by not educating their children, treating their illnesses, or providing them already scarce resources, but we don't. If we did, *that* would be morally wrong. So no, I don't believe requiring people who blatantly disobey our laws, having to undergo minor discomfort in order to protect our country, is morally wrong."

* * *

"We put all sorts of implants in our bodies today," the senior senator from Iowa proclaimed. "If we have metal hips, it only makes sense to have chips too."

"I'm concerned that the benefits of being able to track people clandestinely may be forced upon others. If tracking these illegal aliens succeeds, then it won't be long before we'll use it for released prisoners and sex offenders. If the choice is offered to a person to either stay in prison for another year, or to go on parole as long as they have this monitoring chip in them, then that's not really much of a choice in my opinion," Connecticut's Senator postulated.

"I am not condemning this embedded chip technology. My critique of the proposed technological solution is, whether they are nanotech implants or national ID cards, people will abuse them. That's the fundamental issue of human nature." North Dakota's junior Senator weighed in, knowing he would appear on the news later that evening.

* * *

H.B. 1212 and S.B. 1212 made their way through the long and agonizing process, but the bills were now in the hands of the conferees. It had been said, "If you like lawmaking and sausage, you don't want to see how either is made."

President Curran spoke to a gathering of franchised new vehicle dealers at the Hyatt Regency Capitol Hill. After delivering his remarks and spending time shaking hands with dealer friends he knew from Indianapolis, the President was escorted by Secret Service agents from the hotel.

The explosion shattered hundreds of hotel windows and sent shrapnel in every direction, killing or maiming everyone who came in contact with one of the thousands of ball bearings packed in the bomb. Three Secret Service agents were killed instantly in the blast along with six members of the presidential press corps. One of the dead agents had just shut the door after Sean got into the backseat of the presidential limousine.

The Secret Service referred to the President's heavily armored vehicle as "The Beast." Most details of the car were classified for security reasons. A special night vision system was in a secret location. Special loops replaced the stock door handles, agents held on to them when running alongside the car. Goodyear run-flat tires were fit into extra-large wheel wells. The car was sealed against biochemical attacks. Kept in the trunk was a blood supply of the Sean's blood type.

When the bomb exploded, the bomb casing, as well as any additional shrapnel (nails, screws, ball bearings or other items in the bomb), were violently thrown outward and away from the explosion. When these fragments struck buildings, concrete, masonry, glass, and even people, they may have fragmented even further, causing more damage. Whoever was responsible for this powerful bomb planned to cause as much destruction as possible. The carnage was everywhere. The site resembled a war zone.

The Beast saved the President's life. The powerful bomb was dropped from a ninth floor hotel room, detonating before hitting the ground. That explained the large amount of destruction of both lives and property.

Even though The Beast was positioned under the enclosed hotel entrance, the size of the blast, and the fact that the bomb was delivered from a window directly above the entryway of the registration enclosure, accounted for the devastation. It also explained why the Secret Service failed to detect the device in security sweeps before the President's scheduled arrival. Similar explosive devices were discovered in rooms directly above any entrance the President might have used to enter or exit the building.

* * *

It had been a hard and dangerous slog. Not only did the President escape an assassination attempt where dozens lost their lives and more were seriously injured, but House and Senate members from both sides of the aisle received threatening calls and letters. All but a few were assigned a security detail. Investigations into the attempted assassination and threats to members of Congress pointed to outside sources. This truth significantly propelled supporters of the legislation and helped provide the President with the needed votes for passage.

The Border Patrol Implant Act passed both the House and Senate on a strictly partisan vote. The House gave final passage to the Senate's BPI legislation on a climactic 221-to-209 vote as Republican's muscled the measure through on the strength of the party's big majority. In the final roll call, few House Democrats voted for the bill.

It was a tumultuous sprint to the finish for legislation that had brought Washington many dramas over the last year, ranging from an effort to kill the

President, to the revelation Israel had already employed the device in that country. The final battle on the House floor exposed again the divisions that had driven Congress and the nation over the past year. The Border Patrol Implant would now become the law of the land once President Curran put his signature on the bill.

* * *

It turned out fruit flies permitted the team to develop the *ACCIDENT* much faster than either lab rats or mice. Progress was now speeding ahead. Jack managed to find an answer to an extremely difficult issue without the help of his departed friend, Dennis Reinbold.

"You have to eat an elephant one bite at a time, right, Jack?" Bud asked. He was amazed that Jack had come up with the solution on his own after the Reinbold revelation.

"No, I turned chicken shit into chicken salad," Jack replied, trying to one-up his quick-witted cohort.

With most of the design and development phase now completed, it was time to put the *ACCIDENT* through rigorous testing. But first Max must disclose the plan and his deception to his best friend, the President of the United States.

* * *

The Border Patrol Implant Act became effective upon the President's signature. The Homeland Security Agency was charged with promulgating the rules and regulations associated with implementing the new statute.

Promulgation was the act of formally proclaiming or declaring a new statutory or administrative law after its enactment. National laws of extraordinary importance to the public may be announced by the head of state on a national broadcast. The Border Patrol Implant Act needed no introduction.

President Curran counted on his agency heads for smooth implementation. He was in the midst of a contentious re-election bid. His idea became his campaign promise. That promise became his initiative. Finally, that initiative became a reality, and was named the Border Patrol Implant Act, now and forever dubbed BPI. BPI was the *only* campaign issue.

Sean's opponent was gaining ground in the polls after the assassination attempt "bump" wore off, but a majority still favored the device as a way to deal with America's porous southern border.

The BPI only tracked people who were unlawfully in the United States. Those who came forward could remain in the United States while pursuing citizenship. It wasn't amnesty. It wasn't immediate deportation. It didn't tear families apart. It caused no physical injury, and after people received the implant and were sworn in as new American citizens, the BPI would be deactivated forever.

The opposition didn't agree the device was harmless. They believed the mental effects would be forever lasting, even if a person achieved citizenship. They also argued if a person failed to become a citizen and was deported, he could still be tracked. This, they believed, was blatantly illegal and morally wrong.

* * *

"I've finally been able to identify the device. It is positioned on the right side of the second cervical vertebrae. The device is so tiny, only sensitive imagining equipment can reveal the position. Removing will risk paralysis and even death. The Americans must have anticipated there would be an enormous effort made to remove the devices from their victims," Rudi Assam groaned. He was a leading surgeon employed by the Palestinian terrorist group Hamas. "I discovered what the Americans claimed is true. The device becomes rubbish once exposed to air, so I am unable to make use of the two we removed from the bodies brought to me. Nanotechnology creates barriers that will require more skill and knowledge than I can offer you," Assam said to the onlookers.

"Are you telling us you are helpless? There is no way for you to abolish this poison? How can this be?" One of the Hamas deputies was livid when he was told the news while observing the doctor.

Max and Bud knew how important it would be to prevent reverse engineering of the BPI. This was the last hurdle. The answer to this quandary may have been the finest discovery Solutions, LLC ever developed. Jack's friend Reinbold provided partial elements, but his untimely death required TC's team to search and finally discover the answer.

Max, Bud and Jack were the only people on the planet that knew the precise method and procedure to create the device. They realized early in the trial stage that the implant must be secure both before, and especially *after* implantation.

Their expertise in nanotechnology served them well. Materials used to develop nano-products were not only smaller than microscopic in size, but also possessed physical characteristics not seen in any other manufacturing process. For example, materials used for the BPI were made from baked crystalline sea salt. Therefore, after becoming exposed to any moisture inside the body, the integrity of the material would drastically change once it was re-exposed to air or light.

With nanotechnology and the development of bio-electrics, The Company created a device that would power itself utilizing the bio-electric energy created by the host of the tracker. Since all living organisms utilize electricity to communicate information from their nerve cells, the device safely taps into this unlimited energy source to power its potent micro-processors and on-board communication cells.

The human battery may run down, but nourishment recharges the human body. As a result, TC's team was not concerned about batteries running low, or even running out. The human body is a never-ending power supply. As long as the person was eating and drinking normally, the device would give out its signal for the lifespan of the carrier. When implanted, TC's discovery could provide the exact GPS satellite location, accurate to within five feet, even indoors, which would be automatically sent to the data servers.

As for the actual manufacturing process, TC assigned four separate locations whose tasks were to produce a single component. When completed, the parts were delivered to a federally secure location where the automated protocol prohibited humans from either observing or detailing the final manufacturing process. This protocol was the last stumbling block. Jack's late friend, Dennis Reinbold, had solved this problem.

Chapter 13

The Supremes

"If you cross the North Korean border illegally, you get twelve years hard labor. If you cross the Iranian border illegally, you are detained indefinitely. If you cross the Afghan border illegally, you get shot. If you cross the Saudi Arabian border illegally, you will be jailed. If you cross the Chinese border illegally, you may never be heard from again. If you cross the Venezuelan border illegally, you will be branded a spy and your fate will be sealed. If you cross the Cuban border illegally, you will be thrown into political prison to rot. If you cross the United States border illegally, you get a job, a drivers license, social security card, welfare, food stamps, credit cards, subsidized rent or loan to buy a house, free education, free health care, a lobbyist in Washington, billions of dollars worth of public documents printed in your language, the right to carry your country's flag while you protest that you don't get enough respect." The familiar Hollywood voice came pounding from the television. The political ad was sponsored by YES to BPI.

Money is mother's milk to political candidates. In politics, money doesn't talk, it screams. Candidates for President must adhere to the golden rule; he who has the gold, rules!

The campaign was in full swing. Superpacs were pumping millions of dollars into both parties. President Curran's opposition declared their first act when elected would be full repeal of the Border Patrol Implant Act. The statutory deadline for all illegal aliens to present themselves was approaching. Overlooked by lawmakers during the debate, the deadline would fall just nine days before the federal elections, as if there wasn't enough drama already.

Even though the loudest cries were coming from the Hispanic Congressional Delegation, what polling was available showed the new plan was being embraced even by those who were most affected. The BPI Act awarded U.S. citizenship to people who, just one day earlier, were being hunted down by authorities for possible deportation. It was no surprise these people embraced America's solution to deal with illegal entrants.

* * *

It wasn't the million person march promoters hoped for. It wasn't even a hundred thousand person march. Nevertheless, the media treated the demonstration protesting the use of the Border Patrol Implant like it was the fifty million person march. All the usual suspects were on hand playing to the TV cameras.

The crowd estimated to be no more than twenty thousand flocked around the reflecting pool of the Washington Mall demanding that the government stop the use of the BPI.

Dozens of youths pelted riot police with plastic bottles and small rocks. The police responded with a volley of tear gas which quickly halted the spontaneous violence caused by speeches made from a podium at the foot of the Lincoln Memorial encouraging civil disobedience. Many attendees held banners imploring the government to "Stop Treating People Like Game Fish" and "Immigrants Are People Too."

Demonstrators shouted slogans and carried banners from the Lincoln Memorial to the steps of the Capitol. Mike Packard, executive director of the Fair Treatment for America's Visitors, warned of further protests if the government continued the use of the BPI.

"American people are showing today that they can't accept any more of this abuse of our visitors to our country. If the government doesn't realize this, I'm very afraid that this will lead us to other forms of protest. It will also lead to social unrest." Packard sported the obligatory grubby looking beard and long, messy, stringy, and balding head as he performed to the cameras.

"This President is wrong. These are human beings not over-the-road trucks or airplanes. We don't need to know where these people are at all times. Most are here to make money to send back to their families," Jim Olsen complained. Olsen was a well-known Evangelical preacher-turned-spokesman for any liberal cause.

"But aren't these people guilty of entering our country illegally?" A clearly fast thinking reporter was asking questions.

"Listen, that's no excuse to treat them like criminals."

"But that's exactly what they are Mr. Olsen. Under Title 8, Section 1325 of the U.S. Code, 'Improper Entry by Alien', any citizen of any country other than the United States who: enters or attempts to enter the United States at any time or place other than as designated by immigration officers, or eludes examination or inspection by immigration officers, or attempts to enter or obtains entry to the United States by a willfully false or misleading representation or the willful concealment of a material fact has committed a federal crime." The unusually astute reporter fired back. She was reading her prepared questions from a notepad.

"That's wrong. That's another law we need to repeal, that, and the BPI disaster," Olsen knew he was losing this argument, but was clearly enjoying basking in the klieg lights of the live national TV coverage.

"Mr. Olsen, illegal immigration causes an enormous drain on public funds. Studies of the costs of immigration by the National Academy of Sciences found that the taxes paid by immigrants do not cover the cost of services received by them. We cannot provide high quality education, health care, and…" The reporter was forced to stop.

"Hold on now, young lady," Olsen demanded.

"Please let me finish my question sir and then, please, tell America your answer." Olsen had met his match. The obviously bright and attractive reporter ordered him to allow her to finish.

"Very well," Olsen demurred.

"We cannot provide high quality education, health care, and retirement security for our own people if we continue to bring in endless numbers of poor, unskilled immigrants. Additionally, job competition by waves of illegal immigrants willing to work at substandard wages and working conditions depresses the wages of American workers, hitting hardest at minority workers and those without high school diplomas. Illegal immigration also contributes to the dramatic population growth overwhelming communities across America, crowding school classrooms, consuming already limited affordable housing, and straining precious natural resources like water, energy, and forestland. How do you respond to this Mr. Olsen?"

"So, we tag 'em and let them in anyway. What has that accomplished? You still haven't eliminated the dramatic population growth problem you just said these people cause," Olsen looked embarrassed for the way he answered her questions.

* * *

Homeland Security had already registered and implanted over eight million unlawful immigrants. This number included over seven million undocumented workers and their family members, hospitalized patients and newborns, those incarcerated, and people who had been apprehended after the law became effective.

The Act included ample funding to train and carry out implantation by existing medical providers such as hospitals, clinics, med checks, and other walk-in clinics. Each device cost the government less than a dollar and the procedure used to implant the device took less than five minutes.

The Company decided to incorporate Magnetic Resonance Ultrasound Fusion to determine the precise location to introduce the device. Jack developed a hand-held injector, a simple device consisting of a 5-10 ml syringe with a 12-gauge veterinary-grade needle attached. A push rod is attached to the plunger of the syringe. When the plunger is depressed, the push rod protruded no more than two millimeters past the tip of the needle. The end of the push rod was smoothed and round so that it wouldn't damage internal tissue.

Using this procedure enabled the needle to

puncture the skin at the precise targeted area and inject the BPI in place. After several minutes the device fuses to the C2 vertebrae. The BPI would receive power from the electrometric field generated by the spinal cord and would operate indefinitely.

MRI makes use of the property of nuclear magnetic resonance to image nuclei of atoms inside the body, allowing a trained technician to quickly determine where to position the needle.

Since MRI machines were readily available, and it took only one day to train a technician, the large number of people expected to undergo the procedure posed few logistical problems. But shortly after the law went into effect, a technique was found that eliminated the need for an MRI. Now the process was greatly accelerated and actual implantation of the device would not stand in the way of fully implementing the new provision.

* * *

Max's TBM lifted off Talkeetna, Alaska's runway for the eleven hour plus flight to Austin. Max, Max Jr. and the Glass' wrapped up their five night six day fully-guided float trip the day before. The men covered the sixty scenic river miles of Susitna River before stopping at a wilderness lodge to enjoy a hot shower, re-pack, relax, and get "re-civilized". Afterwards the party boarded a float plane back to Talkeetna. Their raft trip featured world class rainbow trout, king sockeye, pink, chum, and silver salmon fishing. The two guides made sure each day was memorable. As usual, both the boys did the work while the dads told the jokes.

There was plenty of conversation about their previous trip to Costa Rica. Mike Sr. was particularly glad they decided to stay in the U.S. Around the campfire on the second night, Max told both Mikes why he believed his near miss at Crocodile Bay had nothing to do with the choice in destinations. Max had already briefed all his family members about the incident at the Quinn family reunion shortly after the ordeal. Mike Sr. and Jr. were surprised Max's job was the least bit dangerous. But for now, all of it was a moot point; the four had just, for a second time, completed the ultimate fishing float trip Alaska had to offer.

* * *

In the world of criminal investigation, the FBI uses different techniques to solve crimes. Among the most widely used is a "profile matrix." With a profile matrix, the investigator uses a series of questions to find the answers to solve the crime. The questions are simple; who, what, when, where, how, and why. Asking these questions and finding the answers is one of the best methods law enforcement employs in crime solving today.

The what, when, where, and how were obvious. The "who" and "why" were another story. The Border Patrol Implant controversy was likely to be the answer to "why." Dozens of threats were reported ever since the devices' use in secret experiments was announced. Policy makers from both parties received threats of violence while hate mail was delivered daily to every member of Congress. The FBI didn't rule out other causes, but the BPI was by far the best answer to "why." Digital forensics eventually provided the answer for "whom." Bomb fragments, DNA, and fingerprints all led to the suspects.

Mexican drug cartels appeared to be taking a page right out of the terrorist playbook in realizing that the easiest way to infiltrate their enemies was to impersonate them. The discovery came after Mexican Marines found a secret workshop in the northern border city of Piedras, Negras, just miles from Eagle Pass, Texas. In the workshop, the FBI examined hundreds of fake U.S military uniforms. They also found crucial evidence matching this site to shrapnel from the bomb site at the Capitol Hill Hyatt Regency.

It was a tactic that has long been used by radical militant Islamist groups in places like Iraq and Afghanistan. The ties between the cartels and violent terrorist groups like Hezbollah and al-Shabaab of Somalia were well-documented and when put into context alongside other developing similarities between the two factions, it answered the question; the cartels were taking notes from terrorists.

The Mexican government was ill prepared to wage a successful war against the powerful drug cartels. When "asked" by the U.S. to allow American armed forces to "assist" in apprehending the suspected assassins, the Mexican President was all too willing to accept the offer.

"Mr. President, the assassins have been brought to justice," the FBI Director reported. "In a joint mission with the Mexican Marines, elements of our military raided the terrorist enclave and captured or killed the people suspected in the attempt on your life and the murder of so many of our friends."

"This is good news. I will speak to the Mexican President and thank him for allowing us to back him in bringing these criminals to justice. Perhaps we can continue to support him in the future to help fight his war with the narco-terrorists." *Maybe this can be TC's next challenge*, President Curran thought after he replied to the Director.

* * *

Even before the ink dried on the BPI Act, federal lawsuits were filed in numerous jurisdictions throughout the country. Several lower courts ordered injunctions, but those were quickly overturned by their respective district Appellate Courts. Those opposed to the new statute were determined to overturn the legislation, either by defeating the President in the next election, or by having the high court do their bidding by striking down the requirement. The fact was, regardless of who wins the election, without a doubt the U. S. Supreme Court would end up deciding the fate of the Border Patrol Implant Act.

The President's first term was considered successful by any measure. Even though the BPI was Sean's highest profile accomplishment, he managed to navigate the country through an economy still hampered with problems brought about mostly by failed government policy. Since his party controlled both the House and Senate, Sean successfully achieved permanent changes to corporate and personal tax rates. He also took baby steps toward addressing the monumental problem of government spending.

The well-known economist and social theorist, Thomas Sowell, believed elections should be held on April 16, the day after Americans paid their income tax. "That is one of the few things that might discourage politicians from being big spenders."

President Curran learned at a young age what economists have long understood; corporations don't pay taxes, people pay taxes. U.S. workers bore the cost of corporate taxes in lower wages and salaries and higher prices. He, like Sowell, never understood why it was considered greedy to keep the money you earned, but not greedy to want to take somebody else's money. Curran knew taxing corporations made it easy for Congress to raise corporate taxes since the American people seldom objected if it meant they would pay less tax if businesses had to pay more. President Curran succeeded convincing the voters that this was a farce which had been perpetrated on the economy for generations and he was successful in finally putting an end to the masquerade. Minor provisions were included in the BPI Act to make reversing these changes more difficult for future Congresses. This made the opposition that much more determined to have the Court strike down the entire law.

America's federal courts were nearly as politically charged as the Congress. Presidents appoint federal judges for life. A liberal President will likely appoint a liberal judge. Consequently, whenever a controversial issue is heard in lower courts, the rulings would almost always end up making their way to the high court. Many believed the Supreme Court was a "superlegislature", responding to ideological arguments, rather than a legal institution responding to concerns grounded in the rule of law. Regardless, a Supreme Court ruling would be the final word on the Border Patrol Implant Act.

* * *

The FBI filed criminal charges against Elizabeth Keebler. The complaint alleged that, at an October 26, 2018 lunch, Keebler disclosed information related to a potential scientific discovery to two unnamed individuals.

According to contemporary media reports, the two individuals were foreign nationals involved in espionage activities. The complaint also alleged that Keebler disclosed secret information to "an unauthorized person." The report ended by stating Mrs. Keebler was being held without bond pending her arraignment.

"Did Cookie try to reach you?" Bud asked Max.

"Only fifteen times," Max answered. "I was airborne and couldn't receive a signal. I don't blame him for being so upset. We've got to do everything we can to help him, and that includes getting Sean involved. We owe him big time. Hell, it's my fault he's in this situation to begin with."

* * *

Acts of violence continued to erupt in Israel, brought on by the government's decision to utilize the BPI to combat border violations and keep track of foreign workers in their country. But the number of incidents had lessened greatly. The Israeli people favored the BPI because results were providing greater security from terrorism within its borders.

"Our American friends graciously provided us with this marvelous device, greatly assisting us in identifying our country's enemies." The Chief of Internal Security for Israel made this pronouncement while closing the door as a guest made his way into the office. "Paul, I have a proposal ready to be submitted to the Prime Minister for his consideration. Please give me your opinion."

"Bold! Very bold! I'm afraid too bold my friend," Paul Maffei said, after perusing the proposal. Maffei was the Internal Security Chief's friend and member of the

Liberal Party of the Israeli Knesset. "Illegal aliens and undocumented workers are one thing, but convicted sexual offenders, pedophiles, and gang members who are Israeli citizens is quite another." Shaking his head and pointing his finger in a scolding manner, Maffei feigned disgust.

"Why must a society put up with these criminals who have no regard for the law or their victims? We now have a way of knowing where they are at all times, and most importantly, they will know that we know where they are," argued the Chief. "Think of it, Paul, think of the pain and suffering we can alleviate by simply embedding this miracle device into these reprobates."

* * *

The election was only two weeks away. Sean's pole numbers were impressive. He led in every sample, including Hispanics. But an undecided voter, like the class dunce, was a concern to both candidates. The caricatures flourish. People, who can't agree on anything political, find common ground on one point: undecided voters are lifeless, disengaged, and a little bit frightening. Undecided voters validated Churchill's statement, "If you want to know what's wrong with Democracy, all you have to do is talk to an undecided voter for five minutes."

"I think we should require the BPI be used on undecided voters. What do you think Dennis," Sean asked his Vice President in jest. "It's crazy. Both parties spend the lion's share of our campaign funds playing to these people who shouldn't be permitted to vote in the first place."

"You sound like me except I would never say that out loud. I guess that's one of the advantages of being

President, yes?" The Vice President countered.

"Maybe you get that provision in the law when you take over. I don't know of a single member who would oppose the measure if they could vote on it anonymously," Sean and Dennis had managed to become much closer after two near misses with the BPI. Sean now included Dennis in all his controversial discussions. Well, almost all.

* * *

He's my best friend. Sure, I omitted telling him I told Cookie about the project. No way was I going to tell anyone about the ACCIDENT—except Father Bob and the devil's advocates. I suppose he could have me arrested. But then I might tell the world about—, Max was daydreaming while flying the TBM to see the President. The two would be meeting in the Oval Office at the White House.

"Max it's good to talk to you in person," the President said, giving his best friend a hardy handshake.

"So this guy comes home and finds his blonde wife at the kitchen table with the mailman who was eating a piece of cake in his underwear with a dollar bill sitting next to his plate—." Max began telling Sean a joke he was sure he hadn't heard yet.

"Sounds like new material." Sean and Max rarely told each other new jokes; just different versions of old jokes.

"So the guy asked his wife what the hell is going on here. She says to him, remember I asked you what we should get the mailman for Christmas. You said screw him; give him a dollar. The cake was my idea." Sean started laughing so hard, Max could barely finish his story.

"I hope you feel the same way after I get through telling you the news." The two were gathering themselves from their belly laughs before Max made the buzz killing statement.

"You're not going to tell me anything that's going to torpedo my re-election chances are you?" Sean thought he was asking a rhetorical question. "My campaign manager wants to lock me up until election night. He's convinced that's the only way I won't screw up my chances, since our lead is that solid. So tell me, what's so important you can't tell me about it over the phone? Should I sit down before you begin?"

Camp David is the country retreat of the President of the United States and the guests of the President. The presidential retreat received its present name from Dwight D. Eisenhower, in honor of his father and grandson, both named David.

Marine One is the call sign of any United States Marine Corps aircraft carrying the President of the United States. Marine One is sometimes the preferred alternative to motorcades, which can be expensive and logistically difficult.

"Max, it's not Air Force One and sorry, you won't be allowed to fly. But you and I are going to get out of here and figure out what the hell we're going to do about your so called accident." Sean kept talking as he grabbed the phone to make his desires known to the Presidential staff. Max could tell he was nearly as excited about the revelation as Bud and Jack were when he told them. Sean directed his Chief of Staff to make ready Marine One for the flight to Camp David.

"I'm having General Wright meet us there. I hope he'll have some ideas how we can keep this quiet. I guess

The Company's brochure is true; you guys are that good. But be careful Max, flattery is like perfume; sniff it, don't swallow it. How in the hell did you come up with this one?"

Chapter 14

Pre-PRI

Most European nations voted to adopt the use of the Border Patrol Implant in some fashion. In Britain, as in other Western European countries, the devices implanted into illegal aliens most angered the Muslim population, thus the protest was loudest there. Muslims were well-integrated in Britain, but no one seemed to believe it. British Muslims often express a stronger sense of belonging than other citizens. The success of the BPI in America, and especially in Israel, was the determining factor in most European country's voting in favor of its use, including Great Britain. Indeed, it turned out even most Muslims were comfortable with the solution, since it allowed their families to feel more secure. And what was wrong with treating law breakers differently than honest law-abiding citizens?

* * *

After spending one full day at Camp David, Sean, General Wright, and Max succeeded putting in place a plan to allow TC to continue developing the *ACCIDENT*. Max convinced Sean of the importance of the discovery. That wasn't difficult. After all, Max and Sean were not just best friends, they also thought a lot alike. General Wright on the other hand showed no bias one way or the other. He knew what his job was and he intended to carry it out to perfection as usual.

Marine One landed on the White House lawn after dark. Max waited on board until the President entered the White House and the press left the viewing area. He and General Wright made their way off the grounds and away from curious eyes. Max flew back to Austin relieved that Sean not only forgave him for his deception, but also how he embraced Max's finding. Now more than ever Max was confident the *ACCIDENT* could become a reality.

* * *

All three men were struggling with how to test the *ACCIDENT*. They had overcome the excessive time problem in the development phase by employing fruit flies, greatly expediting the process. Jack solved the reverse engineering quandary using an idea he got from Reinbold months earlier. But now they were stuck on how to speed up testing.

"It's like looking from the moon at a highway system in North America and you're trying to understand the traffic," Bud complained. "There are so many paths, and some cars are moving fast, some slow, some over short distances, some over large distances, and all of these things are happening at the same time. We need to break that information down to simple pieces that seem to represent a universal behavior for all the cells we measured. How in the—?"

"Where can we find the greatest incidents of this problem and how can we use this to our benefit?" Max asked.

"Let's work the equation backwards. Picture the desired results at these locations. How could we obtain those findings, assuming the *ACCIDENT* performs properly? Now let's single out the factors most likely causing the problem and isolate them," Jack sounded like a fifth grade math teacher.

"Sure, we don't need to limit ourselves to one species as we did with the flies. We can add as many as we desire. What if we had employed mice and rats, bats and fish, all at the same time? We don't need to be focused on age either," Bud seemed both surprised and delighted with his answer.

"There are ample places to ramp-up, but we are going to need a massive get-out-of-jail free card for this plan," Max said, rolling his eyes. "I know where we can get one."

* * *

"This device is nothing more than branding, the same as you Americans do to your cattle. You are doing the same things to Muslims as you did to your Native Americans and your Japanese citizens," cried Iran's Ambassador to the United Nations. "I implore this august body to condemn this device and outlaw its use on the entire planet." As he finished his speech on the floor of the General Assembly, the American Ambassador approached him.

"Mr. Ambassador, I think you protest too much." The American Ambassador cornered his counterpart from Iran in a quiet hallway at the UN. "We have confirmed your country's involvement in trying to obtain intelligence about this device you have been condemning, even before testing was completed. Indeed, I hope we do not discover it was your agents who are responsible for the death of an innocent man. If you have information you want to share with me, now would be an opportune time." The American Ambassador was taunting his Iranian counterpart.

* * *

"President Sean Curran has been re-elected for another four year term. Even though polls are still open in California and other western states, CBS news can now project the election for President and Vice President has been won by the Curran/Bly ticket." CBS's anchor opened his 2020 Election coverage at 11:35 pm on Tuesday night, November 3, 2020. "The President looks like he will carry all but five states, giving him well over the 270 electoral votes needed to win. This is a somewhat surprising outcome, given the polling data just days ago." The network's talking head had a curious tone in his report. "We will be hearing from the President in just a few moments. Here he is now."

"Good evening my fellow Americans. Vice President Bly and I are humbled by this evening's result. We very much want to continue the work we started. We very much want to bring the nation together. And we very much want to make sure all of us are better off now than we were four years ago. Well tonight's results have given the two of us all we could have hoped for." Sean paused while the crowded banquet hall shouted with joy.

"We will carry on until we finish the work we started. We will bring this nation even closer together. And in four years all of us are going to be better off than we are now." Sean knew he was addressing not only an adoring live audience, but also over one hundred million watching on TV around the country.

"Those who face that which is actually before them, unburdened by the past, undistracted by the future—these are they who live, who make the best use of their lives—these are those who have found the secret of contentment and can make a difference in their lives and the lives of others." Walking off the stage to join his enthusiastic supporters in the celebration, Sean could now finally relax.

* * *

"Aljazeera is reporting a Palestinian man died while doctors were attempting to remove the Border Patrol Implant. Baan Movado, a twenty-four year old day laborer working at a construction site for a new power plant in southern Israel, was reported dead from complications during surgery to remove the controversial device. The implant tracks certain people the Israeli government deem a potential terrorist threat." A CNN anchor working the morning prime time news started his segment with a picture of the Arab language newspaper in the background.

"We knew it would happen, we just didn't know when," Jack told Bud over the phone.

"Yep, there is no excuse though. Every doctor, nurse, medical aid or assistant, not to mention probably everyone else in the world, was told and warned the devise fuses to the spinal cord. Any attempt to remove it will result in nothing but no good." Bud's tone was mocking and full of pride. He was the team member who developed this methodology.

"Maybe it could be that the purpose of Mr. Movado's life was to serve as a warning to others."

Sarcasm was not one of Jack's better attributes, but he nailed this one.

"That may be the funniest thing I've ever heard you say Jack. That was really funny. But you know, I believe you're right."

* * *

"Sir, the FBI believes they are closing in on a suspect. DNA evidence recovered from the victim matched a male named Saud Hakim. Hakim is suspected of working for the Iranian government. We located his whereabouts and are monitoring his every move. The agency is tapping his phone and computer." The Assistant to the Director of the FBI was providing a comprehensive report to President Curran's Chief of Staff.

"Very well, keep me advised. The President is most interested in this case," Sean's Chief of Staff knew the President would appreciate this news.

* * *

"Why didn't you pull me aside and ask me about this less than two days after the inauguration," Sean asked mockingly. He was speaking to Max on a secure line two months after being sworn in for his second term. "That way I could have been sure my second term would end up in the crapper."

"There is no other way, Sean. General Wright believes we can pull this off, at least long enough to verify our results. I know you think it will be impossible to hide the findings, but hey, we've come this far."

"What's this 'we' shit; you got a rat in your

pocket? It's my ass, not yours," Sean complained.

"I take that as a yes?" Max asked.

"Go ahead. I like the four out of the five places you recommended, but lose D.C., okay?"

"Will do," Max replied.

"You've got to break some eggs if you want to make an omelet. This is going to be *some* omelet!" Sean supposed.

"General Wright is one tough customer. If anyone can pull this off he can," Max said. "We need to figure out a way to thank him after this is all over with."

"I agree. So, you say a minimum of two years? I don't see any way of hiding the findings. Oh well, damn the torpedoes; full steam ahead!" Sean ended the call with the famous quote from Civil War Admiral David Glasgow Farragut.

* * *

FBI agents tried to arrest Saud Hakim as he left his motel room. He planned on returning to Iran to answer for his failures. Hakim intended to dispose of his hand gun before arriving at the airport. Instead, when he saw his capture was imminent, he turned the gun on himself.

EMTs quickly began treating the Iranian for a gunshot wound to the head. The spy was just as inept at suicide as he was securing Father Bob at the safe-house. Hakim was very much alive. His botched suicide attempt not only saved his life, but little did he know, he was now on his way to becoming an American citizen. Mr. Hakim became an extremely valuable asset for American agencies charged with protecting the country.

* * *

The Iranian Ambassador tried to look embarrassed over the evidence he reviewed during a closed door meeting with his American counterpart at the UN building. He was handed irrefutable evidence, verifying his country's agents were not only responsible for the murder of Dennis Reinbold, but were also involved in an attempted robbery of Solutions, LLC which resulted in the death of an Iranian national. The U.S. Ambassador delivered this news along with an ultimatum to his counterpart.

"Mr. Ambassador, you have forty-eight hours, beginning this moment, to remove your country's murdering band of spies from the United States. All unauthorized Iranians nationals must be out of the United States of America within this time frame, no exceptions. I am confident you are aware we have extremely accurate intelligence as to your countrymen's whereabouts. Failure to act will result in their immediate arrest." America's UN representative knew his contemporary must and would comply.

"The United States is grateful to Iran for the $10 million contribution made to the University of California at Berkley in the name of Dennis Reinbold." Standing in the shadow of the UN Building, the U.S. diplomat was enjoying himself.

"Details of your country being responsible for the kidnapping of two American citizens and the subsequent murder of one of them will remain classified regardless of the generous contribution made in Mr. Reinbold's name. Mr. Ambassador your country's gift is in no way a quid pro quo." He knew the Iranian Ambassador had no choice but to comply with the acerbically delivered ultimatum.

* * *

After months of speculation, the U.S. Supreme Court ruled 8-1 to uphold the Border Patrol Implant Act in full. Many believed at least parts of the law would be overturned. Had that occurred, the Act would be of no use.

"This law does not take away the rights of any citizen or group of citizens. Indeed it upholds the rights of all. Nowhere in the law does it say a legal immigrant may not become a citizen. It states the opposite. Nowhere in the law does it say all illegal aliens must be deported. It states the opposite. Nowhere in the law does it require a citizen to do anything. Nowhere in the law does it require a citizen not to do something. The law simply allows our law enforcement community to require someone who has entered our country illegally to leave immediately or agree to be implanted with a tracking device in order to monitor their whereabouts; until they either become a citizen or are returned to their own country." Chief Justice Mark Sweeney, dressed in his black robe, stood facing a barrage of cameras at the foot of the Supreme Court's steps. He issued the majority report.

"For decades this problem of undocumented immigrants and illegal aliens has divided our nation. Amnesty programs were declared patently unfair to those who pursued citizenship the proper way. Mass deportation was physically impossible and inhumane to families living in this country for years. This Border Patrol Implant Act does away with all the objections to amnesty programs and mass deportation. The law fits perfectly into the framework laid out by our Founders.

This law fits perfectly within the spirit of both the Constitution and the Declaration of Independence." Sweeney completed his address and directed that any questions be submitted to his office in writing.

* * *

Solutions, LLC was celebrating its thirty-third year in business. The Border Patrol Implant discovery, along with other clients, allowed The Company to flourish. Max repaid the Integra loan and the funding needed to complete testing of the *ACCIDENT* was in place, thanks to Sean. TC now enjoyed international prominence but didn't deviate from Max and Bud's original desire to keep the employee count fewer than one hundred. Although there had been a few retirements and resignations, TC's staff was still made up of longtime employees.

Max was the proud grandfather of a beautiful granddaughter born to Max Jr. and Doctor Marie. Alex married her longtime boyfriend and was still coaching soccer at the Division 1 level. Abby and Max continued traveling to visit their newest family member, AJ, as often as their schedules permitted. All four of Bud's daughters were busy raising his grandchildren. Bud and his wife Jan spent time visiting their family as often as their schedule permitted. Father Bob stayed busy tending to the parish. The new school building project was complete, but the debt incurred from the development was still causing Father Bob sleepless nights. Jack was so engrossed in the *ACCIDENT* that Max and Bud sometimes worried he was too zealous but, they realized, so were they.

As usual, General Wright was always planning for

the worst but the *ACCIDENT* was performing perfectly and testing was more than three quarters complete. Wright occasionally complained about having spent the last twenty-two months traveling to and from the four sites. He announced his plans to retire after the project was completed.

Max also spent a lot of time with Cookie. Liz Keebler was being tried in Federal Court for her actions that compromised the BPI. Sean stayed involved, so both Max and Cookie believed even if the jury found Liz guilty, there was still the possibility of a Presidential pardon.

"We'll pick you up at Mount Comfort. I reserved four rooms at the American Inn in Kohler. We have tee times on all three courses and I promise I'll have you back to the parish no later than 6 p.m. on Thursday." Max explained the itinerary to Father Bob over the phone. He and Bud decided the best way to celebrate The Company's birthday was to get away with Father Bob and Cookie for three days of golf. There may be places on earth as good to play golf, but there were none better than Black Wolf Run and Whistling Straights in Kohler, Wisconsin.

"So, is everything going well? I occasionally run into our devil's advocates. They ask about your so-called accident." Father Bob's curiosity was telling.

"I'll bring you up to date in Kohler. Testing is nearing completion. It's taken longer than I thought but all is well. Bob, I can't explain it, but the results we're achieving are nothing short of remarkable. If all continues to go well—," Father Bob interrupted Max.

"If all continues to go well, your problems will have just begun. Max, when you play with fire, you can get burned." Max was sure he was being lectured by

Father Bob. *If this was anyone else, I'd tell him to kiss my ass*, Max thought.

"We've not crossed the Rubicon, Bob. Only Bud, Jack and I have the formula. We can abort at a moment's notice. It's not like this is the Manhattan Project. The genie is still safely in her bottle." Max knew he was being overly optimistic.

"Max, remember the movie, *Tora, Tora, Tora*? Remember near the end what Admiral Yamamoto said?"

'I'm afraid we have awakened a sleeping giant,'" Max answered.

Chapter 15

De Ja Vu All Over Again

Sean was basking in the glory of a beloved lame duck president. He received the highest approval rating on record for any president at this point in his term. He was nearing his eighth year in office with his legacy already intact based on the success of the Border Patrol Implant. A problem that plagued his predecessors no longer divided the country. The President's initiative and The Company's solution virtually eliminated the enforcement quandary brought on by illegal aliens, or *unauthorized immigrants*, as some preferred.

Countries around the world were employing the BPI to deal with their version of undocumented immigrants and others utilized the new technology to levels still being debated for their morality.

"Are you quite certain?" Sean asked General Wright from the Oval Office.

"I'm afraid so, Mr. President. It turns out you were right. With the dramatic changes taking place it was impossible to avoid the obvious."

"It's time to start making the omelet. I had hoped we could avoid this but you roll the dice; you take your chances." Sean had already anticipated how he would handle this situation. From the outset, he was convinced there would be no way to conceal the ACCIDENT"S test results.

"Mr. President, if I can help in any way—." Sean broke in.

"Well done, General. I should say, well done again, General. I appreciate your professionalism and particularly the way you treated me throughout these initiatives. You served your country well. I wish there was something you could do, but I'll take it from here."

"It has truly been my pleasure. I am honored to have served," General Wright replied. "I'm going to be retiring soon, Mr. President. I wish you well."

"If your ears have been burning, it's because Max and I have been talking about inviting you and your wife to join us for a holiday of sorts. I will make sure you receive the details for your consideration. Good luck and God bless you, General. I hope to see you soon."

* * *

Max, Jack and Bud were huddled around Solution's conference room table, listening on a speaker phone to comments from President Curran, speaking to them on his secure line from the Oval Office.

"I'm going before the American people tomorrow evening," Sean told the three men just one day before a planned Presidential address to a joint session of Congress. "Your discovery is too important to allow this story to take on a life of its own. I'll need any additional information you can provide that's not included in the remarks I sent you. Max, you guys feel free to make any changes to the text, and I mean any. I'll need it by early afternoon in time for a little practice." Sean sounded somewhat panic-stricken.

"I didn't know you had to practice before you made a speech." Max knew Sean could see him giggling through the phone.

"Real funny, don't quit your day job," Sean shot back. His reply lifted the tension from the call and made Jack and Bud laugh out loud, appreciating how close Max was to the President of the United States of America.

* * *

"Neither Government nor Health officials have any answers. 'It's inexplicable,' the Mayor of Los Angeles stated." LA's most watched evening news program began its nightly report by featuring the anchor doing the story from the field. The anchor's remote location took most regular viewers by surprise.

"The medical community has not found any evidence pointing to either physical or mental health issues, but the number of AIDS related births has been nearly nonexistent compared to a year ago. Indeed, this area of LA is experiencing a dramatic decline in all categories of diseases being passed on to newborns. Whispers of some kind of a test being conducted in this area of the city are getting louder."

* * *

For the tenth time in eight years President Curran was standing at the podium in The House of Representatives on Capitol Hill in Washington, D.C. preparing to make what would be the most significant, controversial, and epic address in the country's history. The number wasn't a record, but none of his predecessor's speeches before Congress, including FDR's request for a declaration of war against Japan, would have a greater impact on the nation.

"Mr. Speaker, Mr. Vice President, members of Congress, distinguished guests and fellow Americans, tonight I have an important announcement. I know most of you seated in this room or listening to my voice or watching me are going to be surprised with what I am going to disclose. I begin by asking you to indulge me and reflect on what I am proposing before you condemn either me or my proposal." Sean paused to see the reaction.

"Immediately after becoming President, I embarked on an ambitious course, a course that might offer me and my successor's different options, better options, when faced with complex problems. The controversial Border Patrol Implant was an outcome from taking this path. There can be no denying the BPI initiative had its share of controversy. But at the end of the day, the device provided our nation with not only more secure borders and a less divided country, it also validated that creative technology can be applied to weighty social problems." Taking a deep breath, Sean stopped and noticed how quiet the chamber had become.

"During the BPI development stage the scientists and engineers working on the project discovered, by accident, a safe and reliable method to prevent unwanted pregnancies." Sean paused again, but not because he was receiving applause or to breath, he just stopped.

"I am not announcing the discovery of the next generation birth control pill, and no, I am not proclaiming a new version of a conventional contraceptive that will now be available. This administration will be promoting a device which can be implanted in either a male or female that blocks the natural process of fertilization. The device does not sterilize the recipient, and no, it doesn't harm, nor is it in any way dangerous to a receiver's health, either short or long term. The device simply provides signals to the brain, instructing either the male sperm or the female egg to perform differently. The properties of the implant can be completely destroyed in moments." Again Sean paused, seeking any sign of approval from the lawmakers and guests.

"Now, before I go into more detail, let me tell you how the device has already performed in real time. When I was initially told of the discovery three years ago, I, like you listening now, was taken utterly by surprise. I hold a Master's degree in Chemical Engineering and have spent years in the field of research and development, but I couldn't grasp the capacity of this finding. After reviewing and understanding how the device functions, I instructed the team of engineers to perform rigorous testing. The device exceeded all safety parameters." Sean paused again, still not hearing even a whisper coming from the audience.

"At this point, I believed it necessary to field test the device. I approved the commencement of trials in areas plagued with a high instance of teen pregnancies and areas where generations of people have been doomed from birth to live in poverty, crime, and disease as a result of the never ending cycle of children having children." Sean stopped. He finally received a polite applause.

"When you closely examine what stands as the most serious problem in America, you find it is not high unemployment or inflation, it is not global warming or water shortages, and it is not deficit spending or the national debt. The root cause of poverty, crime, disease, and just about every other horrible trouble man can inflict on himself is, babies having babies." Snapping his head up from the teleprompter, The President stopped because a shriek came from the House floor.

"Negative eugenics, negative eugenics! It was you who prevented all the babies from being born." A Congresswoman from the Los Angeles area shouted, "Shame! Shame!" Over and over she cried shame, until the Sergeant of Arms removed her from the floor.

The President was noticeably shaken by this interruption, but he continued his speech. He explained how the device was field tested and its remarkable results. In attempting to justify his decision, he articulately outlined the benefits society could gain by utilizing this discovery. With passion and confidence he described the horrible pain and suffering brought on by the scourge of children having children.

"I am prepared to shoulder the blame for concealing this program and equally prepared to shepherd its cause. I believe it is the right thing to do and the right time to do it. This is something the country sorely needs. All of us can agree, if we continue to do nothing, the consequences are laid plainly before us. But if we are bold enough to tackle this problem beginning now; our nation will enter a new era of decency and prosperity. God bless you and may God continue to bless the United States of America."

* * *

The President finished his address and walked out of the chamber at a brisk pace, stopping only a few times to shake hands with lawmakers.

The morning papers were trumpeting the President's speech made the night before.

"President God," the LA Tribune front page banner read. ''Implantgate", a new "gate" was added to the lexicon by the Washington Post. The New York Daily news, with its well-known use of large font headlines weighed in with, "PRESIDENT IMPLANT STRIKES AGAIN."

There wasn't much good news being reported, but the President hadn't made the mistake of laying all his cards on the table without first being confident he at least had a competitive hand. He learned that lesson the hard way during the BPI disclosure. The day before his announcement, President Curran first informed the Vice President. After completing that most unpleasant task, he assembled his Cabinet. Finally, he gathered many prominent men and women from his party. Sean knew he needed to "test the waters", instead of blindly going before the country. Over fifty influential leaders already heard about the plan when the President delivered the news publically. Sean received tacit approval to continue to pursue the initiative from those supporters.

Members of Congress representing the Watts area of LA, several cities in Nassau County on Long Island in New York, Carmel, Indiana, a high income suburb near Indianapolis and Atlanta, Georgia, got a friendly judge to issue a restraining order to prevent any more of their constituent's from being "tested." The federal judge also ordered any other jurisdiction active in secret trials of the device to cease and desist. The order was in vain since testing was halted several days earlier after reports began surfacing.

The Border Patrol Implant was controversial. This Personal Responsibility Implant was highly controversial.

The Personal Responsibility Implant, now known as the PRI, came about with the development of the

Border Patrol Implant device. Although the BPI and the PRI integrated similar technologies, the Personal Responsibility Implant had nothing else in common with the Border Patrol Implant. BPI was only intended to track human's whereabouts. The PRI was designed to short-circuit natural electrical impulses generated by organisms inside the body and directed to the brain.

The PRI was implanted in the body at the same location as the BPI; fused to the C2 vertebrae. Both devices receive their power from the electrometric current running through the spinal cord. A trickle of electricity generated by the body is all that is needed to power either tiny machine. The Company's engineers made a major leap in nanotechnology when discovering the ability to design and build a system capable of hijacking certain behavior associated with the homeostasis process.

Homeostasis is a natural process in the body regulating the internal environment to keep body systems functioning well. Max's expertise in nanotechnology exposed him to numerous projects involving the homeostasis process. A body function, such as an organ, uses a relay system which interprets the organs' needs and sends this message to the brain. In turn, the brain sends a response to correct this condition so the body can return to normal ranges. The body's organs and functions have specific receptors sending messages to the brain on the current credit or deficit ranges. The brain sends an appropriate response to either increase or decrease a function so the mechanism returns to normal ranges. It wasn't easy. In fact, isolating the serum that destroys the PRI was the most difficult problem he ever unraveled.

But Max had been pondering and studying how to do something about the diabolical suffering that children having children causes ever since he watched the report of a young man shot dead by Austin police. He cringed upon seeing a seventeen year old child clutching her newborn. He pictured his own daughter living in squalor with the young man who he guessed was born to a mother in her early teens.

The Personal Responsibility Implant device simply made the brain send a different message to the male and female's reproductive system. For fun Bud and Jack characterized the process as men shooting blanks and women passing slugs, or coins that won't work when put into a vending machine.

To reverse the process, The Company's team developed a serum that, when injected anywhere near the C2 vertebrae, triggered the device's main component to disintegrate almost instantaneously. The body simply discards the remaining nano-particles. The team took great care to eliminate the possibility of any other serum being able to disturb the main component.

* * *

"I'm Carrie Mattingly reporting from New York. Scientists have discovered how to eliminate unwanted pregnancies without the use of traditional contraceptives for both male and females. The Personality Responsibility Implant, better known as PRI, uses similar technology as the Border Patrol Implant. The process must be approved by Congress before implementation. Reactions to President Curran's new initiative are as expected as this report shows.

'It could mean that millions of unwanted pregnancies will be eliminated if the Personal Responsibility Implant device becomes law,' said Dennis

Dinn, a Stanford University law professor who studies the implications of biomedical technologies. For technical as well as ethical reasons, nobody expects that doctors will be legally performing the implants any time soon. But some see the implants becoming a reality and question its use. Some experts say it could save billions of dollars currently being spent supporting the blight of children having children.

'I think it's a pretty large advance in the next generation of reproductive technologies for women,' supposed Brad Austin, who studies reproductive development at the University of California, Los Angeles. 'Discussion about policy and regulation needs to begin now.'

"The experiments conducted on the PRI were reported online Thursday in the journal Science by Scientists at Solutions, LLC in Austin, Texas. The same group previously reported work with the Border Patrol Implant, approved for use by the U. S. Congress over four years ago. In the new work, they began with genetically reprogrammed skin cells from both female and male adults. The reprogramming technique, discovered several years ago, made an ordinary cell revert to a kind of blank slate, so it could be chemically prodded to develop into any kind of cell.

"The American researchers have not revealed any other details. The procedure is too controversial for the device's technical aspects to be revealed until enabling legislation is enacted and courts have ruled on its constitutionality. The moral and legal hurdles are so big that some experts are skeptical about the approach ever being used.

'I don't think there's a lot of support here,' said David Mason, who studies the development of human fetuses at the University of Boston.

"Others are more optimistic, but say it won't be easy. 'The PRI is the future,' Austin said. Dinn, the Stanford law professor, speculated that in one to two years, the PRI might make couples more likely to think about fertilization just so they don't act like animals. Some others, however, said they doubt Congress will permit the use of the device.

'I think there's a huge market for it,' said Kris Carter of the Johns Hopkins Berman Institute of Bioethics. 'People are not going to stop having sex, so the use of this device can eliminate unwanted outcomes.'

"The implant also raises a host of medical and ethical concerns. 'I would be worried about the safety of trying to eliminate kids this way,' said Bill Fox, director of the stem cell program at the University of California, Berkley. 'It seems like an experiment on those kids. It would also be complicated and expensive, adding to the question of whether it would really be a good way to treat fertility.' He and others also said society would have to decide how much government regulation would be needed, both for the initial research and its routine use by medical providers. Carrie Mattingly reporting; NBC News, New York."

Chapter 16

Unprecedented

"Hundreds of men and women living in and around the four areas of the country where the secret tests were conducted filed lawsuits. I've never seen more Philadelphia lawyers and Florsheim Imperials hanging around the federal courthouse in Washington, D.C., salivating to gain class status for the plaintiffs in order to consolidate all the cases into one." A TV in the Oval Office carried the report made by a talking head from Stock Market Update.

"Standing outside the courthouse in D.C. would be a very dangerous place today." Bud made the remark to Sean and Max with a smirk on his face. Bud and Max were meeting with Sean in the Oval Office discussing the best way to conduct Max's upcoming testimony. "If an ambulance came by with its siren on anyone in the way would get trampled to death with all those ambulance chasers rushing out the courthouse door. Looks like someone's in for some serious legal plunder."

"Bud, I thought I was the only one who thought most attorneys are parasites," Sean replied.

"Mr. President, is it really fair to destroy the reputation of the five percent because of the behavior of the ninety-five percent?" Bud jibed.

For the first time in a long time, Max was anxious. He was subpoenaed to testify before committees in both the House and Senate that were investigating the same matter, the Personal Responsibility Implant.

"Max, just remember, the whole world is bullshit and paperwork. All these lawmakers have one and only one thing on their mind; they want to get re-elected." Sean didn't even pretend to act like he was kidding.

"And I can ease the pain how?" Max asked sarcastically.

"You know how to work the halls. It's no different here than in Austin, just more and deeper," Sean answered.

"Don't tell my mom I'm a lobbyist, she thinks I play piano in a whorehouse." Max kept up the pretense.

"Max, be proud! Lobbyists are the people we hire to protect us from the people we elect." Sean corrected Max. He was now smiling. The mood was turning slaphappy.

"No, they're the boil on the asshole of democracy," Bud fired back.

"Illigitimum non carborundum, Max, don't let the bastards get you down." Sean was trying to get Max laughing. "The greatest lesson in life is to know that even fools are right sometimes. But not this time, I want you to fight to the death." Sean decided to get back to serious.

"Max, you could just sit there. Silence is often misinterpreted, but never misquoted. But hey, if you get a bad lie, you don't pick up the ball and go home. Sean is right. This matters; the PRI matters." Bud weighed in again.

"My dad always said if anything matters, then everything matters. Don't be ruled by your appetite. If someone says you can have it, but you must take it today, tell them to keep it. Thanks you guys!" Feeling much more confident, Max was now confident he was prepared to defend the Personal Responsibility Implant.

* * *

"Mr. Quinn, isn't it true your company was responsible for delivering this device?" The committee Chairman asked Max the first question, attempting to show off his authority.

"That's true, Mr. Chairman," Max answered confidently.

"If you please, will you enlighten this committee how you envisioned the Personal Responsibility Implant performing?" Max remembered what Sean told him before answering the Chairman's question. *The only thing all politicians are really concerned about is getting re-elected.*

"Mr. Chairman, I have spent my entire adult life in the problem solving business. People who pursue this walk of life believe there are no such things as problems, only solutions. You have been told, as our team was developing the Border Patrol Implant, we came upon this new discovery by accident; that's true. I won't go into all the technical aspects, but suffice to say, there is a great deal of new technology contained in the PRI." Max was reading from prepared remarks.

"To answer your question as succinctly as I can, our team envisions all newborns, both male and female, be implanted with the device. Unless and until a person can either post a bond or successfully complete an evaluation, the device will remain active. After a person has either posted the bond or successfully completed an evaluation, then and only then will he or she become eligible to receive the serum." After answering, Max paused for a moment to see how the panel was reacting.

"The instant the serum comes in contact with the implant the device's main component will disintegrate. This action will completely remove a female's inability to have an egg fertilized, either naturally or using other means such as In Vitro fertilization or artificial insemination. The result will be the same for a male receiving the serum. His sperm will immediately regain the ability to fertilize a female egg." Max's answer was unapologetic in its tone.

"What kind of evaluation are you talking about? And the bond—how much?" The Chairman's inquiry was much more congenial.

"A government report found that a middle-income family with one child will spend about $235,000 child-related expenses from birth through age seventeen. The report found that families with three or more children spend twenty-two percent less per child than those with two children. The savings result from hand-me-down clothes and toys, shared bedrooms and buying food in larger quantities. The estimate includes the cost of transportation, child care, education, food, clothing, health care and miscellaneous expenses, but not higher education." Max again referred to his prepared notes for his report.

"So I suppose the answer to your second question is $235,000 for now, more as time goes by." Max had to pause to take a cleansing breath. "As for the evaluation, I can't be specific. But basically, I believe everyone can agree that a couple desiring to bring a new human being into the world should be able to at least know their alphabet, read and count to ten, and possess a basic ability to know the difference between right and wrong,

Mr. Chairman." Max knew he was being too sarcastic, but he still got a laugh from many of those both on the panel and in the audience.

"Mr. Quinn, as a scientist, do you believe you have a moral responsibility when you experiment with devices designed to block the human reproductive system?" A well-known liberal committee member asked the question in a combative tone.

"First of all Congressman, I'm an engineer. We did however employ several scientists on this project. As their primary professional responsibilities, scientists strive to ensure the integrity of the research record and engineers strive to ensure the safety of the public.

"Wernher von Braun was a German physicist who led the development of rocket technology. During the Second World War he contributed to the development of the V-2 rocket that devastated London. Toward the end of the war he was captured by the United States Army. Are scientists and engineers merely hired guns that provide technical services to whoever employs them?" Max paused. He glanced up to see the Congressman's facial expression.

"In von Braun's case, the contrast is stark, as he worked for both Nazi Germany and the United States. Are scientists and engineers responsible for the uses of their creations? Sir, I am sure of two things. First, there is a God, and I'm not him. Second, yes, I believe all men and women, regardless of their walk in life, should be morally responsible for their actions."

"Mr. Quinn, you're familiar with the term negative eugenics. My colleague from Los Angeles was summarily removed from the House Chambers simply because she correctly characterized your device. Madam Congresswoman, you need not be fearful today. Mr.

Quinn, negative eugenics can be defined as a social philosophy which advocates for the improvement of human hereditary traits through the promotion of higher reproduction of more desired people and traits, and the reduction of reproduction of less desired people and traits. Isn't that exactly what your Personal Responsibility Implant was designed to accomplish?" The question was asked by a congressman from the same state as the Congresswoman who shouted 'negative eugenics' at the President.

"No Congressman! The PRI treats everyone equally. Negative eugenics was a term used often in the Buck v. Bell decision. Justice Oliver Wendell Holmes wrote for the majority that a state statute permitting compulsory sterilization of the unfit, including the mentally retarded, for the protection and health of the state did not violate the due process clause of the Fourteenth Amendment to the United States Constitution. The Personal Responsibility Implant is not even in the same universe as compulsory sterilization. PRI is not sterilization. By the way Congressman, the Buck v. Bell decision has never been overturned. So I repeat my answer, no!" During his entire answer Max stared at his inquisitor.

"So you are testifying that you favor the use of this diabolical devise, Mr. Quinn?" This question came from the now infamous Congresswoman from LA. "Don't you care what people are saying about you and your horrible device? You and your kind are despicable. How can you be so damn hateful?"

"Congresswoman, my father taught me years ago, what other people think of *you* is none of *your* business. So, my answer to your question about what people like you think about me is no. He also taught me that when you throw mud at someone, you not only get your hands dirty, you also begin to run out of ground. And in a final tribute to my dad, he taught me profanity is the use of strong words by weak people." Max replied to her loaded question, while showing his contempt for her arrogance. *Sean would be proud*, he thought.

"So, Mr. Quinn, it's clear you support the use of this device, but all you have described so far are things that will make the problem worse," she blasted back.

"Congresswoman, which is worse, millions of children born each year to mothers not yet seventeen years old, or the millions more who will be born to these newborns before they turn seventeen, or the millions of unborn aborted each year in America, or the—." Max was interrupted by the Congresswoman screaming, "Stop"!

After the Chairman regained order, Max went on to describe how the PRI could virtually eliminate not only the shameful number of abortions being performed each year in America, but also how billions of dollars in resources would be freed up. Billions of dollars being wasted from the cost associated with children having children, including crime, health, and welfare expenditures, and the too numerous to mention advantages to the culture at large. He provided data showing the problem is widespread.

"Women of all ages have unintended pregnancies, but some groups, such as teens, are at a much higher risk. Studies show that forty-nine percent of pregnancies in the United States were unintended, but four out of five pregnancies among women aged nineteen years and younger were unintended," Max once again paused from being interrupted.

"Did you develop this device to exclusively

address teen pregnancies?" Finally Max was asked a question by a Congressman from Texas who he knew.

"Congressman, teen pregnancy is closely linked to a host of other critical social issues including poverty and income, overall child well-being, out-of-wedlock births, irresponsible fatherhood, health issues, education, child welfare, and other risky behavior. There are also substantial public costs associated with adolescent childbearing. Consequently, teen pregnancy should be viewed not only as a reproductive health issue, but as one that works to improve all of these measures." Max had to pause because a cameraman slipped and fell right in front of him.

"Simply put, if more children in this country were born to parents who were ready and able to care for them, we would see a significant reduction in a host of social problems afflicting children in the United States, from school failure and crime to child abuse and neglect. So yes, Congressman," Max again answered confidently.

"But why a device that prevents a woman from getting pregnant? We already have numerous forms of birth control available, free to anyone unable to afford them. Why must her body be invaded with a device when she can choose conventional birth control methods?" *Sean was right, there is a lot of low IQ stuff going on in here;* Max thought, after a Congresswoman from Michigan asked yet another stupid question.

"May I answer my esteemed colleague's question Mr. Quinn?" A Congressman from Florida spoke up.

"Sir, you can answer as many questions asked of me that you want. Believe me, I'm okay with that." Max wasn't surprised when the entire panel, the guests and the press present in the committee room all erupted in polite laughter. *Thank you, dear Lord*, Max prayed to himself.

"Mr. Quinn testified that every child born would receive this implant. Therefore it is not just females who are affected. And please Madam, we must all admit, your suggestion that everyone should simply take advantage of available birth control methods is why we are here in the first place; it fails miserably." After his answer, it was clear to all that he was deriding his colleague.

"Mr. Quinn, I know you're growing tired from this inquiry. I for one congratulate you. Your effort to solve this national plague is to be commended, regardless of whether or not this bill becomes law." The Committee Chairman's comment surprised Max. "But I have one more question for you, and then we can adjourn. Can you tell this committee the difference in babies born to teens versus babies born to—let's say—women older than twenty?"

"Mr. Chairman, babies born to teenagers are particularly vulnerable. Even when taking into account various social and economic factors, teens experiencing an unplanned pregnancy are less likely to obtain prenatal care, and their babies are at increased risk of both low birth weight and of being born prematurely. These babies also face a range of developmental risks including poorer physical and mental health, and compared to children born as the result of an intended pregnancy, they have significantly lower cognitive test scores.

When these children born to children are compared to children born to more mature women who generally grow up with two parents, children in the one-parent families are more likely to be poor, drop out of high school, have lower grade-point averages, lower college aspirations, and poorer school attendance records. As adults, they experience a myriad of problems." Max ended his testimony; certain he had not made any serious gaffes.

His appearance before the committee lasted over three hours before he was allowed to leave, in order to repeat his performance in a Senate committee.

* * *

"Your Honor, we the people find the defendant, Elizabeth Keebler, guilty on all counts." The announcement was made by the jury foreman to the federal judge hearing the case of The United States of America vs. Elizabeth J Keebler. Liz was tried and convicted on three counts of providing the enemy with secrets vital to American interests. The convictions added up to a life sentence.

In the United States, the pardon power for federal crimes is granted to the President under Article II, Section 2, of the United States Constitution, which states that the President "shall have power to grant reprieves and pardons for offenses against the United States, except in cases of impeachment." President Curran granted a Presidential Pardon to Cookie's wife. Liz's trial was under a gag order; therefore it did not receive a lot of media coverage, taking a lot of the heat off the President.

Cookie was overwhelmed with relief. Liz may be self-centered and narcissistic, but he wasn't perfect either. Besides, now the couple could work on improving their marriage after this trying ordeal. Max too was most grateful to Sean. He knew if it weren't for Cookie's help, the *ACCIDENT* might never have been completed.

Max chose not to tell Cookie about his deception. *What good would it do to tell him the funds I needed were not for the President's project,* he supposed?

* * *

"Ladies and gentlemen, please help me welcome the President of the United States." Applauding as Sean appeared on stage, America's number one late night talk show host opened his hour long program to a packed house. "Mr. President, you're two terms have turned out to be good for most Americans, in that most say they are doing well. But this so-called PRI, why mess up your legacy?"

"It is hard in this world to do well. It is hard to do good. When I hear a claim that a person or an institution is going to do both, I reach for my wallet. You should too." Sean tried to add a little levity to his answer.

"Mr. President, your Personal Responsibility Implant idea has certainly caused a ruckus to say the least, wouldn't you agree? Can you tell us what you think this plan can accomplish? Laws never made man a whit more just."

"Jay, I want you to close your eyes and imagine the word picture I'm going to paint. Go ahead, close your eyes, please." Sean stretched out his hand towards the host face as if to help him close his eyes. "You're driving on a street in a rundown inner city, low-income neighborhood, neglected by police and with inadequate law enforcement services. Negotiating with police is as much an everyday activity as dealing with the local gang. How are you doing there?" Sean quipped as he panned the audience. He was trying to keep the moment from getting too serious.

"You've seen this picture depicted hundreds of times in movies and TV series. Young, unemployed, angry, dope-dealing high school drop outs, selling drugs and guns, hanging out on a corner, terrorizing the neighbors and the neighborhood. As you continue driving, this scene is repeated over and over. If you were to stop and ask any one of these young people how old was their mother when they were born, it's likely you would learn she was under seventeen. Continuing your drive you notice an unusually large number of pregnant girls hanging around with their gang member boyfriends. Go ahead and open your eyes now, Jay." The President playfully instructed the host and continued his serious explanation.

"Jay, I believe if this widespread malady, children having children, continues to go unchecked, hopeless situations like I just described will only increase, relegating literally millions of human beings to a life of crime, poverty, hopelessness, and despair. Whatever you feed grows. Whatever you starve dies," Sean paused for the host to reply.

"Mr. President, polls show this bill has very little chance of passing."

"As Warren Buffet would say, if you're picking stocks, I wouldn't pick that one. I think the bill has an excellent chance."

"So you believe your idea can put a stop to this problem you call children having children?" Jay asked, looking like he wished he hadn't asked the question.

"Jay, my proposal requires both men and women to either post a bond or pass a simple exam before the device is deactivated, allowing normal reproductive functions to resume immediately. So yes! I believe we now have the technology to all but eliminate unwanted pregnancies and the diabolical results they have on our society and culture at large.

"Do you think these people I described— hanging around with no hope for the future— chose this life? Of course not! No one would choose that kind of existence. My plan doesn't deprive anyone of life, liberty or the pursuit of happiness, indeed it strengthens opportunities for all," Sean had to stop. The mostly young audience was making rowdy screams, high fives and fist pumps of approval.

"Jay, I want you, and all of you in the audience and at home, to please listen to me very closely. Ladies and gentlemen please hear what I'm saying. The Personal Responsibility Implant does just that; requires men and women to be responsible when it comes to bringing new life into their world." Sean finished to a rousing standing ovation from the studio audience.

* * *

Not in a very long time had the Catholic Church's hierarchy scheduled such a public hearing. The Pope believed this new discovery may be much more dangerous to the soul than birth control pills. In 1968, Pope Paul VI issued his landmark encyclical letter titled "Human Life", which reemphasized the Church's constant teaching that it is always intrinsically wrong to use contraception to prevent new human beings from coming into existence.

The Catholic Church believes contraception is wrong because it's a deliberate violation of the design God built into the human race, often referred to as "natural law." The natural law purpose of sex is procreation. The pleasure that sexual intercourse provides is an additional blessing from God, intended to offer the possibility of new life while strengthening the bond of intimacy, respect, and love between husband and wife. The loving environment this bond creates is the perfect setting for nurturing children.

"There can be no denying the pain and suffering poured out because of unmarried children giving birth to children," the Archbishop of New York City said in opening remarks at the conclave. "The Church has constantly taught that it is always intrinsically wrong to use contraception to prevent new human beings from coming into existence. This device is clearly a contraceptive. This device clearly prevents new human beings from coming into existence. But this device is different.

"In the past, our teachings were always directed toward adults, both married and single. The scourge of children giving birth to children is destroying our culture. In the United States, we were able to prove that if you give people something for nothing, you will cause the problem to worsen. Our welfare laws were creating generations of beneficiaries that never knew there was a better way to live through work, not welfare. The U.S. changed this destructive law and consequently changed the culture. This new device, appropriately named the Personal Responsibility Implant, can potentially eliminate a problem the Church has never considered."

* * *

The Wall Street Journal reported that a powerful lawmaker is calling for Senate hearings following a lawsuit charging the Curran administration on the grounds that they approved illegal human experiments, including some that exposed minors to procedures potentially life threatening.

Sen. James Hughes, D-OK, called it extremely disturbing that scientists may have exposed people to a potentially life threatening experiment. The allegations first surfaced after President Curran announced his Personal Responsibility Implant initiative and additional information was obtained through Freedom of Information Act requests. Those findings led to the lawsuit and now Hughes' call for hearings.

"Indeed, the administration may be criminally liable for its conduct," Sen. Hughes said at a news conference today. Hughes, the ranking member of the Senate Committee on Environment and Public Works, wrote in a letter to the committee's chairman, Sen. Roby Swanson, R-Calif. "The President deliberately placed the administration's desire to move its project forward; it just validates the problem that the Curran mission is not about public health. The law and the rules that the administration has violated are not just technical, trivial regulations, they ran afoul of spirit of the law," Hughes, who compared the research to the Tuskegee syphilis experiments and to those conducted in Nazi Germany, told CNNews.com.

"These are among the most sacrosanct federal regulations in that they are protecting human subjects in medical experiments. No study subject was told what these things do," he added, citing the Common Rule, a set of ethics guidelines governing experiments on people. "It's shocking," Hughes concluded.

Hughes suggested the administration may be criminally liable for its conduct. Curran's press secretary, in a statement, said all human studies conducted by its scientists were, "independently evaluated for safety and ethics and all results are peer-reviewed."

The report ended by stating the Department of Justice is representing the United States in the litigation. "Although the administration isn't discussing the allegations, President Curran is on record about the safety the test subjects were provided."

* * *

Tens of thousands of demonstrators descended on Capitol Hill protesting the government's proposed Personal Responsibility Implant bill, illustrating the network of activists that had emerged in opposition to President Curran's policy. Demonstrators cheered during a rally at Freedom Plaza in Washington. Organizers said they believed people from all fifty States came for the Reproductive Freedom March on Washington.

Crowds filled nearly every pocket of open space near the west lawn of the Capitol, many standing and listening without a view of the stage. They marched from Freedom Plaza, adjacent to the White House, as shouts of "No Implant" echoed through downtown Washington, and marchers dressed as assorted animals while banging drums. Some people stayed stranded on Constitution Avenue as the program began near the Capitol, unable to find room to watch the speakers.

A spokesman for D.C. Fire and Emergency Medical Services estimated the crowd in excess of seven hundred thousand people. Local and federal law enforcement authorities didn't provide crowd estimates. The gathering was largely peaceful. Speakers and demonstrators said they opposed Curran's so called PRI bill making its way through Congress.

"It's not about national security, it's about Curran seizing our freedom", read one sign.

Former House Minority Leader, Doug McKibbon, a Michigan Democrat, roused the crowd when he criticized the President for treating people like animals, suggesting that the President had violated his "Commitment of Fidelity to the United States Constitution."

President Curran's Personal Responsibility Implant proposal had sparked heated debate over whether the plan was indeed a national security issue.

"Ladies and gentlemen, welcome to Little Bighorn!" Mr. McKibbon made this declaration to a wave of roaring applause, professing hope that the President failed in his quest for reproductive control. "If we're able to stop Curran on this, it will be his Little Bighorn," Mr. McKibbon told activists. "It will break him. While some are prepared to write the obituary on the ability for Americans to freely reproduce, I believe we are on the verge of a great American awakening. And it will begin here, and begin now, and begin with you."

While Sean's critics were flooding the streets near the White House and the Capitol, the President was in California, speaking to a rally that police estimated to have drawn fifteen thousand people, to drum up support for his new implant initiative. While Sean didn't directly acknowledge the protests back home, he did refer to his opponents.

"Now, what we've seen in these past months is the same partisan display that has left so many of you disillusioned in Washington for so long," Sean said to applause. "Too many have used this opportunity to score short-term political points instead of working together to solve long-term challenges." President Curran finished by saying, "Change should consist of true reproductive reform for America."

Chapter 17

Can't Uninvent

Sean invited Father Bob and Max to the White House for a reunion of sorts. Almost eight years had passed since the three men spent time alone together and all three had experienced life changing incidents. Father Bob's kidnapping and escape; Max's accidental discovery of the technology contained in the PRI and his ordeal in Costa Rica; the attempted assassination, and of course Sean's position as the most powerful person in the world. The three friends wouldn't run out of things to talk about.

"This really shy middle aged guy with horrible stinky feet who's never had a sexual relationship in his life meets this really shy middle aged woman with a chronic case of halitosis who's never has a sexual relationship in her life in the hotel bar where they were vacationing. Their libido is running high." Sean began his joke and asked Max if he heard it.

"Haven't heard it," Max replied, looking at Father Bob for his reaction.

"Me neither," Father Bob said, smiling.

"So several hours and many cocktails later they end up in her room. He immediately made his way into the bathroom in order to dispose of his smelly socks and wash off his feet. When he finished she then rushed into the bathroom in order to scrub her teeth and cover-up the offensive order caused by her condition. Afterwards, as they were face to face for the first time, she said—I need to tell you something before we go any further. He interrupted her and said— let me guess, you ate my socks." After Sean said the punch line, Max and Father Bob were laughing so loud he was sure the Secret Service was going to come crashing in with guns blazing.

"One of your best," Max laughed. "Where are you getting your material these days, from Senator Hughes?" He knew how much grief Sean was getting from his adversary.

"That jackass! He is proof positive that you can't fool all the people all the time. Dennis is going to have his hands full." Sean warned his Vice President to keep his friends close and his enemies closer if he is successful in his bid to succeed him as President.

The three were served dinner in the President's suite in the North Wing dining room. Father Bob talked about his kidnapping in detail when pressed by Max and Sean. He explained how Reinbold responded to the interrogation tactics used by the Iranian spies. His description agitated both men. After the meal was over, Sean asked Max if he had it to do all over again, would he pursue the Personal Responsibility Implant technology as vigorously. He asked Father Bob if he personally took the same position as the Catholic Church had on the device.

The best friends visited late into the night. Sean's invitation included a stay over. Father Bob got the Lincoln Bedroom and Max slept in another not so famous White House guest room. The next morning brought news about support increasing for the President's PRI bill making its way through Congress. Sean bid his buddies' farewell as Max sped back to Austin in the TBM, while Father Bob took a flight back home to Indianapolis.

* * *

The era before the Civil War was known as the golden age of debate, when oratory, the art of public speaking, flourished in Congress. But the quality of oratory in Congress had declined substantially. Modern visitors to the galleries, who expected to hear great speech-making or dramatic debates, were often disappointed to find someone reading a dry and technical speech to a largely empty chamber. Regardless of the empty chairs, members spoke to establish a record of support or disapproval of some legislation, as their words were recorded in the Congressional Record and were broadcast on television.

"These are children giving birth to children. Their offspring are responsible for most of the crime in our country. Their offspring are beneficiaries of most of the welfare dollars. Their offspring represent most of the unemployable. Their offspring receive most of the Medicaid budget. Their offspring spread most of the sexually transmitted diseases. Their offspring account for most of the high school dropouts. And their offspring are mostly responsible for bringing into existence the next generation of babies born to children; carrying on this scourge indefinitely. We finally have a solution to this crisis. Future generations will judge us on how we tackled the big problems. The future is now." One of the bill's House sponsors made the declaration while giving a floor speech to a nearly empty chamber.

"How can we take the precious gift of motherhood from our daughters? How can we strip our sons of the right to carry on their family name through their children? How can we deny anyone the right to procreate?" The same Congresswoman from California who was ejected from the House Chambers during the President's speech screamed into a microphone in the same nearly empty chamber.

"If the number of abortions can be reduced, that is reason enough to vote in favor of this bill," a Congresswoman from New York declared. "There are 1.2 million unborn babies aborted each year in our country. Why? The reasons they would give you are these: It's a matter of freedom; a woman has a right over her own body. Well, not true. That baby inside her is not her body. That's somebody else's body. That's not her body," she said with raised voice.

"They say women shouldn't be victimized by men. Bull! You're not a victim if you lie down with a man." Her voice was now filled with sarcasm. "They say well, the child may have some genetic defect or some issue. Look people, we all are defective; it's only a question of degree." She persisted in her sarcasm.

"They tell us we have to do some eugenic abortions to eliminate birth-defective children, because of cost." She made this comment in a quiet, almost reverent tone. "They want you to believe women need total reproductive freedom. Women must have abortion as a backup to contraceptive failure they say. Murder as a backup?" She screamed into the microphone. "And by the way, in their world, this would all be paid for by *our* tax money." She appeared to be getting madder by the minute.

"They believe it's good to do this because it kind

of controls population. Really? We already know all those things. Nineteen seventy-three, it was January twenty-second when this horrendous decision came out of a Supreme Court that certainly should have known better." She wasn't finished yet.

"The Fourteenth Amendment of the Constitution says, '*No person shall be deprived of life.' 'No person shall be deprived of life without due process of law.'* What's the due process for an infant in the womb, legalized murder?" she screamed again. "The court ignored the reality of life beginning at conception, which *is* when life begins. And at that point you have a person. Criminals in our history have been prosecuted successfully for killing unborn children in an attack on a pregnant woman. A person can be prosecuted even today for killing an unborn infant in the womb of a mother—but not the mother. A mother *can't* be prosecuted for killing that infant. I support passage of this bill because it will at least protect the unborn in what should be the safest place in the universe. A culture that cannot be absolutely horrified by such repugnant things is dead."

"At first I admired you conservatives for the fine words you preach opposing a woman's choice. Then I thought, no, I envy you. I wish I felt the same. But the more I thought about it, the more I realized, I *resent* it!" A leading liberal Congressman from Minnesota clenched his fist as he began his allotted time at the podium.

"Reproductive choice can be the only thing that stands between a woman and poverty. There is a reason that the one billion poorest people on the planet are female. In sub-Saharan Africa and West Asia, women typically have five to six children, which leave them powerless to provide for not only their own families, but themselves. It's the mother's body, she should decide what happens," he paused, seeing a friend walk into the chamber.

"Reproductive choice can be the only thing that stands between a woman and death. Women who face deadly consequences of a pregnancy deserve to choose to live. Teen girls, whose bodies are not yet ready for childbirth, are five times more likely to die. Not only do seventy-thousand girls age fifteen to nineteen die each year from pregnancy and childbirth, but the babies that do survive have a sixty percent higher chance of dying as well." He stopped to pick up his prepared remarks which had fallen off the lectern as he was flipping through the pages.

"Every baby has the right to proper care and love; if this is not possible, abortion should be okay. Doctors, not governments, should always be the people to make medical recommendations and opinions. Would you allow the government to tell you if you could have a kidney transplant or a blood transfusion? Of course not! The fact that we even consider, let alone allow, a government to regulate a medical procedure is both illogical and foolish. If fifty million people say a foolish thing, it is still a foolish thing." The Congressman paused. He too was speaking to an empty chamber.

"The politicians pro-lifers so ardently support are only after one thing: self-interest. The majority of them are not pro-life because they *agree* with you, they are pro-life because they *know* you will continue to vote for them, and they *know* that making women remain pregnant not only takes away their power, but it also keeps them busy, in line, controlled. The more people they have to rule over, the more they have to work and buy things. Surely the woman and her family have rights, not just the unborn baby? In the case of under-age pregnancy, the girl may not have really understood what she was doing, and should not lose her education and career opportunities over one mistake. Life doesn't really start until birth, or at least until the fetus is viable." He finished as a large African American man moved to the lectern on the right.

"You're wrong sir! Your statement has only enough truth in it to make many people believe your lies." The Southern Baptist Minister-turned-Congressman from California boomed from the podium. "I abhor my colleague's stand on legalized abortion in our country. I am committed to do everything in my power to work to overturn this horrific Supreme Court decision. Sir, I must give you a handful of things to think about, just some principles and I won't take too much time. It is vitally important what you laugh at. It is vitally important what you weep at. What breaks your heart tells God who you are. What makes you laugh tells God who you are," the former Minister began.

"Number one, conception is an act of God, God personally creates every life. You're not an animal. You're not a biological accident. You're not tissue at some point and then you become a person. You're a creation of God, by God, who weaves together the genetic code, who intimately sees the unformed fetus and who guides the entire process." He sounded like a true baritone and paused for a drink of water.

"You're not a mortal. No life is mortal. May I say this quickly? Every life conceived is immortal. Every single child conceived lives forever. It doesn't matter if you're married, if you're having sex with someone you're not married to, if you were raped, if it was incest, it doesn't change the creation of God. Life is created by God. It is not up to us or anybody to determine if life should be prohibited from coming into existence. It's God's; and God *doesn't* make mistakes." He was staring directly into the CSPAN camera focused on him. "This bill should never become law regardless of the problems it may solve. Not until the human heart is changed can we end the scourge of children having children."

* * *

All ninety-eight of The Company's employees were on hand for Jack's retirement party. A month earlier, Jack turned in his resignation. Max made a limited effort to change his mind even though he recalled Jack's desire to take a sabbatical before the President's project was announced.

"You remember the night all of us were sitting on the porch at the Masters?" Jack asked Max.

"Yep, you and Father Bob got into a deep discussion about the existence of God," Max answered, not telling him he saw Father Bob use the same explanation many times.

"I had a lot to drink, so I thought I would put him on the spot. Well, you were there, he blew me away. Ever since then, I decided to learn more about God, and especially Christianity," Jack paused, looking for approval.

"Jack, that's great! It is the big picture you know. I had to learn it the hard way," Max said approvingly.

"I decided I'm going to spend some time in Rome and visit the Holy Land, so I can experience firsthand what I felt that night." Jack was smiling after he answered, and looking very much at ease with his decision.

Jack's retirement party carried on until close to

midnight. He was beloved by everyone at TC and his co-workers showered him with love that evening. Max and Bud knew The Company was never going to be the same, but there was something strange going on that neither of them could put his finger on. The next afternoon Max called Bud.

"The guy says he's going to explore Christianity out of the clear blue. He's going to Rome? What do you make of all that Max?" Bud asked, already thinking he'd come up with the answer.

"I know. I thought, why does someone who is serious about looking into the existence of God never mention it before now? We were at the Masters eight years ago. Doesn't make sense," Max agreed.

"Weird dude! It's a bean problem," Bud said, knowing he'd get a rise out of Max.

"Okay, what's a *bean* problem?"

"Human beans, you know, Jack has a problem with human beans."

"You're right, probably just Jack being Jack," Max again agreed.

* * *

The Personal Responsibility Implant Act passed by the narrowest of margins. The vote was bipartisan, but only three more members in the House and two more Senators cast their vote in favor of the measure. For a change, party affiliation had nothing to do with individual member's votes.

Never before had a bill become law with the provision it would not become effective unless the Supreme Court ruled it was Constitutional. There was the famous case of a former Speaker of the House once pleading with her colleagues to "pass a bill so we know what's in the bill", but never a conditional clause like the one contained in the PRI Act. This was unprecedented with a capital "U"!

The U.S. Supreme Court was the ultimate authority on Constitutionality and had the right to make the final decision if they received the case on appeal. The Court was primarily an hermeneutical agency; the court looked at a current law to see if it was in harmony with the Constitution. Recently, the Court's new approach relied not on what the law may have meant in the 18th Century, but how it applied to contemporary community standards today. Unfortunately this judicial activism rendered the Constitution to a relative document, subject to change and change and change. In the case of the Personal Responsibility Implant Act, the Court was charged with deciding if the law *should* become law; again, unprecedented with a capital "U."

The nine Justices were scheduled to take the bench for the last time before their summer recess. Most would head out of town for the summer, leaving the country to digest one of the most anticipated decisions in memory: the Court's opinion on the constitutionality of the Personal Responsibility Implant Act.

The Court had only two questions before it; was the Act constitutional and, was Congress within its power to "punt" the question to the Court? The question keeping the White House, Congress, and everyone else in the country on pins and needles was whether the mandate—which would require virtually all future Americans to be implanted with the device, and pass a competence test or post a bond— was constitutional. Could Congress, using its power under the Constitution, make people perform one of two options before being allowed to bear children?

But before the Court could decide whether the mandate was constitutional, it must first decide whether it could even rule on this question at all. The potential obstacle to the Court's review of the mandate was the fact that Congress passed a law that provided that the Supreme Court determine if the new law was constitutional *before* it could become effective. Most scholars believed this unprecedented move placed new responsibilities on the Court that the Founders never intended.

The matter would end if at least five of the nine members of the Court were to conclude that the mandate was unconstitutional. The Court would not discuss, much less rule on, whether Congress's move was constitutional, nor would there be any reason for the Court to weigh in on what parts of the law, if any, could survive.

After oral argument in March, most Court watchers believed that the Court would not regard the Congress deferring to the Court as a bar to reviewing the mandate. But if that issue went the other way, that verdict would postpone a decision on the mandate until well after the next presidential election.

Finally, as long as the Court didn't conclude that the entire PRI must fall, it would have to resolve one more issue: did another provision of the Act violate the Constitution because it effectively required new immigrants to be implanted? The lower court agreed with the federal government that it did not, and the Justices seemed to be leaning that way at oral argument.

* * *

Chief Justice Sweeney wrote for the majority. In a

9 to 0 ruling, Justice Sweeney said the Court rejected the argument that the device did not infringe on the rights of citizens.

"The Court agreed Congress has the power to pass laws protecting citizens from hazards that can adversely affect the prosperity of the nation. The Court accepted the theory that it is the duty of the Executive to take advantage of any means available to act on conditions which are a clear and present danger to the nation's sovereignty. But the Court now rules unanimously, sighting the Fourteenth Amendment." Judge Sweeney's pronouncement was sternly made into cameras focused on his every word.

"The Constitution holds in Section 1 of the Fourteenth Amendment, all persons born or naturalized in the United States, and subject to the jurisdiction thereof, are citizens of the United States and of the State wherein they reside. No State shall make or enforce any law which shall abridge the privileges or immunities of citizens of the United States, nor shall any State deprive any person of life, liberty, or property, without due process of law, nor deny any person within its jurisdiction the equal protection of the laws.

The Court also relies on the first paragraph of the Declaration's Preamble, '*to which the Laws of Nature and of Nature's God entitle them.*' Therefore we judge the law to be unconstitutional. The Laws of Nature and Nature's God cannot withstand the state condoning the abolition of people's ability to conceive. Regardless of a clear and present danger to the United States brought on by children having children, the Personal Responsibility Implant may not be applied in the United States of America now, or in the future." Judge Sweeney finished.

* * *

"The U.S. Supreme Court's ruling striking down the Personal Responsibility Implant Act championed by President Sean Curran reignited an intense debate, with some Democrats and Republicans celebrating while others railed against what they contended was dangerous intrusion on the ability of government to protect the nation," informed an ABC News reporter.

"The 9-0 ruling was a defeat for Curran, causing disappointment at the White House. 'Today's decision was a defeat for people all over this country whose lives are less secure because of this ruling,' Curran's Press Secretary said in a televised White House statement.

"Meanwhile, the ruling quickly became a rallying cry for proponents who criticized the high court's reasoning and vowed to bring back the Personal Responsibility Implant Act. Emily Francis, spokeswoman for Personal Responsibility Now, said that last night via Twitter more than $3.2 million was raised in the hours after the decision was announced.

'Our government exists to protect the Constitutional rights of the people. Those rights are protected by the Constitution and its Amendments as the law of the land,' the Executive Vice President of the Conservative Coalition of America said.

'Only the people have the incontestable, unalienable and unencroachable right to change the laws which they have established. The elected and appointed officials may not change the law of the Constitution; neither can the courts change the law. Not even the Supreme Court can change any law. Courts only judge situations to which the law applies. Courts may not judge the law. Not the courts, not the officials, not even the

Supreme Court, have the incontestable, unalienable, and unrecoverable right to change the law of the land, only the people. They do it through their elected officials of the many States. But for such power to make laws to exist in the hands of a few appointed men, untouchable by the people, that is the exact thing our Founders denied. They set up the Constitution so only the Congress should have the power to make laws, and the Congress is elected by the people.'

"This is Joan Rosner, ABC News, reporting from the White House."

* * *

"Good evening fellow Americans. I am speaking to you tonight about yesterday's Supreme Court decision regarding the Personal Responsibility Implant legislation passed by Congress two months ago. As you know, there was a provision written into the measure requiring the Supreme Court to consider the constitutionality of the statute before the Act could be implemented. The Court has ruled. The law has been struck down." President Curran was speaking from the Oval Office in a live television address to the American people.

The President venerated the Founders foresight establishing three separate but equal branches of government. He delighted in the Court's judicial restraint and the Justice's determination to consider the facts and avoid outside pressure from either opponents or proponents. Curran admitted on several occasions that he was disappointed.

"I've learned success is the ability to go from one failure to another with no loss of enthusiasm. It is a mistake to try to look too far ahead. The chain of destiny can only be grasped one link at a time."

About the controversy the Border Patrol and Personal Responsibility Implant's technology stirred, the President said, "Creative technology can induce fear of the unknown. Our century will see many more discoveries like these devices. But as with this Supreme Court ruling, Justice must prevail. Justice is the firmest pillar of government. When it crumbles, all others follow."

Sean knew this nationally televised address would likely be his last. The election was less than three weeks away. Regardless of the Court's decision, he intended to take this opportunity to give a farewell speech to the American people, by thanking them for their support and prayers over the last eight years.

"American Presidents must lead and do so sometimes at great personal expense. Leadership sometimes demands standing against the tide. Opposed by the majority and all the power and influence, it's easy to be convinced the best course is going along with the crowd. You start thinking; can all those people be wrong?" Sean was looking very Presidential.

"Standing your ground is a daunting task and lonely road and American Presidents, along with Jeremiah, Isaiah and Amos in the Old Testament, are special individuals. We're not asking if the people agree with us. We stand our ground, and are adamant. We are convinced and prepared to take it on the chin if need be." Sean spoke confidently into the camera.

"I'll share with you a comment my favorite professor in college often told us, 'A kicking mule makes no headway. Stop complaining, it gets you nowhere.' The Supreme Court has the final say in this matter, and the Justices have spoken. So let's get back to work." Sean closed with, "Good night and God bless America."

The President's address received the highest rating ever for a speech made from the Oval Office in prime time. Press reports were giving Sean high marks across the political divide.

"Everybody loves that kind of leadership. Everybody recognizes the tremendous commitment in leadership and conviction and being prepared to stand alone in a tide of compromise and appeasement," opined a CBS White House correspondent.

"Exercising his role as President stands up, as it were, on the great ramparts of history, and calls to the people." The most liberal news spokesperson on the air closed his segment with words that surprised even his strongest critics.

* * *

From the outset, only Max, Bud and Jack knew all the particulars of both the Border Patrol Implant and the PRI. Of course the BPI was now being utilized throughout the world, and secrecy was abandoned for efficiencies. But processes and details regarding the PRI had been closely guarded by The Company for no other reason than to limit the number of people who could reproduce the device in the event it would be outlawed.

It wasn't required, but President Curran believed it was necessary to be on hand to witness the destruction of the Personal Responsibility Implant device. The unanimous Supreme Court ruling should have been enough to convince its supporters to move on. Unfortunately the debate raged on. Sean believed his appearance at the event to support the termination of the initiative would help heal the wounds left behind, and lay to rest the PRI once and for all.

* * *

Father Bob met the TBM at Mount Comfort Airport. Max needed to talk to him, and it couldn't be done over the phone.

"Max, whether you're Catholic or Protestant or Muslim or Hindu or any other belief system, there is only one truth, every life is created by God and created in His image, to bear His image. Every creation is the special object of God's loving care." Father Bob wasn't waxing philosophical this time.

"In the New Testament, in the gospel of Matthew and the gospel of Luke, we learn that the Holy Spirit created Christ in the womb of Mary without a human father. When did Christ come into the world? Did He come into the world in His birth? Did Jesus come into the world in Bethlehem? No, Jesus came into the world in His conception. Every creation is an act of God and every person created is in the image of God." He paused to ask Max a question. "Max, this PRI, it prohibits conception. Do you think that is the same thing as denying God? The Church is clear in its position on birth control. Isn't this the same thing?"

"Bob, I didn't, but I should have considered the tremendous effect this device could have from other points of view. Frankly I was focused on the pain and suffering that children having children brings to all of society," Max replied.

"I think the Supreme Court made the right decision. No device is the answer. The Justices may not have decided for the same reasons I would have. Bottom line, God is in control. We should strive to obey his commandments." Father Bob's response led Max to think that even Father Bob was struggling with the issue.

"Why do you think babies are in the womb for nine months? Why do you think they're in that protected place, a place that should be the safest place on the planet? So what the Scripture teaches us then is that conception is an act of God, each person is in the image of God, and it's not up to us to do anything that changes this." Max was wrong; Father Bob was strong in his convictions.

* * *

Max and Abby, Cookie and Liz, Sean and Karen, and Bud and Jan departed Austin-Bergstrom International Airport aboard Integra's G650. Sean's Secret Service detail remained close by. The luggage compartment was filled with golf clubs and bursting suitcases.

The four couples were en-route to KAVX where they would be met by a limo to transfer them to Avalon Bay on Santa Catalina Island twenty-two miles off the coast of California. There they would board an Ocean Alexander 155 Megayacht christened "Took Care of Business."

Maggie Ehrgott met her boss onboard. She and Tess Puglielli had been working with the crew and Secret Service for the last ten days to ensure the cruise would go as planned.

Cruising to Cabo San Lucas, Mexico, would take approximately seventeen hours. The yacht anchored in the Sea of Cortez a mile off shore from the Las Ventanas al Paraíso, one of Max and Abby's favorite places to relax in Cabo when they weren't staying on a one hundred fifty-five foot luxury mega yacht.

Just as Max promised Cookie five years earlier, the four men were going to golf 'til they dropped. Retired Major General Mac Wright, his wife Kathy, and Father Bob would be joining them a few days after their arrival at the Gulf of California anchorage. Traveling with the former President of the United States had its perks, playing a fivesome or sixsome on a golf course anywhere in the world would be one of them. Maggie arranged for the wives to receive the best the southern tip of the Baja Peninsula had to offer. The ship was reserved for an entire month, but if that would not be enough time for all eleven friends to overdose on happiness, the "Took Care of Business" was available for as long as they desired.

"So do you know how you can tell you're an extreme Redneck?" Father Bob began telling his joke. All the guests onboard were enjoying watching the sun begin to set from the upper deck of the fabulous ship.

"You're an extreme Redneck when you let your twelve- year-old daughter smoke at the dinner table in front of her kids. The Blue Book value of your truck goes up and down depending on how much gas is in it. You've been married three times and still have the same in-laws. You wonder how service stations keep their rest-rooms so clean. Your junior prom offered day care. You think the last words of the Star-Spangled Banner are 'Gentlemen, start your engines'. The Halloween pumpkin on your porch has more teeth than your spouse. You can't get married to your sweetheart because there's a law against it. And finally, you think loading the dishwasher means getting your wife drunk."

"Some guys can tell jokes and some guys can't," Max whispered to Bud. They both laughed anyway after Father Bob finished telling his joke.

"When you and I first spoke Max, I could have

made a lot of money betting my plan would fail. Whether it's a big secret like the President's, or a tiny secret like the ones little girls try to keep, a secret is only safe as long as one person knows it. If more than one person knows it, well it isn't a secret anymore is it? I don't want any of you guys to beat up on yourself. I'd like to have a nickel for every time I screwed up. Like I said from the outset, plans rarely unfold the way you draw them up." General Wright didn't know he had been betrayed, but that wasn't important, since he was almost certain someone would. "You can do the best you can, and that's all the better you can do."

Max knew why he was feeling anxious and uneasy. His company, along with his best friends, truly changed the world with the Border Patrol Implant. Maybe it was time to stop and smell the roses, put the Personal Responsibility Implant behind him. *I thought for sure*, he daydreamed. "Oh well, we'll see," he said out loud.

Chapter 18

God Help Us

"The State Department is reporting that Israel has been employing the now infamous Personal Responsibility Implant, or so-called PRI, in their country for over a year," NBC's Nightly News anchor opened the broadcast with this shocking report.

"No way, Max! No fricken way! There simply ain't no way. We both watched *everything* being destroyed. It would be virtually impossible for the device to be duplicated." Max thought Bud was protesting a bit too much.

"No, it's not impossible. I'm afraid the more likely answer is they got the data from Jack." Max's response to Bud had an ominous tone.

"No way! Why? How?"

"Think about it, Bud. Remember when you and I spoke with him the day he turned in his resignation. He came with some song and dance about wanting to pursue an altruistic path; Green Peace or some other tree hugging group. I was afraid you were going to make me burst out laughing the way you were making faces behind his back. We had no idea what the hell he was talking about. He said he was going to travel to Rome and visit the Holy Land to learn more about Christianity because of Father Bob. We didn't buy it, remember? But we didn't think anything sinister was going on either. We figured Jack was just being Jack." Max paused when Bud nodded his head in agreement.

"That son-of-a-bitch would have had plenty of opportunity to strike up a relationship with one of their engineers. Hell, he was there for at least two months." Max made his thoughts known while studying Bud's reaction. "Bud, you know Jack is a zealot. He never wanted to be confused with facts. He told me he thought the PRI was the most important discovery made in decades. Remember when I first told you guys about the finding? You called it an accident; and the name stuck? Jack nearly hit the ceiling. You and I both know how upset he became when the Supreme Court struck down the use of the device." Max was studying Bud's face, looking for a tell during his answer.

"So how did the little prick get the plans?" Bud asked a rhetorical question, since he knew all three men were capable of reproducing the device.

"My guess is his photographic memory. Besides, how else could the Israelis obtain the technology? The chances of someone accidently making the same discovery is beyond remote." Max realized Bud was not at all suspicious.

"I see what you're saying. It all makes sense when you connect those dots. But you know Max, when I was standing there watching everything being destroyed, I honestly believed it would simply be a matter of time until somebody built a similar device. That's the nature of technological findings. You can't uninvent! *Eventually* someone will reproduce the PRI," Bud prophesied. Even though he secretly worried, *I hope eventually isn't too late.*

* * *

"Bless me Father for I have sinned—." Max was making his confession to Father Bob, immediately after Sean concluded his confession from the opposite side of the confessional box.

The three men walked silently to the Rectory. Without saying it out loud, Father Bob vividly recalled watching Max and Bud enter the same confessional over forty-five years earlier, after they confessed to robbing St. Thomas More's chemistry lab. Only this time he was not watching, the two men had confessed their sin to him.

"I've got two pieces of good news," Father Bob announced, after the three got comfortable in the Rectory living room.

"I could go for some good news," Sean replied.

"Max, you remember me telling you about my Marriage 101 project on the plane to the Masters?"

"Sure do. I loved it," Max replied.

"Long story, but I got it published. A well-known company got a hold of it somehow and—voila! I'm a published writer. I'm donating all the proceeds to the Foundation. After all, it was the students who provided a lot of the copy."

"That's great Bob." Sean congratulated Father Bob by giving him and Max a high five. "So what's the other good news?"

"Out of the clear blue, I received this anonymous donation. I still can't believe it. It's the largest amount any parish in the diocese ever received. It's inexplicable, but it wipes out all the debt on our new school, plus there may be a significant amount left to add to the Foundation."

All three were enjoying a snifter of Courvoisier

after Father Bob's cook left the Rectory where she served the three men her specialty, roasted rack of lamb.

"How much was this mysterious contribution, Bob?" Sean asked.

"One million two thousand five hundred dollars." Still in disbelief, Father Bob continued to be dumbfounded. "Peculiar amount, don't you think?"

"That's terrific. I'm guessing whoever made that gift either has a massive guilty conscience or believes it may help him get to Heaven, or both," Max guessed. His mind was racing as he recalled past events.

"Let's change the subject. Max, you must speak to Jack. He deserves the truth." Father Bob made his dictum to both men.

"Bob, you have to understand. Both of us strongly agreed it was way too important to allow the Personal Responsibility Implant to die a natural death. When Max came to visit me at the White House, we decided regardless of how Congress voted or the Supreme Court ruled, we were going to make sure the new technology lived on. The Israelis offered us the best opportunity." Sean kept looking back and forth between Max and Father Bob as he made his case.

"Bob, you told me some people don't deserve the truth. I know this wasn't one of those times. But first of all, Bud was right when he said you can't *uninvent* new technologies." Max knew he was trying desperately to justify his and Sean's deception.

"We both are convinced the scourge of children having children must be stopped. It is accelerating the culture's decay and destroying our nation. This curse is being passed on to future generations. Birth control fails. Schools are part of the problem. Churches are part of the problem. The media culture shares the blame. Parents are culpable. There's plenty of blame to go around. But that doesn't change the fact. America is like the frog placed in cold water that is slowly heated. It will not perceive the danger and will be cooked to death." Max finished his justification.

"Death, destruction, and pain are part of our natural world. Com'on Boys, this is Bob Dugan you're talking to." Father Bob looked at the two with an almost playful grin after his challenging comment. "You're giving rational thought to a predicate without a subject."

"Okay, we give." After looking at Max shrugging his shoulders in total confusion, Sean too didn't understand where Father Bob was going with this snippet of philosophical truism.

"You two want your cake and eat it too."

"Thank you, Doctor," Sean sarcastically replied.

"Both of you have achieved enormous success. I'm sitting here with a former two-term President of the United States and one of the world's foremost chemical engineers. Men in leadership positions must set examples. But that doesn't change the facts. America is strong because America is good. That will change when America is no longer good." Father Bob was now taking both Max and Sean into the deep end of the philosophical pool.

"Think about how many people you have known who did their best, but always wanted to do more, because they were haunted by a sense of failure. Be good and true. Be patient. Be undaunted. Leave your usefulness for God to estimate. He will see to it that you do not live in vain." Father Bob paused, noticing both men appeared remorseful.

"Character is like a tree. Reputation is the shadow it casts. Be more concerned with your character than your reputation. Your character is what you really are while your reputation is merely what others think you are." Father Bob believed the two were truly repentant for their actions. He went on to tell Max and Sean something they already knew, but likely forgot because of their passion for the PRI.

"Government is like fire, handy for a servant, but dangerous as a master. A government big enough to give you everything you want is strong enough to take everything you have." Father paused again. He pointed his index finger at an article he had framed of Max, Bud, Jack and Sean holding a test tube that contained the PRI.

"Remember the five simple rules to be happy. Free your heart from hatred. Free your mind from worries. Live simply. Give more. Expect less. Doing the right thing is hard, and speaking the truth is dangerous. Many have been abhorred for it, some killed, one crucified." Father Bob looked at each of the men while speaking. "As for the Supreme Court's decision, I realize now, love spoke louder than logic, and prevailed!"

* * *

"China Ends Controversial One Child Policy" was the banner headline in The Wall Street Journal. Bud was reading the paper while sitting at his desk with his feet propped up on his credenza.

Holy shit, he thought. He continued reading the account.

"Since the government's successful employment of the Personal Responsibility Implant technology discovered by the Americans, there is now no longer the need for the One Child program," a government spokesman told the Journal under the condition of anonymity.

"ZhanWeing, Minister of the State Commission of Population and Family Planning, confirmed that China's new Implant policy is consistent with the nation's plan for population growth and would continue indefinitely. He denied rumors the technology was stolen from the US."

Bud put the newspaper down. He stood up and stared out his window, noticing a departing airliner in the distance. He'd willingly accepted the offer the Chinese had made to him. His golfing buddy, Tony Clark, arranged to have five million dollars deposited into an untraceable Swiss Bank account. Bud immediately sent an anonymous donation of $1 million to Father Bob for his new school fund. He added twenty-five hundred dollars, which represented the amount he and Father Bob forgave Max and Cookie in a gin game at Augusta over eight years earlier.

Bud gained comfort knowing he would have provided the technology for free after the Supreme Court struck down the law. The money wasn't important. The PRI was important. The Chinese offer was a means to an end, an end Bud believed was vitally important. Continuing to stare out his window, he daydreamed—*you know dipshit, if you can't lead, and you can't follow, get the hell out of the way. Think about all those babies who won't be slaughtered thanks to me. Think about how much healthier our world will be thanks to me. I know I did the right thing. History will prove me correct. It was only a matter of time until somebody designed a similar device. That's the nature of technological findings. You can't uninvent. Eventually someone will reproduce the PRI.* Bud had made sure...*eventually* wasn't going to be too late.

* * *

"Jack, it's good to see you again. You look well." Father Bob directed Jack into the Rectory's living room. "Would you care for something to eat or drink?"

"No thanks, Bob. I'm still a little jet lagged. I just got in yesterday. I appreciate you taking the time. Isn't this where one of you guys tells the other a joke?"

"It's not exactly a rule, but the three of us have made it a habit over the years; make that a bad habit." Father Bob was surprised with Jack's question.

"I've got one that may be timely," Father Bob said, feeling a bit odd with Jack's request. "A scientist told God that he figured out how to create life. God was impressed and asked the man if he would show him how he did it. The scientist agreed and proceeded to bend over and grab a handful of dirt. God slapped the dirt out of the man's hand and told him to get his *own* dirt."

"Well done. Timely is right," Jack said smiling.

"Sorry, that's all I could come up with in such short notice." Father Bob was still a little taken aback with Jack's request.

"Bob, when I emailed you my request, I had just left Vatican City. My mind was swirling. I've been a strict atheist all my life. Not until that night in Augusta did I ever seriously consider the existence of God." Jack paused while he sat down across from Father Bob.

"That was a long time ago; over eight years, yes?" Father Bob guessed.

"That's right. But after the Court weighed in on the PRI, the timing appeared right for me to leave Solutions. I couldn't believe the law was struck down. My original plans included doing some work with Green

Peace, but after recalling our exchange in Georgia, I felt I needed to search for answers. That's when I decided to visit Rome and the Holy Land." Jack appeared more comfortable than Father Bob had ever seen him before.

"I spent a great deal of time studying in Rome. Did you enjoy the city?" Father Bob asked, recalling the years he spent pursuing his Doctorate of Philosophy in Europe.

Jack continued recounting his travels, but finished by asking Father Bob what he suggested he do for the next phase on his journey to abandon atheism for theism.

"What question do you believe you need a response to?" Father Bob answered Jack's question with a question.

"Bob, one of my favorite writers is H.G. Wells. I was surprised when I read one of his quotes. It went something like this, 'I am an historian. I am not a believer. But this penniless preacher from Galilee is irresistibly the center of history'. What do you make of that?" Jack asked in an almost childlike tone.

"Jack, science has been your life. You and many of your contemporaries have not only rejected the existence of God, but have done so with a vengeance." Father Bob sensed Jack was ready to be confronted with the truth.

"Please explain what you mean," Jack replied. His response was somewhat provocative.

"Has anyone ever provided proof of God's *inexistence*? Not even close. Has quantum cosmology explained the emergence of the universe or why it is here? Not even close. Have the sciences explained why the universe seems to be so finely tuned to allow for the existence of life? Not even close. Are some physicists and biologists willing to believe in *anything* so long as it is not religious thought? Close enough. Have rationalism and moral thought provided us with an understanding of what is good, what is right, and what is moral? No way! Has secularism in the terrible twentieth century been a force for good? Not even close to being close. Is there a narrow and oppressive orthodoxy of thought and opinion within the sciences? No doubt! Does anything in the sciences or philosophy justify the claim that religious belief is irrational? Not even in the same zip code. Is scientific atheism a frivolous exercise in intellectual contempt? Spot on!" Father Bob finished his pointed criticism and saw that Jack was hanging on his every word.

"Please go on, Father Dugan."

"Cosmology is the argument of cause and effect. You see Jack, there are only two worldviews of the universe; either God *is,* and that makes sense, or God *is not,* and then we've got problems. As Christians we accept *one* miracle, God is, then everything else makes sense. An atheist denies God is, and has to have a miracle for *every* other thing. We look at something that is perfected, or finished, or done, and we say it's a design and it must have had a designer. You can take your watch apart and put all the pieces in your pocket and shake your leg forever, and you won't ever hear it tick. You know, when you have something that works, somebody has to have made it work. If you see a piano, you don't assume there was an elephant that ran into a tree, with a guy sitting in the tree playing a harp, and it all fell together and there it is—the whole thing, ivory, wood and strings. Ridiculous! Absurd! Design implies a designer. Do you follow me?"

"Your logic is dizzying, but at the same time refreshingly clear," Jack answered.

"Jack, if you go down to the beach and see the first three letters of your name written in the sand, you immediately postulate intelligence behind the writing, don't you? An intelligent person or thing created those letters, right?"

"Of course, Father."

"Let's say you're invited to peer through your microbiologist buddy's electron microscope. You see before you the double strand of DNA unfolding and spitting off its codons – AACTGCTGCCCAG – all three point one *billion* of them, in exactly the right order. Jack, what is the origin of that? You and your colleagues say chance and necessity. Really? Seriously? But they see three letters scribbled in the sand, and immediately think intelligent design?" Father Bob paused, once more seeking a reply, but could see none was coming.

"You see Jack; an atheist believes it is a legitimate question to ask a theist who created *your* creator? A theist can answer his question with the same question, who created *your* creator? Both the atheist and the theist don't go back forever; they come to an ultimate fact. For the atheist, the universe is his creator. For the theist, God is his creator; God is eternal; He never came to be. Jack, my friend, the key question you must answer is this: not *is* there an ultimate fact, but which fact *is* ultimate."

* * *

Max and Jack were seated at the custom made conference room table inside Solutions, LLC home office. Most of TC's employees stopped by earlier to wish Jack well, since they hadn't seen him since his retirement party.

"Jack, I sincerely apologize for placing the blame on you. I took the path of least resistance and I am truly sorry. I hope you can forgive me. It was selfish, arrogant and small," Max confessed. He had quietly blamed Jack for disclosing the PRI formula to the Israelis. His rumor caused a great deal of trouble for Jack. Before he could finish, Bud came charging into the room.

"Jack, rumors of your death have been greatly exaggerated. I understand you have been to Europe searching for God; and you found him?" Bud was shaking Jack's hand and patting him on his shoulder while making his energetic inquiry. "We miss you man, it's a drag here without you. You never cease to amaze me, Jack. Brain won't come close to replacing you, but I would have never guessed, you, of all people, would recommend him for our new project. I remember—"

"Hold on, don't *even* go there Bud. We've all heard that story too many times." Max interrupted Bud before he could re-tell the time he had to break John Henn and Jack apart.

"Yep, well it's good to see you too, Bud. And yes, I did find God, and I recommend you do the same before it's too late." Jack was smiling and looking toward Max while answering Bud's question. "John's changed. He'll be a great team member. It turns out Brain provided Reinbold with a vital link that helped Max develop the serum used to destroy the PRI. Aren't you glad I asked Dennis to help?"

"I'll be dipped in shit, any other surprises?" Bud asked Jack, noticing Max nodding in agreement. "You know, I always liked Brain, even though he looked like someone put a Cuban out on his ugly mug. Too bad his wife is a butter face. Everything looks good but her face."

"OK, that's enough smartass. Jack and I were just

talking about all the times we met right in this very spot. We did some good work here, you know. Bud's right Jack, we do miss you. I'm really happy for you." Max knew Jack had accepted his apology, notwithstanding Bud's interruption.

"It must be five o'clock somewhere. I say we toast to something," Bud insisted, pouring two fingers of Blue into three glasses.

"Gentlemen, here's to my good buddies, I've got to tell you, I don't miss seeing you guys every day," Jack said.

"That makes at least two of us," Bud replied.

"It's not been the same since you left," said Max.

"I know how disappointed you guys were when the Supreme Court struck down the Act, but not as much as I was. But I'm not any longer. I've finally learned that I must always be willing to listen and then also be willing to change. I discovered a lot about how God operates. He doesn't make mistakes." Jack held up his glass after finishing his toast.

"I'd like to propose a toast to Solutions, LLC and to welcoming Brain back into the fold. Jack, there's no way he will ever fill your shoes," Bud said, smiling at Jack with an appreciative stare.

"Okay, I have one more. Pour a little more in my glass for this one. Fill yours too Bud. Here's to Father Bob's new school project. He told me he received an anonymous donation. Sounds like some unbelievably nice guy with a serious guilty conscience paid off Bob's entire debt." Max raised his glass and smiled at Bud; winking at him at the same time.

* * *

"Come with me, Max. I want to show you something," Bud said, walking toward the door moments after Jack left the building.

"Hold on. I think we need to talk, don't you?" Max answered in a way that confirmed Bud's suspicions.

The two men got into Bud's car and drove less than three miles. Neither spoke a word to each other. A few minutes later, Bud stopped the car and pointed to a large billboard situated a half block from one of Austin's largest high schools.

"What do you think?" Bud asked, without looking at Max.

"So, are you finally going to get to sail to Tahiti with that all-girl crew?" Max asked his question in a slightly belligerent tone. "How much did you get?"

"Max, you know better than anyone, I don't give a damn about the money. Sure, I like to spend other peoples', but that's different, especially when it's the Chinese. Clark offered me—"

"Hold on! Clark? Tony Clark? The guy we met in Ireland. The same guy we played with in Palm Springs? Clark is Chinese? What the —" Max was flabbergasted.

"Yep. Clark worked for the Ministry of State Security of the People's Republic of China. He's a spy. Nice guy though, really fooled me."

"Really fooled you? That may be the greatest understatement you've ever made. Tony Clark is a spy?" Max asked, still in shock.

"He offered me five million bucks. I told him he had to throw in the taxes and he's got a deal. I guessed you knew when you told me Bob mentioned the contribution. You lost the bet by the way; I didn't try to expense that twenty-five hundred. I didn't do it for the money, Max. I did it because it was the right thing to do."

There was no remorse in Bud's proclamation.

"Tony Clark! Wow! So tell me, what I'm looking at," Max asked, staring up at the billboard.

"I bought five hundred of them. They're positioned close to five hundred of the largest high schools in America. I leased them for two years. And they say four million bucks doesn't go very far these days. Remember, you said you thought it was a good idea? Well, do you still want in?" Bud asked, sensing his explanation was enough for Max.

"If you had only told—," Max was interrupted by Bud.

"If a frog had wings, he wouldn't bump his ass every time he jumped."

"You prick! It never ends does it? Sure. What's my buy in?"

"I'll let you in cheap. I looked over our new project. I believe it has even more potential than the *ACCIDENT* and the President's gig combined. All I need from you is your trust. I did this for the right reason, Max, not for the money."

"Okay, so let's go hit the ball," Max said, knowing he would eventually tell his friend about what he and Sean had done. But Bud was on target; it was the right thing to do, wasn't it?

The two shook hands before Bud drove away. Max raised his head once again to read the multi-colored and brightly lit billboard shouting the phrase Max heard his friend and partner recite nearly a decade earlier.

DON'T BE STUPID – CHOOSE TO NOT BE POOR
Finish High School
Don't Have Children In Your Teens
Don't Get Married While You Are A Teenager

18427639R00154

Printed in Great Britain
by Amazon